You Never Forget Your Worst

And He's the Best I've Never Had

MILLIE PEREZ

Author's Note

Hello lovely readers! You Never Forget Your Worst is an interconnected standalone in the Never Forget duet. You do not have to read *You Never Forget Your First* in order to read Nikki and Antonio's story (although it is a much more enjoyable experience to see all your favorite people from book one make an appearance in this book).

This book is "open door" with explicit sexual scenes. If you are a fan of "closed door" books, like my first book, fear not, for I have written this book in a manner in which spicy scenes can be skipped without missing out on any plot.

Therefore, if you prefer sweet over spicy, please feel free to skip chapters 28, 29 and 45. If you prefer spice, please read those chapters over as many times as you like!

I have also placed content warnings below for your consideration.

Happy reading! xo Millie

<u>Content Warnings</u>

- Discussions of policing in America (topics related to police brutality, working in the force as a person of color, leaving the police force, FBI investigations into organized crime)
- Death of a parent (off-page)
- Graphic, consensual sexual content.
- References to kidnapping and stabbing (off-page, non-descriptive, from first book)
- On-page alcohol consumption
- Absentee father (abandonment before birth)
- Needles (receiving a tattoo- not descriptive)
- On-page therapy session related to mental health, parental expectations, immigrating to America in childhood.

For those who are on a journey to find a place where they belong.
Let this story be your home.

PROLOGUE
SEVEN YEARS AGO – NEW YEAR'S EVE

"Hey, Nikki, are my nipples pointing in the same direction?" my best friend, Amelia, shouts over the loud club music.

I can't help but laugh at the absurdity of the question. To be fair, Amelia is wearing a very tight black latex dress. I had to cover her body with baby powder to shimmy her into it, then use baby oil over the latex to make the dress even shinier. A whole lotta hoops to jump through for a New Year's Eve dress, but given that Amelia is nursing a broken heart, I'll take one for the team and stay vigilant on nipple watch. Plus, she started day drinking way too early, so at this rate, she's working overtime staying vertical.

"Yes, your little boobies aren't cross-eyed at the moment," I tease.

Amelia huffs. "Well, sorry. We mere mortals can't compete with these." She makes grabby hands toward my bejeweled chest, but I swat them away.

My dress consists of hundreds of tiny, interconnected mirrors that catch the light and create a sparkle effect everywhere I turn. I'm wearing a nude bodysuit under, giving the illusion that I'm naked under this dress, which hits right above my knee. My long blond hair is down in loose waves, accompanied by a red lip that makes my blue eyes pop.

Sexy disco ball at your service.

"Girl, we've been over this already. I'm the tits of the relationship, and you're the ass. Together, we make the dream team." I angle my drink toward hers and clink them together.

"Otro más, another shot!" Vanessa, Amelia's non-blood-related cousin, shouts. Amelia and the rest of the ladies in her cousin crew shriek and rush toward the bar.

I pull Amelia's arm and talk loudly into her ear. "It's a couple hours until the ball drops. I'm going to check out the bars on the other floors since I've never been here before. I'll be back by midnight to celebrate with you."

She frowns. "Boo, no! I'll come with you. Or just stay with us. I don't want you wandering alone. My cousins are so excited to finally meet you, and they're technically your cousins since we're basically sisters now, ya know?" She hiccups.

Even in her drunken stupor, my best friend has the kindest heart. But the truth is, her family flew down to celebrate New Year's Eve with her as her farewell to Miami before she moves back home to New York City, and I already feel like an interloper since I'll be tagging along and moving in with her. Besides, I wouldn't mind having a moment to myself to bid my hometown's nightlife goodbye.

I want her to let her hair down and have fun with her family, but she'll never let me go willingly at this point in the night. So I give her the bait that will allow me to break away. Amelia being the hopeless romantic of the duo, I pat her arm and say, "A girl needs to do her rounds in order to find a New Year's kiss, Amelia."

She smiles widely, and I can see the romantic comedy unfolding behind her eyes. "Ohmygosh you are totally gonna find the love of your life tonight. And then you'll have the most magical kiss ever, and then he'll follow you to New York, and then—"

"Too far, girl. I said someone to kiss, not compare retirement plans with."

She pouts like a petulant child. "But if I'm never going to find true love, I need you to do it so I can hear firsthand what it's like. Because at the rate I'm going—"

"Okay, this is turning into sad drunk territory. And I did not get my hands all oiled up for you to spiral tonight. So I'm going to hand you off to someone who's gonna put you on water duty for the rest of the night." I look over all the bobbling heads and dancing bodies. "Wait, isn't your brother supposed to be here by now?"

She frowns. "He texted me earlier saying his flight got canceled due to a small snowstorm up north. He should be able to fly in tomorrow night at the earliest." She folds her arms across her chest.

Bummer, I was really looking forward to meeting Antonio. Amelia talks about him like he hung the moon. I'm an only child, so I always dreamed of having a loving sibling. Plus, I'm hoping to make a good impression since Amelia is my best friend and I fully intend to be considered their *plus one* sibling for life.

Looks like introductions will have to wait. I steer Amelia over to one of her more responsible cousins and inform her that she should be on a food and water diet for the rest of the night. We're no longer in college, and I have no desire to hold her hair back while she gets sick. She's notorious for having terrible aim.

After I confirm that Amelia has a bottle of water in her hands and is surrounded by her family members, I take off toward the higher levels of the club to see what adventure awaits me until midnight.

I

NIKKI
PRESENT

"You can't be serious. You almost died, like, two seconds ago. I'm not leaving your side for a vacation at a time like this." I wave my hand up and down her bedridden body where she's lying next to me in her massive king-size bed. An absurd number of sugary snacks create a barrier between us as we digest everything that's gone down in the past few weeks.

Last month, Evan Cooper, Amelia's billionaire boyfriend, offered me a golden ticket. He was so grateful that I played a role that eventually led them to spending Thanksgiving alone together in his cabin, he offered me a trip of a lifetime.

Anywhere. Anytime. All expenses paid for me and my now newly ex-boyfriend, Justin. We planned on taking Evan's private jet to an exclusive posh resort in Bali. But I haven't even thought about the trip since Amelia was attacked over a week ago. And not just attacked, but kidnapped and held at gunpoint by the man who was her very first kiss when they were kids. Thank God her brother and Evan got there in time to save her. Though by then she'd been stabbed and had nearly died.

"Nikki, I'm fine. My recovery is pretty straight-forward. Plus, Evan is my literal shadow. I don't think I can handle two of those right now."

"Rude!" Evan shouts from the kitchen.

Amelia playfully rolls her eyes. "See? I'm under constant observation. I'll be fine." I give her an unimpressed look, so she continues. "Nikki, I'm serious. Everyone dropped everything to be at my bedside during Christmas, and I love and appreciate you all for doing that. But right now, I need to feel useful. I'm stuck in this bed all day watching *The Real Housewives of Miami*." She puts her hand up before I can interrupt her. "Which is my favorite thing in the world to watch, but it's not the same while I'm bedridden. I need to do something. Anything. So please, pretty please, let me plan this vacation for you. It would make me feel so much better knowing that I have something to do. You know how much I love planning our girls' trips! Plus, forget Bali. I found the perfect place for you, and the private jet will get you there in under four hours." She pleads with her hands in a prayer pose.

"Wow. You're not above playing dirty with my guilt, are you?"

"Nope." She pops the *p*.

"Amelia, I love you, and I think that I hit the best friend jackpot the day we met, but I don't think going on a trip I intended for Justin and me is the best thing for me at the moment."

Amelia's eyes fill with compassion. "You've been so wrapped up in my chaos that you've been avoiding talking about your breakup. The rundown you gave me at the hospital while I was still on morphine is foggy at best, so I'm gonna need you to fill me in when you're ready to talk."

"There isn't much to say." I sigh. "He wanted me to move

to Florida, to live on his family farm. And I'm not in my small town–romance era."

"Nikki," Amelia warns.

"Okay, fine. Look, Justin is a great guy. Probably the best boyfriend I've ever had. We lived together and moved through life pretty seamlessly. But when I looked at my future, I could tell you how many clients I intended to add to my private practice, and I could recite the internships I'm running for the psychology undergrad students at Fordham. I could visualize what I hoped my future apartment would look like and what cities I would love to vacation in."

I take a small bag of Skittles and pull out all the red and orange ones to eat, then dispose of the rest. "I can even see myself being the best auntie to your future billionaire babies, because that's totally happening." I chuckle. "But I just couldn't see him. I couldn't see us together long term. And that's not fair to him. I would never make him choose between me and his family farm. Especially knowing that I couldn't see a future for us, even after spending a year together." I shrug sadly.

Amelia squeezes my hand. "I'm so sorry, Nikki. I really thought you and Justin were endgame. But I'm happy that you have clarity on your decision." She smiles softly.

"To be honest, I didn't know if I was making the right decision. I'm thirty years old, I'm settled in my career, I had a steady, responsible, and loving boyfriend. Yet somehow, I couldn't take that leap with him. I kept waiting to feel this overwhelming sense of loss after he left to spend the holidays with his family. But I just felt… nothing." I turn to face Amelia, crossing my legs under me. "It shouldn't feel like that, right? I should be elbow deep into a bucket of ice cream, watching rom-coms. Or at the very least, I should be crying a bit, shouldn't I?"

"He wasn't the one," a male voice rumbles.

I startle as I see Evan leaning against the doorway with a glass of water and a prescription bottle in his hands.

Look, Amelia is my best friend, and I would never betray her, but I would have to feign blindness to deny how annoyingly attractive Evan is. I'm still getting used to my best friend dating a Chris Evans look-alike, but for now, I push those thoughts away while I focus on the romantic mumbo jumbo he's about to spew.

I scoff. "The one. So stupid." I watch him as he makes his way toward Amelia, his eyes filled with devotion. "Unless it's you two shmucks."

Evan speaks again. "Justin seemed like a good guy, Nikki, but he wasn't the one for you. It was clear as day." He shakes out two pills from the prescription bottle and hands them to Amelia, then passes her the glass of water. "He wasn't enough for you."

That causes both Amelia and me to do a double take and widen our eyes at his declaration. "Care to elaborate, Dr. Phil?" Amelia asks after taking her pain medication.

Evan sighs. "Look, Nikki, you're the shrink here, so this shouldn't be rocket science to you. But Justin? He was more of a lapdog. Someone who could keep you company day to day but never challenge you. And if you're anything like Amelia, I know for a fact that it would've never worked in the long run. You're both strong-willed women, but sometimes," he looks at Amelia in mock seriousness, "and only a very small number of times, you need someone who isn't afraid of calling you on your shit."

Amelia gasps.

"I said only sometimes!" Evan dodges an elbow from Amelia as he takes a seat next to her, pulling her into his side while placing a chaste kiss on her forehead.

I groan. "Save the Hallmark moments for after I've left for

the day. We're talking about my failed love life here." I lean forward and place my head in my hands.

"Well, well, well. Another one bites the dust."

I stiffen when I recognize the familiar, deep, velvety voice of the last person I want bearing witness to this conversation. I send up a silent prayer in vain, because when I slowly lift my head, there he stands.

The man who makes no effort to hide his disdain for me.

The man who has consumed my thoughts on lonely nights.

The man who is the absolute worst.

Amelia's older brother, who also happens to be the man who gave me my worst New Year's kiss ever, because it was tainted by my lies.

I close my eyes momentarily to brace myself for the inevitable. A larger-than-life man with height and muscles that easily rival those of Dwayne "The Rock" Johnson. With year-round tan skin, short, soft brown hair, a clean-shaven face, and caramel-colored eyes. A panty-dropping smile that turns into an immediate scowl when I'm in his presence. Thighs that could be compared to tree trunks and… and now I'm thinking about climbing him like a tree. Crap, focus girl.

I finally straighten and begrudgingly give him my full attention.

Standing by the foot of the bed, wearing his typical winter uniform that consists of a backward Yankees hat, dark hoodie, jeans, and white Nikes, along with a smug look on his face, is none other than Antonio Nuñez. The bane of my existence, and the only man who has the power to be my undoing.

"Antonio, play nice," Amelia chides.

Antonio chuckles as he makes his way to her, only breaking eye contact with me once he's at her side. "How are you feeling today, sis?" He places a kiss on her head and drops a small brown paper bag on her lap.

"I'm okay." She opens Antonio's offering and beams up at

him. "You brought me Doña Gloria's empanadas! *Ah!* You're my favorite brother ever!" She holds her arms up, and he easily lowers himself to give her a quick hug.

"Only one, because I know you can do some real damage with unlimited access to those. Gloria says hi and hopes to see you soon."

"Why don't I know about these magical empanadas my woman loves?" Evan scoffs.

Antonio levels him with a glare that only a best friend like Evan would be able to survive. "Take it easy on the *my woman* stuff, Casanova. Give a brother a minute to warm up to this… change of dynamic."

Evan gives Antonio a pat on the shoulder. "Sorry, Tony, but this has been a long time in the making. Hard to reel all that back in." He winks at Amelia.

Between the disgustingly cute couple and the man ignoring my existence, I realize that this is my cue to get the hell outta here. I slide off the bed and grab my scarf from where it's hanging off the nightstand next to me.

"And here I thought I was about to get the four-one-one on the adventures of Nikki's love life. Or lack thereof."

"Tony!" Amelia starts.

I take a deep breath before I speak. "Two," I say as I loop my scarf around my neck while meeting Antonio's gaze head on.

"Pardon?" He raises an amused brow.

"I gave you two free passes to make snarky remarks about me and my love life. And I've so generously gifted you those opportunities, because, although you have the emotional intelligence of that empanada Amelia is inhaling, you are the bonehead who saved her life. So yeah. Two is all you're getting. Try for a third, and I promise I won't hesitate to hit below the belt."

Antonio shakes his head while blowing out a breath. "Singledom makes you cranky," he mocks as he places his hands in his pockets and slowly starts to round the bed toward me. "And threatening a police officer? No need to get so pissy. If you stick to your usual rinse and repeat schedule, I'm sure the next Mr. Right will make an appearance any day now." He smirks as he finally comes face to face with me.

Or more so my face to his chest.

Evan whisper-shouts, "This is going to get ugly," while theatrically placing his hands over Amelia's ears.

She swats his hands away while counting down softly. "Three… two… one…"

She knows me too well.

While that comment did hit a nerve, I'd never let it show. I'll attack first and save the tears for the long, hot shower calling my name.

But for now, it's time to knock this man down a peg or two.

"I'm sorry. Shouldn't you be at work right now?" I look at my wrist, where my nonexistent watch is. "Oh, right." I wince dramatically. "You've been downgraded to errand boy around here since you've been suspended." A flash of *something* crosses Antonio's features at the mention of his work troubles, but he quickly covers it up with his signature scowl, so I carry on. "Well, look on the bright side. You can use the next few weeks to work on your people skills. Maybe even convince an unsuspecting woman that there's more to you than popcorn muscles and a badge." I give his chest a few patronizing pats.

Geez. Definitely no popcorn muscles here. Feels like I'm slapping a marble counter.

Before I can pull my hand away, he grabs my wrist and… *growls*? Did this man seriously just growl? What kind of acoustics does he carry in that massive chest of his?

While I continue my internal tangent, he leans in close. Too close for me not to notice his thick, dark eyelashes. The kind women would pay hundreds of dollars for. They're currently unmoving since he has his gaze pinned on me. "I may be suspended, but I can still put you in handcuffs," he says so low I'm the only one who can hear him.

I gasp and try to pull away, but he keeps my hand pinned to his chest.

"Okay, that's enough, Tony. Leave Nikki alone," Amelia shouts.

"Oh, come on, Amelia. We're all friends here." He quirks his lips. "Right *Nicolette?*"

A zap of electricity, along with a deluge of old memories, comes flooding to the forefront of my mind. My mask of indifference slips for just a moment, but it's long enough for Antonio to notice, given the look on his face.

"Stop it! You guys and your constant bickering. It's stressing me out!" Amelia whines.

Evan immediately gets up and caresses her cheek. "You look a bit flushed, babe. Why don't we all clear out and let you take a nap?"

"No! I don't need a nap, Evan." She starts waving her hands between Antonio and me. "I need… I need… huh." Her face morphs from annoyed to serene.

"Babe, are you okay? Your smile is giving off the Joker vibes. Super cute and sexy, of course. But yeah, a little creepy," Evan stutters.

Amelia smiles widely while looking at Antonio and me. "Guys, I love you both *so* much."

The three of us groan in unison. This is how she starts when she has a big ask.

"Oh hush. This is more for you two than for me. But I really would appreciate it if you went along with it."

"Spit it out, Amelia. And just know the answer is probably no if it includes Nikki," Antonio says.

Amelia sits up higher on the bed. "Antonio, you know you're my literal lifesaver, my favorite brother—"

"Only brother," he mutters under his breath.

"Okay, fine." Amelia drops the sweet act and goes full scary Latina mother in two seconds flat. "Nikki is right. You need something to do now that you have all this free time."

"Imma stop you right there. The moment you start a sentence with *Nikki is right*, that's my cue to—"

"*Callate la boca* and let me finish!" Amelia shouts.

The rest of us are stunned into silence. And far too terrified to move a muscle.

Amelia clears her throat. "Like I was saying. Tony, you need something to do. Or better yet, you should be rewarded for saving my life, not sulking over a suspension that's only happening due to 'optics,' as your department claims. So I'll cut to the chase." She gives Evan a quick look, one that even he, in his love-stricken state, can't decipher. "Evan and I are sending you *both* on an all-expenses paid vacation."

"And here I thought I was special," I say as Antonio sputters, "What? Absolutely not."

Evan's eyes widen to cartoonish proportions. "Um, babe. How about we discuss this first before—"

Amelia steamrolls Evan and carries on. "You are special, Nikki. Coincidentally, the people in this room are the most important people in my life. Which is why I'm asking… actually, no, scratch that. I'm notifying you that you will be going on a one-week vacation. Together."

Momentary silence fills the room before Antonio starts laughing uncontrollably. "Good one, sis. You almost had me there."

Amelia doesn't crack a smile. In fact, she crosses her arms over her chest and challenges his gaze.

"Sis, c'mon. you've got to be joking, right?" He looks at me. "She's joking. She can't be serious." He clears his throat. "Right?"

I roll my eyes and take pity on the man. I zero in on my

best friend, who looks like she's gearing up for a fight. "Amelia." I smile broadly. "Love you lots. But this is a bit much. Your brother and I can barely tolerate being in the same room. How do you expect us to go on a vacation together, of all things?"

"The same way he's holding your hand to his chest while your arm is slack. It's been like that for the past five minutes." She pointedly looks at where we're connected and shrugs. "But who's counting." I barely register the smug look on her face before Antonio and I both take massive leaps backward to create distance between us.

What the hell?

Did we really have most of that conversation with Amelia and Evan while… touching?

And why is my heart trying to beat out of my chest?

Simmer down, broad.

Amelia laughs and continues. "Look, guys. You've both been there for me during this insane time, and I appreciate it so much. No one deserves a vacation more than a woman getting over a breakup and a man who risked his career to save his little sister." Her eyes start to well with tears. "Antonio, you haven't taken time off in years. *Years*. And Nikki, we already offered you this trip, and you said yes. You can't back out now. Please let Evan and me do this for you guys."

I chance a glance at Antonio.

Why is his chest rising and falling as rapidly as mine? What kind of weird twilight zone did we enter that has me considering going on vacation with this man?

Evan kisses Amelia's hand and continues for her. "Look, guys, this might actually be a great thing for you both." Antonio and I mirror each other by giving Evan a dubious look. "Hear me out first." He puts his hands up. "You'll be flown out on my jet, so you'll have no time to kill each other in an airport security line. Then you'll get your own rooms on what I'm sure will be a massive resort, and you'll probably only see each other in passing. Or, if you're lucky, when the trip is over and you meet up on the plane. Just think of it as carpooling to different vacations happening at the same location." Evan shrugs.

Damn it. When you put it like that, it really doesn't seem like a big deal. I bite my thumb as I ponder what my rebuttal should be. Surely Antonio would never agree to this. When I look over at him, his eyes are already on me.

He takes a deep breath. "Amelia—"

"I almost died, Tony. You saved my life." Amelia looks down at her hands and then delivers the final blow that will seal our fate. "Mom would want you to go," she whispers.

All heads in the room bow, and shoulders slump.

The ultimate trump card. Antonio and Amelia's late mother, Anna.

We all know there's no fighting this, and Amelia knows it too, given the tiny smirk she's so desperately trying to hide.

I run my hands through my hair, then place them on my hips. After taking a few deep breaths, I nod and wave at Antonio. "Well?" I ask expectantly.

Antonio closes his eyes and groans. When he straightens, he looks at me and nods.

We all turn toward Amelia.

"So, babe, where are we sending these two misfits off to?" Evan asks.

A mischievous grin takes over her face. "Buckle up, you two. You're spending New Year's Eve in the Dominican Republic."

2

NIKKI

I THOUGHT FLYING PRIVATE MEANT I WOULDN'T HAVE TO WAKE up at the ass crack of dawn.

Yet here I am at six a.m., being driven into the private airport entrance by Evan's driver, Teddy.

"What's the point of being rich if you can't even sleep in?" I mumble mostly to myself, but Teddy chuckles.

"Miss Amelia wanted to make sure you got the most out of your trip, and leaving this early means you'll get there before lunchtime."

I look out the window, and I can't lie. Leaving cold and dreary New York City for the beautiful beaches of the Dominican Republic isn't a hard sell. Even if I have to share the plane ride with Mr. Satan's Spawn himself.

When I got home yesterday, I had no idea that Amelia meant that we would be leaving *the next day*. Color me surprised when there was a knock on my door later that evening. It was one of Bergdorf Goodman's personal shoppers. I knew Evan had a lady named Maribel who worked wonders there, but I'd forgotten that he had the kind of pull that could bring people to your doorstep. The woman introduced herself, took my measurements quickly, and left me with cute new carry-on luggage. *She* was the one who broke the news that my new wardrobe would be awaiting me on the private jet today and told me that I should only pack my toiletries and essentials in the carry-on.

I immediately called Amelia, but Evan answered. Apparently, after planning our entire trip in record time, Amelia passed out for the rest of the day, thanks to her pain killers. Evan filled me in on the rest, and now, here I am.

We pull up next to a plane, and Jesus Christ, Amelia was not exaggerating when she said Evan's jet was huge.

I'm still gawking at the monstrosity as Teddy opens my door with a knowing smile. "Your chariot awaits, Ms. Nikki."

I accept his extended hand and get out of the SUV. After taking a deep breath, I decide that this trip will be one to remember. And I can reel in the verbal ass-whooping I was planning on giving my bestie for giving me less than twenty-four hours to prepare for it.

I watch as a male flight attendant makes his way up the stairs of the plane with my luggage already in tow.

I smile at the red carpet leading up to the stairs and shake my head.

"Okay, let's blow this popsicle stand. Thanks for the ride, Teddy." He tries to shake my hand, but I pull him in for a bear hug. I've pinned his upper arms to his side, so he has no other recourse than to awkwardly pat my back.

"Have a nice trip. I'll be here to pick you up when you're back." With a small salute, Teddy turns around and opens the driver's side door.

"Welcome, Ms. Nikki. We're ready for you to board." I turn around to see a cute blond flight attendant. Her hair and makeup are impeccable. What time did she get up to look this put together?

I offer an awkward wave and realize that I have this woman

standing in the freezing cold while she waits for me to get a move on.

"Ah, of course. Yep. Super ready! Lead the way, please." I wave toward the plane.

"After you. I insist." She places one hand on her stomach and points toward the plane with the other like one of those airline demonstration videos.

"Oh. All right. Okie dokie," I say as I make my way to the plane. Gosh, I would suck as a rich person. Why am I so awkward right now?

I've successfully made it up the stairs and onto the plane when my jaw drops.

Holy cannoli, this plane is stunning. Are there *Architectural Digest* magazines for planes? Because this one would take the cake.

I'm afraid to touch anything. Everything screams money. From the massive ivory-colored seats to the lavish couches and tables that adorn the sides of the plane.

The male flight attendant opens a closet next to me and offers to take my coat.

"We also have your garment bag and luggage that were delivered from Bergdorf Goodman. We'll make sure the gown travels safely by keeping it here during the flight." He offers a warm smile.

"Gown?" I whisper, but before he can respond, a door at the back of the plane opens, and out walks Antonio.

How does he still look like a giant in this massive aircraft? More importantly, why does he look insanely attractive in a gray hoodie, black track pants, and Nike sneakers?

Our eyes meet, and his impassive face turns into a scowl.

Right on schedule.

"You're late. As usual," he says as a greeting.

"Well, good morning to you too, plane buddy. How'd ya sleep? How's the fam? Good, I hope." I offer a fake smile and make my way toward the closest window seat. To my surprise, Antonio takes the seat across from me.

I raise my eyebrow at him as he leans forward. "Let's just set some ground rules here. I agreed to go on this trip for Amelia, but I'm not gonna be some overqualified bodyguard for you in the event you have too much to drink or lock yourself out of your room."

"Aw, Tony, are you worried about me getting a hangover?" I ask sarcastically.

"Wouldn't be the first time you couldn't handle your liquor," he says as he looks out the window.

My guilt stuns me into silence, and before I can respond, the female flight attendant interrupts us. "Can I get you guys anything before we take off? Coffee, tea, or perhaps some champagne?" She smiles sweetly, but only has eyes for Antonio.

I roll my eyes. Not like she would notice anyway. "I'll have champagne; lord knows I'll need it."

"Nervous flier?" she asks.

"Nope. Just celebrating being in such great company." I wink in Antonio's direction.

The flight attendant uncomfortably shuffles from one foot to the other. "And a glass for you, sir?" She clears her throat, not knowing what to make of us as we openly stare each other down.

"Why not? It's not like it's six a.m. or anything." He shrugs, then turns his megawatt smile on. Just for her.

The poor woman almost faints right then and there. "Co-coming right up. I'm Cortney, if you need anything," she says three octaves too high for such an early hour.

I watch as she walks to the front of the plane and starts opening a bottle of Veuve Clicquot.

"It's Antonio."

I turn my attention to Mr. Grumpy Pants. "Huh?"

"You called me Tony. Only my friends and family call me Tony," he says pointedly.

I release an unattractive snort.

This guy can't be serious. I mean, I get it. We didn't get off on the right foot. But it's been seven years. We've both clearly moved on from that night. I mean…

"Here you go. Cheers!" Cortney says delightfully. She starts to walk away but stops and turns her attention back to us. "Oh, make sure to keep hold of those glasses. Captain says we'll be flying through some light turbulence this morning." Then she disappears.

Thanks, Cortney. But I could have already called the fact that this would be a bumpy ride.

3

NIKKI

Four hours later, I finally unclench my ass cheeks.

It felt as though we flew through a hurricane, not the light turbulence Cortney warned us of. If this is any indication of how this week is going to go, I should probably go ahead and book myself a one-way on a cruise ship to start slowly sailing back home.

"We've landed. You can stop white-knuckling the armrests. I'm sure you've left a dent in the fabric," Antonio says smugly.

I release my death grip and run my hands up and down the fabric. Don't need Evan to threaten me with an upholstery bill.

"How were you able to sleep through that? I thought we were going down at least three times." I huff as the flight attendants start the deplaning process.

Antonio shrugs. "It wasn't that bad."

Okay, sociopath.

A man decked out in Dominican customs gear walks onto the plane and makes a beeline for us.

Whoa, holy hot balls. This guy looks like he could be related to Antonio. What is in the water here? And can I drink it without being chained to a toilet?

"Pasaportes?" the customs hottie asks with a wink in my direction.

Fanny flutters: Activated.

As I openly check out Officer Ortega, Antonio makes quick work of handing over our passports and the documentation we had to fill out. During the flight, he took my passport from my bag and filled out my customs paperwork when I was unable to open my eyes due to paralyzing fear.

Officer Ortega opens my passport first and smiles. "Nicolette McClane." He raises his eyebrows. "Oh, como *Die Hard.*" He laughs.

Fanny flutters: Deactivated.

I hate my legal name.

I hate how it's just another part of a life based on lies.

And I especially hate the *Die Hard* references. Which is why Officer Ortega can go ahead and wrap up this process and get a move on.

Antonio seems to notice my shift in mood and quirks a questioning eyebrow in my direction.

My cheeks flush at his perceptiveness. In my attempt to hide my physical reaction, I roll my eyes with extra flair and hope that he'll ignore me.

Like he usually does.

After we've completed the process, Officer Ortega tries to make small talk with me while I politely nod and smile. I'm dying to stand and stretch since I spent the last four hours wound tighter than a spring, but he's currently blocking my exit path.

As if Antonio can read my thoughts, he unfolds himself and stands at his full height, then moves to stand next to my new chatty sidekick. With a firm pat on his shoulder and a few words exchanged in Spanish, Officer Ortega nods at us, welcomes us to the Dominican Republic, and hightails it off the plane.

That's odd.

"What did you tell him?" I ask as I stand to stretch. *God, that feels good.*

Antonio ignores my question and wiggles my passport in front of my face. "Just remember to keep one thing in mind. You have an American passport, and you have that Malibu Barbie thing going on, so the men here will be like white on rice for you."

I scrunch up my face. "Huh?"

Antonio sighs deeply as he drops my documents back into my open purse. "Your passport, your all-American look, they're like beacons to the working-class men here." He brushes past me to walk toward the plane exit. "You're their golden ticket out of this country. A fast-track to a green card. So remember that the next time you turn into putty with a simple wink."

He's bolted off the plane before I've even had time to gasp.

That asshole.

How dare he? As if I was putty.

Okay, maybe a teeny tiny smidge. But that interest burned out faster than it started. Plus, what is it to him anyway?

I swear that man is insufferable.

At least I'm officially done with him until this vacation is over. That thought alone is enough to spring me into action and haul my ass off this plane. It's time to finally enjoy paradise.

My excitement is short-lived when I spot Antonio loading himself into a very sleek, very tiny, black helicopter.

You've gotta be kidding me.

Cortney meets me at the bottom of the plane stairs as the helicopter's propellers start to come alive. "The resort you're going to is only accessible by boat or helicopter ride. Helicopter is the fastest. You'll be there in ten minutes." She smiles softly. My face must be giving away how hesitant I am to get on another aircraft after the flight from hell.

"Um, yeah. Okay." I nod, mostly to myself, while she guides me to my next ass-clenching adventure. "Okay, I can do this. Just ten minutes."

I take a seat by the open door, making sure to leave the middle one vacant for Antonio's grumpy attitude. He's too busy staring out his own window to pay me any mind anyway.

Once my door is closed and locked, I'm instructed to put on a headset with an attached mic. "Bienvenidos a La República Dominicana," the helicopter pilot chirps in my ears. I smile and nod in his direction. Just as I'm about to regale him with my nonaccented *gracias*, the aircraft makes a swift vertical move, and we're in the air. My hands immediately grab the seat cushions on each side of me, and I accidentally let out a very non-ladylike squeal.

I try to focus on the beautiful palm trees and crystal-clear waters coming into view below me, but I can't seem to shake off the nerves from the earlier plane turbulence.

Without warning, Antonio takes hold of my left hand. For a split second, and without my permission, my heart swoons at the idea that he's attempting to soothe my frayed nerves.

"Interesting." He raises our joined hands. "With your track record, it's astonishing that you haven't conned a man or two into giving you an engagement ring."

My eyes widen to comical proportions. "*Excuse me?*"

He tugs my hand closer to his face and examines my ring finger closely. "See, not even a small tan line on this finger. Must be one of life's unsolved mysteries."

I tear my hand out of his grip and give his shoulder a hard shove.

His body doesn't move an inch, except for the smug look that forms on his face.

"What is wrong with you? Who says shit like that to women? And when did I say I wanted to be engaged or even married?" I scoff. "How barbarian of you."

"So marriage isn't the goal? Could have fooled me with the revolving door of hopefuls. Taking serial monogamy to the next level."

"Wow. That's real rich coming from Mr. Love 'Em and Leave 'Em. Pardon me for having meaningful relationships instead of a *revolving door* of one-night stands."

"I have a full transparency policy. Women know exactly what they're signing up for when they spend the night with me."

I roll my eyes. "Tarzan chest banging and grunts?"

"The best sex of their life." He smirks.

I can't contain the laughter that bursts out of me. "Oh wow. You really are something, aren't you?" I swipe away a single tear. "I'll tell you what. If what you're packing below the belt is a fraction of the size of your ego, then maybe you're not a total dud in the sack." I pause. "But all signs are pointing to the most common clinical diagnosis."

His smile widens. "Lay it on me."

"Little dick syndrome." I put my hand on his thigh and wince dramatically. "And I'm sorry to report, but the condition is permanent."

Antonio surprises me by throwing his head back and barking out a glorious laugh. "Oh man, say it isn't so, doc." He puts his hand over his heart. "You wound me." His laughter starts to die down. "Although I must say, your hand seems to want to verify for itself. For scientific purposes, of course."

Before I get lost in the fact that my hand looks so tiny placed on his thigh, I snatch it back and return it to its rightful place on my lap, then straighten in my seat. At that exact moment, the helicopter decides to take a sharp turn and drop.

I forcefully close my eyes and clench every body part humanly possible. Kegels included.

It's amazing how many ways I curse out Amelia in my head during these few rocky seconds. I'm so enthralled in my imaginary assault that it takes me a minute to realize that my hand is back in Antonio's. I open my eyes, and before I attempt to regain custody of my extremity, Antonio asks, "How many?"

Huh?

He takes in my Scooby Doo expression and lifts my hand as he continues. "Show of hands; how many cats do you intend to adopt to keep you company since marriage is off the table?"

I swear I can feel laser beams forming in my eyes as I give him what I hope to be the most intimidating look possible.

But I'm sure I probably look constipated instead.

Antonio is staring at me like he expects an actual answer. How is this guy possibly related to my sweet angel friend Amelia?

He squeezes my hand and squints. "I can see two. Three tops. You know, with New York City apartments being so tiny and all. But if anyone can pull it off, I know it's you." He fakes a smile.

I squeeze my hand in his. Hard. Hoping my nails are creating satisfying half-moons on his tan skin.

His smile reaches his eyes this time, and he whispers, "There she is."

Just as I'm about to transfer all my prior imaginary insults planned for Amelia to him, I feel a light jolt. "We've landed. Welcome to paradise. And in my opinion, two cats are ideal," the helicopter copilot says in a British accent.

Awkward.

Antonio releases my hand so fast that it ends up falling on the seat between us. "Finally. Consider my distraction tactics as my good deed for this trip. Don't expect it on the way back."

What the hell? "You mean you being your usual asshole self and all that hand holding? Yeah, thanks, but no thanks."

We remove our headsets and unbuckle ourselves in silence. Until Mr. Needs to Have the Last Word speaks. "You know what? You're right. Next time, instead of engaging in mind numbing-conversation with you, I'll just let you white-knuckle your way through the helicopter ride. No sweat off my back." He shrugs.

"Oh please. That was just a way for you to once again talk shit about my dating life while also boasting about your sex life. At least you were man enough to agree that you're not packing much heat." I turn to face him, only to realize he's already hopped out of the helicopter.

I reach for the door, only for it to slide open and reveal Antonio standing in front of me. How is he still taller than me while I sit on an elevated helicopter? "For the record, *Nicolette*, you brought up my penis size in the conversation, not me. So what does that tell me about where your mind's at?"

I open my mouth to respond, but my brain is too busy replaying the tape back and realizing that I was the one who mentioned it first.

Dammit.

He leans all the way into the aircraft. Until his lips are faintly brushing my ear. I suck in a breath at his proximity. Looking at Antonio is hard enough sometimes, but being wrapped in his scent should be straight-up illegal. I need to take a trip to the perfume department because I need to find a way to track down this scent that can only be described as ruggedly masculine man.

I turn my head to look at him and realize I've made a big mistake.

His usual scowl is replaced by tender eyes and soft lips. The fanning of his eyelashes almost puts me in a hypnotic state, where I don't even realize that I'm leaning into him.

But he does.

And just as quickly as before, I have a front-row seat to his walls being put back up. Right where they've always been.

He reaches behind me and grabs his baseball hat that was left on the seat between us. Of course.

He clears his throat as he straightens himself. "And for the record, If I wanted to keep my hands off you while keeping your mind on my penis, all I had to do was tell you that I'm a size fourteen shoe." He pulls a pair of sunglasses out of his bag and places them on his face as he salutes me and walks off toward to resort doors.

Size fourteen? Holy hell. He must be lying.

I hop out of the flying torture chamber and try to get a good look at his shoes. Not like I would be able to tell, but those sneakers do look massive. Just like the rest of him…

What the hell? What am I thinking?

Gotta keep my head outta the gutter if I'm going to survive this week.

Luckily, all I have to do now is check in, pick a cute outfit… and change my underwear. Then all traces of Antonio will be erased until this vacation is over. Until then, I'm off to find the nearest drink with an umbrella in it. Dream vacay, here I come.

4

NIKKI

MIAMI

"What can I get ya?" the handsome bartender asks as he leans across the bar.

"Vodka soda with a splash of cran."

"Coming right up." He knocks twice on the lit-up bar top before making his way toward the other end.

I need this drink, my first of the night. I've been babysitting Amelia all day. Hardly an inconvenience for me since she's always there for me, day or night. But when Amelia starts drinking, she wants everyone to drink with her.

So I may have only had orange juice in my mimosa and water shots instead of vodka. I knew we would be partying tonight and staying out past midnight. Therefore, I made the judgment call to hide my lack of drinking so she didn't feel guilty for letting loose. We all have those moments, especially in our early twenties, and I'm more than happy to let my girl do her thing. Safely.

I turn away from the bar to face the crowd. The booming

bass vibrates on my skin as my dress twinkles below the club's strobe lights. Crowded bodies move to the sensual beat while keeping a close eye on the massive digital clock above the DJ booth that's currently counting down the minutes until midnight. Miami definitely knows how to do nightlife, and there is no shortage of beautiful people.

I was born and raised here, therefore jaded by the novelty of it all. I quickly learned that, for a lot of the people in this city, their lifestyles are just a bunch of smoke and mirrors.

That's why I'm so excited about my move to New York. I can't wait to leave the swamp humidity and experience all four seasons. Abandon I-95 traffic for walking the cool city streets. And most of all, to finally create physical space between me and my mother and our strained relationship. Unlike me, she has yet to learn her lesson about not falling prey to all of Miami's vices. And unfortunately for her, this city is crawling with her kryptonite. Wealthy and emotionally unavailable men.

I, on the other hand, take a different approach when it comes to relationships. I like practicality and understand that nothing is meant to last forever. So I avoid putting my fate in someone else's hands. Not everyone needs to be swept off their feet and I quite like having mine firmly planted on the ground.

I know. Someone out there is probably thinking "who hurt you, girl?" And honestly, the answer is no one. My mom went through enough emotional turmoil raising me as a single mom that I made the educated decision to abstain from the messy, the unpredictable, and the most volatile emotion on the planet. Love.

Don't get me wrong, I'm a full marshmallow on the inside and am very much capable of love, but I like to think that I hold the capacity to "put a cap on it." Not let it overflow and run my life.

Case in point, Amelia. Poor thing is a mess after breaking up with her on-again, off-again boyfriend. Someone who is clearly not suited for her, and she very well knows this. And yet you can expect her to be out of commission for a minimum of twenty to twenty-five business days because she needs to "mourn the relationship appropriately."

I'm perfectly fine with *giving* love to the men I end up in relationships with, but I will never allow myself to fall in love. I mean, the fact that I have to *fall* already seems like such an unsafe concept.

So instead, I'm the one who loves less and leaves first.

"Here's your drink." The bartender slides the drink toward me as I dig into my clutch to grab my debit card.

"It's on me," says the jittery man to my left. His eyes are wild, and he can't seem to stop moving his weight from one foot to another.

Growing up in a party city, you quickly learn to look for the warning signs, and this guy is definitely on an upper. Must have partaken in some nose candy in the bathrooms earlier in the night and is looking for someone to ride the high with. Or just someone to ride *him*.

"Oh, thank you, but I'm all set." I push my card toward the bartender and widen my eyes a bit, giving him the universal girl signal to ignore the man beside me. He nods and reaches for my card as the guy next to me tries to intercept with his own card.

"Come on. One drink, babe. It's New Year's Eve." He tries to smolder at me but instead gives me a squinty look with a slight eye twitch.

"Like I said, I'm good. Thanks anyway." The bartender reaches to my right, and I'm able to finally hand him my card. He nods and holds my gaze for a second, secretly letting me know that he'll keep an eye on the situation.

I honestly hate that I live in a world where a silent language needs to be created in order for a woman to feel safe out in the world, but this isn't my first rodeo. This is my city, and I can tell this guy isn't a local, so I'll be damned if a tourist puts a damper on my last New Year's Eve in my hometown.

Without ever taking my eyes off my drink, I go to grab it, but yet again, this guy intercepts.

"Sweetheart, let me take care of you tonight. This party is just getting started, if you know what I mean." He sniffles and rubs his reddening eyes.

I fully cover my drink with my right hand as I face him, not giving a damn if I'm being obvious about the fact that I absolutely think this guy would spike my drink. "Listen, buddy, I'm not interested. Best you focus your efforts on drinking some water and staying hydrated. You're looking a bit thirsty." I couldn't help myself with that last bit. I really do try and hold back when it comes to guys like this because they're so unpredictable. But what can I say? I have a mouth on me.

Right on cue, his bruised ego makes an appearance as his dilated pupils darken and he invades my personal space. Before he can get any closer, I feel the hair on the back of my neck stand, and a dominating presence looms over us. For some reason, my body isn't reacting to it as danger. The loser next to me must not notice, because he's still sneering in my direction.

"I'm going to need you to step the fuck away from her." A deep, rich voice speaks from behind me. So close I can feel him everywhere, with his breath cascading down my neck, even though he isn't actually touching me.

I keep my focus on the drink in front of me while urging my body to stand straight instead of leaning back into the magnetic pull this faceless stranger has on me. Startled, the man next to me moves back an inch and volleys his attention from me to the mystery man behind me. "Oh, are you gonna lie and tell me she's your girlfriend or something? Don't worry, she doesn't need rescuing from me. We're just ironing out our plans for the night, so if you don't mind—"

"I mind," he declares, as his dominance vibrates off his chest.

I'm no damsel in distress, but damn if those two words don't have me weak in the knees and looking for his white horse to ride off into the sunset, or Collins Drive in this instance.

Without giving the man a chance to speak, my mystery man behind me continues. "And for the record, I don't need to lay claim to any woman in order to protect her from creeps like you. So in an attempt to level the scales for all the men out there, I'm going to step in. Every time. For every woman. Regardless of who she is to me. Now, I'm going to tell you one more time to step the fuck away from her." He pauses for a moment. "Make me tell you a third time, and you won't make it till the New Year. Test me."

Whoosh. And that, ladies and gentlemen, was the sound of my panties incinerating.

At this point, my curiosity can no longer hold out. I turn in place, and my breath catches. The music fades to the background, and I don't even notice the moment in which the creep skedaddles. My eyes are on the mountain of a man who stands in front of me. I'm in heels, and I only reach the barrel of his chest. He's dressed in all black. Shoes, slacks, and dress shirt. The top buttons tease me with the view of a muscular chest. I crane my neck and immediately find myself drowning in deep caramel brown eyes. All traces of roughness have been erased from them. Only concern remains.

"Are you okay?" he asks.

I nod. "Uh yeah. Thank you for that," I say, breathier than intended.

He notices and smiles, because, of course, he must know the effect he has on women. And with the alpha man rescue act? Oh God. I never stood a chance.

He chuckles. "I'm just going to order a drink and then I'll

be out of your hair." He hesitates. "But can I know your name? I'm not trying to swoop in and be the next creep in line, I promise." He smiles, and I turn into complete mush. The man has the most beautiful smile I've ever seen, wide and bright, with the most adorable dimple on his right cheek. *And that voice.*

But as much as my lady bits are going wild, you can never be too careful. Even serial killers can be handsome. So I give him the name I tell all men at clubs. "I'm Nicolette." Which is not a lie; it's my legal name. But no one has ever called me Nicolette. I've always been Nikki. Yet it always feels safer to have a stranger call me that instead of the name my loved ones use.

"Nicolette," he says with reverence, a hint of a Spanish accent slipping into my name. In that moment, I'm contemplating never having anyone call me Nikki ever again. "Nice to meet you, Nicolette. I'm Tony."

Tony.

He holds out a hand so massive it could be a baseball mitt. I slip my small hand into his to shake but still when my body feels like it's burning up in flames. Slowly, the sensation runs from my hand, all the way up my arm, until I can feel it all the way down to my toes.

I look up at him and watch an unreadable expression flash over his face and his mouth gape slightly. I can feel the moment he sucks in a breath and lightly squeezes my hand. All attempts of normal handshakes are clearly forgotten by both of us.

Our connection is broken by two knocks on the bar. The bartender looks at me and my untouched drink. "Need me to change that out for you?" He gives a pointed look to Tony, then my drink.

I give him a genuine smile. "No, thank you. I'm all right. But can you get my new friend here a drink? On me?" The bartender visibly relaxes, knowing I'm no longer in danger.

"Absolutely not. I can buy my own drink, and yours, for the

matter. Put her on my tab." Tony releases my hand, then reaches into his back pocket to grab his wallet. The motion causes his shirt to stretch around his bulging biceps and allows his cologne to reach me. God, is this what a man is supposed to smell like? I feel like my peers are still weening off using Axe body spray.

Focus, girl.

I turn on my sass. "Are you saying that a woman can't buy a man a drink? It is the twenty-first century, you know." I fold my arms over my chest and pop a hip out.

Tony tracks the movements as a grin takes over his face. "Oh, I wouldn't dare say that." He chuckles. "I just mean that any woman in my presence is always taken care of."

I raise an eyebrow, fully aware of the innuendo he's throwing down. "Well, then, how about if, for tonight, you allow me the pleasure of taking care of you, *Tony?*"

He tilts his head while rubbing his lower lip with this thumb, as if thinking over my offer. The little shit thinks he's making me sweat.

He turns to the bartender. "You heard the lady. I'm a kept man for the night." He turns to me with playful eyes. "I'll have whatever IPA you got." The bartender nods and grabs a bottle from the mini fridge behind him. He uncaps the beer and slides it over to Tony without either of us breaking eye contact.

We tilt our drinks toward one another. "So what should we toast to?" I ask.

He looks away pensively for a moment, a smile playing on his lips. His eyes return to meet mine when he says, "A night we'll never forget."

5

ANTONIO
PRESENT

SAMANÁ, DOMINICAN REPUBLIC

I think I almost hate-kissed her.

Is that even a thing?

I'm a thirty-five-year-old man for fucks sake. I don't hate kiss.

Not even five whole hours of travel time, and I've already proven that coming here with her was a bad idea. Although the look on her face does offer some consolation. She's affected by being around me as well.

If only she would remember.

Nope. Not going there. And while we're at it, I need to stop calling her Nicolette as if it's going to kick start her memory. I haven't uttered that name in what feels like a lifetime, yet here I am, letting it roll right off my tongue. You'd think that seven years would be enough time to get over… nothing. Absolutely nothing happened, and that's what I've got to keep reminding myself of in order to survive this trip.

This goddamn trip.

Why couldn't Evan and Amelia ship me off to a different island? It's not like they're strapped for cash. My little sister has no idea that my best friend is about to make her a billionaire via marriage. Can't believe that's a real sentence in my head.

And while I appreciate the people I love looking out for me, I truly don't know what I've done to deserve having to pay this penance. I saved my sister's life from a raging lunatic, and she ships me off with the one person I can't stand being in a room with.

The woman who leaves a trail of broken hearts wherever she goes.

The woman who gallivants through life like she's untouchable.

The woman who is the absolute worst.

Which is why I need to constantly remind myself of who this woman will always be to me.

The woman who won't fucking remember.

As I near the entrance of the hotel, I can hear Nikki straggling along behind me. I focus on the cabana style entryway as I step up a handful of stairs. Once the rest of the hotel has come into view, I'm greeted by a man in a suit... and about a staff of twenty people. Shit, is this a cult?

"Good morning, Mr. Nuñez and Ms. McClane. Welcome to the Barlowe. My name is Frobish, and I am the manager of this oasis, here to assist you with all of your needs for the duration of your stay. Behind me is our staff. They will work around the clock to make sure that your every wish is our command," he says in a thick Russian accent. He then flicks two fingers in the air, and two men with trays that hold tiny white sugar-cube looking things walk up to us.

Before we're given any instructions, Nikki dives in and pops one into her mouth. The choir of muted gasps lets me know not to take her lead.

With her mouth full, Nikki states, "Oh. Um, yum. But I had one of these earlier, so I'm just gonna…" She spits it into her hand and drops it onto the tray.

Classy.

One of the tray-holding men clears his throat, then proceeds to produce a tea kettle out of what seems like thin air and runs it over the cube. The hot water causes it to grow… into a hand towel? Once it has reached its full size, this magician pulls out tiny tongs and hands me the steaming towel.

As I run it over my hands, I can smell lemon and lavender. I can't help but chance a glance at Nikki, whose cheeks have taken on a rosy color. "Interesting. Did you eat a hand towel before your omelet on the plane or after?" I smirk.

"Anywho. Lovely place you got here. But this guy, with his big ole feet and big ole bunions, probably wants to check in and take a nice long nap in his room. Isn't that right, Tony?" She taps my arm.

And there she goes, calling me Tony again.

"Bunions. Really, Nikki?"

Frobish chuckles quietly. "This isn't a normal vacation experience, Ms. McClane."

"Nikki."

"Of course, Ms. Nikki. Your documents, payment, and everything else we need were collected at the time of booking. Once you deboarded from your plane, our systems corroborated your identities. So now all that is left to do is to join me on the golf cart so that I can show you the over-the-water bungalow you and Mr. Nuñez will be sharing during your stay."

I hear an immediate hissing sound. And if not for Nikki being right next to me, I would have thought a tropical snake had made its way to greet us.

"What the hell are you doing, Nikki?"

"Sorry." She blushes. "Just wanted to make sure I heard Frobish's beautiful accent correctly. Just adding an *s* to *bungalow*. You know, bungalowsss. That's all. Please carry on." She nods at Frobish. He looks at her as if she's grown a second head.

I don't blame him.

"Actually." Frobish Americanizes his English a bit more. "You heard my beautiful accent correctly. We have you both staying at the best bungalow we have to offer. Provides the best sunset view on the island." He preens.

Wait, what?

"I'm sorry. There seems to be some kind of misunderstanding. Nikki and I are supposed to be in different rooms. On opposite sides of the island, preferably. Can you double check that you've got the right reservation?"

Frobish gives an order in Russian, and the staff behind him quickly disappear.

"Mr. Nuñez, when the bungalow suite was booked, it was under both of your names. One suite was booked. Not two individual ones." He picks up a tablet from a side table and flips it toward me to show me our reservation details.

He's right.

"Well, I'm sorry, but that just won't do. Can you just put me in another suite? Doesn't have to be a fancy bungalow. Anything on this island is fine." Nikki shrugs nervously.

Frobish clears his throat. "We are an exclusive thirteen suite resort. There are no more available suites Ms. Nikki. It is December twenty-ninth. This week has been booked solid for almost a year. The only reason we were able to accommodate you was due to a last-minute cancellation, and a Ms..." He looks down at his tablet. "Amelia Nuñez paid four times the suite's value to assure she skipped the waitlist and secure this room."

I'm going to kill my little sister.

"Okay, I'll deal with Amelia after. Can you please direct me to another resort? As beautiful as this place is, I'll have Nikki stay while I go elsewhere. Just give me a name, and I can call them myself."

Frobish winces. "Like I said, it's two days before New Year's Eve. We are the only hotel on this small island, and everything from here to Santo Domingo is booked. I'm afraid that, unless you fly back today, your only option is to stay in the suite together. But I promise you, our three thousand square foot bungalow will leave nothing to be desired. There is more than enough room to accommodate the both of you."

"Oh, Well, yeah. Okay. Beggars can't be choosers and all that." Nikki stiffens. "Not that this place is a consolation prize or anything. It's stunning. So pretty. Very romantic. If I wasn't stranded here with Mr. Bunion—"

"Nikki, for the love of God, please shut up."

"Yep. Uh-huh. Doing that now." She nods repeatedly.

Frobish gestures for us to board a small golf cart. Nikki and I ride side by side in silence.

This can't be happening.

My chest tightens at the idea of sharing a room with Nikki.

I have to keep telling myself it'll be fine. Closer quarters than ideal, but he did mention it being three thousand square feet. That's larger than the average home in Florida. I wouldn't be surprised if there were multiple bedrooms. Or, at the very least, a pullout couch. Fancy hotels love over-furnishing rooms. Yep. It should be all good. Nikki and I will probably be out at the beach the whole day anyway, so we'll only have to cross paths once it's time for bed.

Again, not ideal.

But it's not like there's anything I can do about it.

The golf cart comes to a stop in front of our over-the-water bungalow. I was so spaced out I didn't even realize we'd driven over a skinny bridge that has led us far out into the ocean, although the water doesn't seem very deep.

The bungalow suite itself looks like something straight out of Amelia's Pinterest boards. I'm sure I've seen videos of places like this all over Instagram, but a small screen doesn't do it justice.

And as predicted, it's massive. Looks like it's two stories too. So steering clear from Nikki shouldn't be a problem. The realization has me easing the tension in my shoulders.

The three of us hop off the golf cart, and Frobish leads the way. He opens our front door with a flamboyant *voilà* and steps aside for us to enter first.

Nikki gasps. "Holy—"

"Shit," I say.

Unlike Nikki, I'm not looking at the panoramic views of the ocean. Or the clear view into the bathroom on the second floor. And I'm sure as hell not focusing on the outdoor area, which has a netted hammock, a hot tub, and a massive pool on our deck.

Nope. I'm looking at the final nail in my coffin. The one mocking me from the center of the room. The one slight detail that's going to be the death of me.

One. Fucking. Bed.

No couch in sight. Not even a measly footstool. Why did this resort decide to go full minimalistic for a massive bungalow?

While Nikki is busy picking her jaw off the ground, Frobish smiles at us expectantly.

I wave my finger in a circle around us. "So I'm guessing there's no other sleeping area on the roof? No rollaway cot?"

Frobish literally clutches his pearls... on the brooch he's wearing.

"Mr. Nuñez, we are not a, as you say, *rollaway cot* type of experience. But as you can see, there is a California king bed in this suite. More than enough room for the both of you." He nods toward the bed. "Now, I shall leave you to get settled. The white button by the door calls your personal butler, and they will provide you with anything you should need."

"Like another bed?" I mutter under my breath.

Frobish acts like he didn't hear me, but the tic in his jaw says otherwise.

He nods at us as he makes his way out of the room, closing the door with a soft click.

Nikki and I stand rooted in place with our eyes locked on one another. I don't know how many minutes pass before the spell is broken by the ringing of Nikki's phone. I can see a picture of Amelia's face light up on the screen. We don matching scowls, and for the first time since I can remember, Nikki and I are about to be on the same team.

6

NIKKI

AMELIA HAS LOST ALL COLOR IN HER FACE BY THE TIME WE'VE finished filling her in on our whole debacle. "Oh my God, you guys. I am so, so sorry! I don't know what happened. I'm a master at planning trips. I have no idea how I could have messed this up so badly." She rubs a hand back and forth over her forehead.

"I do," Evan chimes in smugly. "You've been a little out of it since you've been on pain meds. I had just given you some when you went into full planner mode. I tried to reel you in a bit, but you cursed at me in Spanish."

"I would never." Amelia gasps.

Evan levels her with a mild glare. "I know what *pendejo* means, babe. And it's not a term of endearment."

"Proud of your Spanish comprehension, Evan. But can we get back to our problem here? How the hell am I supposed to spend the week here… with *her*?"

I should be offended by Antonio's disdain while speaking about me, but I agree with him. There is no way in hell that we'll survive a week of this. I need to get the hell outta Dodge ASAP.

"Look, guys, this is my mistake. I'll get on my computer right now and book another place for you. I can't believe I've royally fumbled the bag on this one. Really, I'm so insanely sorry about this." Amelia looks truly dejected. Poor girl has been through the ringer, and I know that gifting us this trip meant so much to her.

Antonio blows out a breath. I can tell he's thinking the same thing. If there's one thing we have in common, it's our love for Amelia. And even though I was mentally cursing her out for putting me on a helicopter, I would never actually want her to feel bad about this. Especially now.

"Amelia, don't sweat it. Honestly. The resort is beautiful, and the restaurant we drove past looks delectable."

"So delectable that Nikki ate a hand towel upon arrival —oof."

I elbow Antonio's side. "You really did pick and plan an amazing vacation. So don't worry about us. Maybe we can fly out and cut the trip short?"

I look to Evan on the screen, but he shakes his head. "We can look at commercial flights if you'd like, but I gave my pilot and crew time off for New Year's. And I truly doubt that after all you've experienced, you want to endure drunken New Year's Eve holiday travel—"

"Not necessary. Like Nikki said, this place is great. We'll manage."

Amelia's eyes go about as wide as mine. Is Antonio finally not acting like a total tool?

"Besides," he starts, "I saw a very luxurious hammock that I'm sure Nikki is dying to spend the night in. Right, champ?" He bumps my shoulder.

"Champ," I mouth to Amelia on the screen as she stifles a laugh.

Evan looks thoughtfully into the camera and says, "You know, this kind of reminds me of—"

"Bye, guys. Love you! Play nice!" Amelia yells quickly before ending the call.

That was abrupt. And odd.

I put my phone in my pocket and face Antonio. This feels awkward now that we're sitting side by side in silence. So, of course, I have the deep need to make it even worse. "Alone at last, huh?" I fake chuckle.

Antonio looks at me like I've officially lost the plot, then points upstairs. "I'm going to take a quick shower. Be gone by the time I'm out." And with that, he starts taking the stairs two at a time.

Well, alrighty, then. Don't have to tell me twice. I ignore the massive luggage Bergdorf Goodman packed for me and go straight to my trusty carry-on. After checking that Antonio can't see me from upstairs, I throw on my red bikini and a white cover-up and slide my feet into my flip-flops. I grab my toiletry bag and look at my reflection in my compact mirror as I apply some light makeup and throw my hair up in a ponytail. After a quick swipe of tinted lip balm, I grab my tote bag and drop in a few essentials, including sunscreen. I have no intention of returning to this room until bedtime, so I'm bringing all I need with me.

I consider it a success when I'm out the door before he's out of the shower. Taking a deep breath, I tell myself for the millionth time today, that this is the beginning of a great vacation. At this point, I have clearly crossed over into delusional territory, but I *am* the queen of *fake it till you make it*.

I only manage a few steps out our front door when a golf cart pulls up in front of me. "G'day, ma'am, I'm Chris. I'm here to provide you a ride to anywhere you need to go." The young man smiles. He doesn't seem a day over twenty.

"Oh, I'm okay. Just walking to the pool over there. I'm a New Yorker. We know how to use our legs and walk everywhere."

Chris chuckles. "Oh, I'd love to go to New York sometime. How about you hop on board and tell me all about it?"

That line might have creeped me out had some other guy said it, but coming from Chris, it sounded so earnest, so I oblige. "Sure. But first you have to tell me why I have yet to run into a single Dominican staff member," I say as I hop onto the golf cart next to him instead of the bench behind him. He goes to protest, but I wave him off as I start to recall.

"First, it was the pilot. He had a British accent. Frobish clearly has a Russian accent. And now, and please forgive me if I'm wrong, but is that an Australian accent I'm picking up from you?"

Chris laughs. "That would be correct. Born and raised in Sydney. And as for the others? I assume they saw the same job postings as me. This place put out ads that offered to pay relocation and visa costs, along with documentation prep and good pay to come work here. At first, I honestly thought it was a joke. But turns out, Mr. Barlowe wanted to make this place feel like its own little world rather than just a small island in the Caribbean, so he threw money at all of us to help make that vision come to fruition."

"Wow, that sounds… a little weird. I'm not gonna lie. But this place is beautiful, so I won't complain," I say as I take in the breathtaking surroundings.

Crystal clear water and white sand surround us as we drive on a skinny bridge toward the impressive cabana that houses the hotel lobby. Perfectly lined palm trees surround the entire property, along with the most beautiful bayahibe roses in every meticulously landscaped bush.

Chris lowers his voice as he continues. "Want to know the weirdest part?" Obviously, kid. "None of us know what Mr. Barlowe looks like. At first, some of us thought he wanted to stay anonymous so he could come to the resort and check up on us when we least expected it, but from what I hear, he hasn't stepped foot on this resort since it was built. Rich people are mad, aren't they?" He quickly turns a deep shade of red. "My apologies, ma'am. I meant—"

"That does sound batshit crazy to me." I laugh, and the relief on his face is palpable. "Besides, I'm not rich, so no offense taken. My friend sent me here as a gift."

His eyebrows shoot up. "Well, then, I guess I need to find me some better mates!" We both laugh as we pull up to the walkway that'll lead me to the resort pool.

"Thank you so much for the ride, Chris. See you around!"

He tips his Barlowe Resort & Spa cap at me and smiles before he drives off.

I make the quick walk toward the pool and stop once it all comes into view. To my left is a stunning restaurant, decorated in whites and blues with wood accents. Dainty chandeliers adorn the ceilings along with tasteful string lights. It makes me feel like my TJ Maxx cover-up doesn't quite make the dress code, so I continue to my right, where the enormous pool is surrounded by ivory and tan loungers. With a handful of over-the-pool cabanas.

Geez. Is this place against placing anything on solid ground?

My eyes land on the view beyond the pool which leads to the clear blue ocean water that I will definitely be taking advantage of later.

I realize that I'm grinning like a fool, and I already feel out of place as it is, so I quickly pick the lounge chair closest to me and settle in. The pool is mostly empty aside from a cute family of three that's hanging out in one of the cabanas. A little girl, who must be no older than five, spots me from the cabana and offers me an exaggerated smile and wave. Her brown hair slips out of her pigtails in the process. I can't help but laugh at her infectious enthusiasm and offer her my own goofy smile and wave.

Our interactions are interrupted when a server comes my way. "Hello, Ms. Nikki. My name is Kelsey. Could I interest you in anything to drink or eat?" *American? No, Canadian accent.*

"Oh, um, sure. Can I see a menu?" I look around me to see if I missed it.

She smiles sweetly at me. "We don't use menus by the pool. Just tell me what you'd like, and the staff will make it for you."

I sit up straight on the lounger. "Hold on. Anything?" I snap my fingers. "Just like that?" I ask, gobsmacked.

Kelsey giggles again. "Yes." She snaps her fingers like I just demonstrated. "Just like that. Chris was right. You are funny."

"Huh, how did you know… never mind." News here must travel quicker than a small town. Noted.

"Just tell me what you typically like to drink and eat, then we'll do all the magic. Trust me."

After I rattle off the most random list of my likes and dislikes, Kelsey takes off toward the restaurant.

I stand to take my cover-up off, and once I'm left in my red bikini, I feel eyes on me. I turn back toward the restaurant just as I connect my gaze with a man who exudes power. Tall, dark, and dangerous. Black hair with a bit of graying by the temples, along with more pronounced crinkles by his eyes as he keeps me pinned in place. His stride doesn't break as he stays locked on me on his way to the restaurant bar.

Discretion isn't my forte, so I force myself to turn around and take my spot on my lounger before I start salivating. Who knew I'd be into older men?

I rummage through my tote bag for my sunscreen and e-reader. Looks like I'll be reading some age-gap romance by the pool today. I slip on my sunglasses just as Kelsey returns with a drink in hand that looks like it could be a fire hazard.

"Um, Kelsey. Is there smoke coming out of that drink?"

She giggles. "There's dry ice in it. Makes the whole drink

bubble up. But don't worry, it's harmless," she says as she hands me the drink.

I take a wary sip and am pleasantly surprised. "Wow, this is delicious. You guys really know what you're doing back there." I take a longer sip of the pink and bubbly martini.

"Actually, the drink we intended for you, along with your lunch, is still being made. That drink was sent over by the gentleman at the bar." She coyly tips her head toward the restaurant.

Oh.

I turn in my lounger to see the hot older gentleman in question smirking at me. He raises his drink in a silent toast, and I return the gesture with a smile. Our silent conversation ends too soon when Kelsey clears her throat. "So, is it safe to say that the man approaching is Mr. Nuñez?" she asks nervously. Probably thinking he's my boyfriend, and I'm out here flirting with a guy that could be his dad.

Oh, mental note to look for that trope for tomorrow's pool read.

"Well, Kelsey, if the guy coming this way has a permanent scowl and is giving off grumpy man vibes, then yes, that should be him." I pause. "Oh, and call him Tony. He hates being called anything else." I laugh inwardly.

"Uh, I wouldn't exactly call it that. Much more like hot bad boy about to throw a woman over his shoulder vibe. I mean, respectfully." She blushes.

Huh?

I turn over to get a peek at who she must be confusing Antonio with and almost spill my entire drink on my chest.

HOLY FUCKITY FUCK.

What? When? How?

Please, God. Why me?

These are the only thoughts able to penetrate my mind while my brain refuses to catch up to the fact that the face that I know to belong to Antonio is attached to a shirtless, muscular, tanned, and *tatted* body. I repeat, tatted! I can literally feel my nipples harden the closer he gets. When did Antonio get tattoos? How did I not know Mr. Straitlaced had ink adorning his bulkiest muscles? I've already had dirty thoughts about the tree trunks he calls thighs, but there's a massive tiger tattoo wrapped around one of them, and now I can't stop thinking about wrapping my hand around—

"Hello, Mr. Tony, is it? My name is Kelsey. May I get you anything?" Kelsey smiles timidly.

Antonio looks down at me and gives me a full body scan before shaking his head subtly. He's clearly not happy with me now that I gave Kelsey the wrong impression about calling him Tony. "Hi there, Kelsey. Yes, *please* call me Tony." He winks at her. Fucking winks! "Can I have a Presidente beer and maybe a food menu?"

She beams at him. Simmer down there, Kels. "Absolutely, Presidente coming right up. And as for food, how about I bring you a variety of plates, tapas style? I'll bring more of whatever you like and will let the chef know what's not your favorite so we can get your food profiles figured out."

Antonio smiles. "Sounds amazing, Kelsey. I'm sure I'll be happy with whatever you bring me."

Wow, so this man does know how to be pleasant. He's just incapable of being cordial with me. Cool. Awesome. Fantastic.

"Be right back!" She takes off flying toward the restaurant. When I look over at the bar, my older mystery man is gone. Bummer. I needed something else to look at other than Antonio.

The devil himself sits in the lounger next to me and makes himself comfortable.

"Really? I thought you'd pick the lounger farthest from me." I raise an eyebrow.

Antonio removes his sunglasses and places them on the side table between us. "We've got some ground rules to set, so we might as well get it out of the way now." He shrugs nonchalantly.

I take off my sunglasses as well. "Are you joking? More ground rules? Have I not been through enough? I haven't even been rid of you for thirty minutes. Can you just, like, sit somewhere else and let me be? And put on a shirt while you're at it. There are children here!" I huff.

Antonio laughs and smiles widely. God, that smile is devastating. Maybe I should be grateful he doesn't unleash it often, because man, oh man.

"I'm sure you can try your very hardest to not openly gawk at me, and I'll make a point to not look below your neck. Deal?" I scoff at his audacity and fold my arms under my chest, which may or may not have made my boobs look even more pronounced. Antonio's eyes dip momentarily. "Real mature." He shakes his head. "Anyway, as I was saying, we need ground rules. Simple stuff that'll get us through this vacation."

A male server comes by to bring me the drink they had intended to make for me. "Hello, Ms. Nikki." His eyes dip to my boobs. "Here is a pomegranate martini." He smiles as he holds it out.

Before I can reach for it, I feel a towel being thrown over me, in time to see Antonio towering over the server as he grabs my drink. "Thanks, bud. Mind checking on that beer for me?"

"Y-yes, sir. Coming right up." He scurries away.

"What the hell? Don't be rude. And why did you throw a towel over me?"

"Because you're cold."

"No, I'm not."

"Well, then care to explain those?" His index finger moves side to side as he points at my chest. Guess my hard nipples *are*, in fact, visible in this top. Fabulous.

I clear my throat. "So, ground rules. Let's discuss." I nod and look forward.

He chuckles darkly as he hands me my drink while also nodding at my half-finished one on the side table. "Double fisting by noon. Can't say I'm surprised," he mutters.

I sit up straighter, forcing the towel to pool at my waist. "Okay, let's hammer this out once and for all. What is your issue with me? And why do you think I'm some kind of drunk? Have Amelia and I had a couple of crazy nights where we've been overserved… by bartending for ourselves? Absolutely. But I am in no way in need of a trip to the Betty Ford Center anytime soon. I can promise you that."

"Well, if a person tends to black out after drinking, that doesn't exactly make them the poster child for responsible drinking."

"Black out? Are you joking? That's only ever happened to me a few times. And they were in my early college days when I didn't know the rule about mixing drinks! And—"

Wait a minute. Could he be referencing the night we met? The clench in his jaw makes me believe I might be right.

But why? That's ancient history. I would be surprised if he even gave that night a second thought. Especially after all these years.

"Doesn't matter. Not my problem what you do on your own time back home, but since you're sharing a room with me, I'd like to make sure you don't get too wild." He pointedly stares at my two drinks.

"Like I said, it's not a problem. Besides, I didn't even order that other drink. A guy at the bar sent it over with Kelsey, your new best friend." I roll my eyes.

Antonio rubs his jaw roughly. "Unbelievable." He shakes his head. "Hope this goes without saying, but no bringing random men to our room." He stares off toward the beach.

"Who knows, maybe you can room with the guy who bought you the drink and save us the trouble of cohabitating."

I rear back as if I've been slapped in the face. "You're a pig."

"Not the first time I've been called that as a cop. Figured you'd call me something more creative." He smiles humorlessly.

I blow out a breath as I place my sunglasses back on my face and stand to pick up my things. Didn't anticipate storming off this early in the trip, yet here we are.

Before I make to reach for my bag, Antonio grabs my wrist. "Stop."

"Let go of me right now." He lets me pull out of his grasp easily and holds his hands up in surrender.

"Look, I went too far. I'm… I'm sorry. Just sit so we can talk. Please?" The sincerity in his voice brings me to a halt.

I was ready to wring his neck, but the *please* made me too curious to walk away. I move in front of him and sit back down reluctantly. "Talk. Nicely," I bite out.

He rubs the back of his neck nervously. I should be focused on the fact that all signs of cocky assholery have been erased. Instead, I'm hoping that my dark-tinted sunglasses hide the fact that I'm staring at his massive biceps.

"Fuck. I came down here so we could, like, I don't know, make a truce or something. I'm sure neither of us wants to spend a week coming for each other's necks. Let's just try to be civil. Maybe even try to play nice?" He offers a small smile.

I snort at the idea of Antonio Nuñez being nice to me. "For the record, I have no problem being nice to you." He gives me an unbelieving look. "Most of the time. The only reason I ever snap at you is because you're a dick to me. It's like you have this perception of who I am and treat me accordingly. You don't even know me, Tony."

"It's Antonio."

"And here I thought we were playing nice." I fake pout.

Antonio closes his eyes and takes a deep breath. "You're right."

Say what now? "Um, can you repeat that? I think I heard you say I was right?"

"Don't push it, Nikki." He points at me. Now it's my turn to put my hands up in surrender while biting down on my smile. He looks down at my lips as I do, then runs a hand through his hair. "We don't know each other very well. Maybe we should fix that. At least for the sake of this trip."

I cross my arms over my chest and tap my chin, pretending to contemplate his offer. Like I'd pass up on the opportunity to best Antonio with questions about his broody self. But it can't hurt to make him sweat a bit. Hmm, wonder how he looks while sweaty…

Hard stop, girl.

"Okay, I think we can manage that." I shrug, and Antonio visibly relaxes.

Kelsey arrives with Antonio's beer and a few small plates. She lets us know she'll be back shortly with more food. Once she's out of earshot, Antonio starts. "So, why did—"

"Nuh-uh, me first. The tattoos. When did all this happen?" I wave at his body.

He shakes his head, but I can see that he's amused by my enthusiasm. "Got my first in college. And I've added one or two a year since. Nothing crazy." He takes a bite of a bougie-looking puff pastry and nods in approval. "So—"

"No, wait. There's a part two to this question. How did Anna let this fly? She was so strict about her kids not getting tattoos. So much so that when she watched my Instagram story of Amelia and me out in Miami getting matching best friend tattoos, she called Amelia up immediately and shut that shit down. Too bad it was *after* mine was halfway finished. Do you know how lonely it is to get a bestie tattoo with no bestie?" I exclaim.

Antonio genuinely laughs at this, and I don't appreciate the warm and fuzzy feelings that stir in me. "I remember that day. Mom was furious. Serves you right for posting it on social media. Evan told me he was able to locate Amelia out one night because you kept posting your location. Not safe, by the way," he lectures. "But to answer your question, I kept it a secret for a while. Got tatted in spots she'd never see." I wiggle my eyebrows suggestively. "Not like that, you perve." I giggle as he continues. "But one day, I reached for something and the sleeve of my T-shirt rode up and she saw it. I can't tell you how many times she made the cross motion over her body and asked God for my forgiveness… and my mom wasn't even that religious." He smiles sweetly at the memory. "Anyway, once she realized they weren't going to scrub off, she made me promise to only have them in places that wouldn't be visible in dress shirts and pants. And to be honest, I thought it was a reasonable request. I've never wanted my tattoos to be the first thing people see when I walk into a room. They're for me…" He pauses. "And I guess for the lucky onlookers that get to see me with my shirt off while on vacation." He fakes seriousness.

I look from side to side. "Wait. Was that you trying to make a joke or something? Have we progressed to that level of friendliness already?" He stuffs his face with a lobster taco so he doesn't have to answer me. "So what's your favorite tattoo?"

"Nope. My turn. What tattoo did you get the day Amelia backed out?"

"You're going to think it's stupid, and I kinda like this peaceful vibe we got going on, so I don't wanna give you any new ammo against me."

"I won't say anything. I promise." He plates another lobster taco and places it in front of me. Is this a literal peace offering? Well, shit. Looks like I'm taking it.

I shift to my side and raise my left arm, revealing the small tattoo that rests high on my ribcage. "It's one-half of a heart." With a jagged zigzag running down the middle. No bigger than a quarter.

Antonio leans in for a closer look and lifts his hand. He hovers for a moment, just about to make contact with my skin, before deciding against it, and leans away. "Why half?"

It takes me a second to confirm that he's not mocking me, so I put my arm down and face him again. "Amelia and I met at a party during our freshman year. We instantly connected and stayed attached at the hip that night. We avoided all the frat boys and instead danced the night away under a cheap disco ball. At the end of the night, we ripped some tinsel foil curtains and made each other friendship bracelets. We vowed that day to buy the real thing, the kind that have broken heart charms that, when connected, spell *best friends*. A few years later, that idea morphed into getting it tattooed. But as you know, your mom put the kibosh on that while I was still in the tattoo chair. So I asked the tattoo artist to leave the inside blank." I shrugged. "So it may be silly, but it marked the beginning of our friendship and the night I'll forever be grateful for. Plus, not being a complete version of something kind of resonates with my life, but that's a story for a different day." I take a bite out of the taco to distract from my slip at the end.

"We're gonna have to circle back to that at some point." He takes a sip of his beer.

"Maybe, maybe not. Answer my last question that you avoided. Which is your favorite tattoo?"

"You know there's more we can chat about than body art in order to get to know one another."

"I know, but you've avoided this question twice now, so naturally, I'm like a dog with a bone." I shimmy in my chair.

"It's not a dance in your chair kind of story, and I'm pretty sure it'll bring down the mood." He pauses as I keep taking bites of various finger foods. "Last warning."

I sit up straight, wiping my mouth with a napkin, and give Antonio my full attention. "Well, if it's your favorite, I still want to hear about it."

He blows out a heavy breath. "It's the angel wings below my neck." He throws his legs over the opposite side of the lounger and turns his body fully until I can see his back. At any other moment, I would have taken the time to appreciate his back muscles. But the second he said angel wings, I felt a lump forming in my throat.

"It's beautiful," I say, barely above a whisper.

He turns back around and studies my sullen expression. "Told ya it would bring down the mood." He offers a forced smile.

I reach forward and put my hand on top of his and give it a little squeeze. "Tell me why it's your favorite."

He holds my gaze, and for the first time in a long time, I feel like there are no walls standing between us. It's just us in that moment, and for a split second, I'm almost taken back to the night we met. But before those familiar memories come flooding back to me, he starts. "Before my mom was admitted into hospice, she was bedridden at home. I went to visit her every day. During her last few weeks, she made a joke about not caring if I got more tattoos after she passed. I asked if she would be offended if I ever got one in her honor, since she was initially so against them. Turns out she said she wanted a front-row seat to my next tattoo before... before she was gone." He swallows deeply, then meets my eyes. "But first, she had two rules she wanted me to follow." He smiles softly. "I could never get a woman's name tattooed on my body. That was a big *hell no* for her. The only amendment to that rule was if I had a family with this woman, but she still thought it was safer to err on the side of caution and just not do it." He chuckles. "The other rule was that my future tattoos should only be about things that are deeply meaningful to me. She was referring to a couple of my early spontaneous tattoos. That rule didn't really matter, because no other tattoo would compare to the one I would get for her, and I vowed to myself that it would be my final one." He stares at the pool as he continues. "So I was able to convince my favorite tattoo artist to come to my parents' apartment and do this piece at my mom's bedside. She held my hand during the whole process. I never felt the needle. Just the faint grip she held on to me with." His eyes shine with unshed tears. "She was gone before the tattoo fully healed."

I will my tears to stay at bay, but it's futile. I make quick work of wiping them away and stand. Antonio regards me cautiously as I hold out a hand for him to join me. Once up, I ask, "Can I hug you, Tony? I feel like you could use a hug. Or maybe it's just me who needs one?"

After a few seconds, Antonio nods once. And that's all the permission I need to wrap my arms around his center. When my cheek presses to his chest, his body tenses. I realize then that hugging while he's shirtless might be uncomfortable for him, and that I probably should have thought about that before I initiated this. As I lift my cheek to take a step back, he wraps one arm around my lower back and the other behind my neck. His fingers cradle my head while also threading through my hair. I sink into him once more just as I feel him release a deep breath.

This feels nice.

"Hey, Nikki."

"Yeah." I sigh dreamily.

"It's still Antonio to you."

Oh, for fuck's sake.

7

ANTONIO

SEVEN YEARS AGO – NEW YEAR'S EVE

MIAMI

Thirty minutes later, we've gotten all the small talk out of the way and have found the rooftop patio. The fresh air and background music are a welcome relief after being crammed inside the loud club.

We snag a love seat barely big enough for the both of us and pull it to the far corner, away from loud conversations.

"How cute are these mini disco balls everywhere?" she asks in delight as we get comfortable in our seats.

I did not come here looking to spend the night with a woman, but I'd be lying if I said that one look from Nicolette didn't almost throw me on my ass.

Clearly, the woman is drop-dead gorgeous. My hands itch to touch her silky blond strands and hold her petite body close to me.

But her eyes?

Her big blue eyes pulled me in and have kept me captive ever since.

It feels like things are reshuffling in my chest to make room for her, as insane as that may seem. I've just met the woman, but my heart and mind seem to have made an agreement that they don't want to go back to living a day where this woman is a stranger to me.

Her vibrant smile and effervescent personality are keeping me hostage, and I don't mind it one bit.

Nicolette.

Nicolette.

Nicolette.

My Nicolette.

Jesus Christ. I need to snap out of it. I know I haven't been in a relationship in years, but I'm hardly pressed for female companionship. At least for one night only. But this? This is different. As much as I would love to see her writhing beneath me, my dick isn't the driving force behind my madness.

It's my heart. I know it is. It's been dead for years, only to beat to life the second I laid eyes on her.

Nicolette.

"Tony?"

Shit. Even the way she says my name drives me wild. Something as simple as "Tony" on her lips is enough to set my soul on fire. "Yeah, sorry?"

"So, you're a tourist." Those words should remind my heart to simmer down. I don't even live here. But I've never been a man to turn down a challenge.

"Yeah. I live in New York. Just down here to visit family for a couple of days."

Her jaw drops. "Where in New York? It is a big state and all."

I chuckle. "New York City. Manhattan. Upper West Side. Do you want my building number and access code to get in, or would that be too much?" I smirk.

Her eyes go wide as her mind seems to calculate this information.

"Oh, wow. That's kinda crazy," she whispers while rubbing her throat.

I lean in closer. Not because I can't hear her, but because I just want to be closer to her. "And why is that crazy, Nicolette?" I ask, my voice taking on a gravelly tone now that she's close enough to touch.

She leans in an inch, holding my gaze. "Because I'm moving to New York City. Manhattan. Upper West Side. In *two* days."

My muscles tense. My initial reaction is to call bullshit. No way can that be possible. But the flush in her cheeks, the stunned look in her eyes, and her slightly trembling hand tell me she's not lying.

"Can it really be?" I ask, just to be safe.

She nods. "I just wrapped up grad school. Well, most of it. I have two online classes left and just need to complete my clinical hours. I'll be doing that at a nonprofit in downtown Manhattan. I'm only staying in the Upper West Side because it's where my roommate found us a decent apartment." Her breathing has picked up, and she's taking quick, short breaths. She's just as affected as I am. Is she feeling what I'm feeling? Does she feel as crazy as I do in this moment?

This is pure insanity, but there's no stopping me now.

I eat up the space between us and place my hand behind her neck. "This is the moment where you tell me to stop," I whisper over her lips as they open slightly. "This is when you tell me to pump the brakes, and I will respectfully do so and go at whatever pace you're comfortable with. So what do you say, Nicolette?"

Her eyes bounce from my lips to my eyes, and her smile broadens a fraction. "But it's not midnight, and I was really hoping to get a New Year's kiss, Tony," she teases.

My restraint is a hair's breadth away from snapping.

The hand on her neck holds steady as my thumb brushes along her cheek, and I give her my final warning. "You let me kiss you now, and I'll be the only one claiming your kisses from now on. You won't be getting rid of me at midnight. Do you understand what I'm saying here?"

She raises a brow as she bites her bottom lip. Her eyes gleam with mischief. "Do your worst."

She's barely gotten her last word out when I'm crashing my lips onto hers. With my free hand, I scoop her up, careful not to expose any part of her in her dress, and sit her sideways on my lap, never once breaking the kiss.

This goddamn kiss.

A life-changing kiss.

The kiss to seal the deal.

The kiss that confirms what I never, even in my wildest dreams, would have imagined.

That I've fallen in love at first sight.

8

ANTONIO
PRESENT

I'm playing a dangerous game here.

One minute, I'm deliberately pushing Nikki away, and in the next, I'm crushing her against my chest. I can't believe the thought of another man sending her a drink sent me into a douchebag tailspin. As if I haven't seen her in multiple committed relationships throughout the years. *It still stings though.*

I don't know how she does it. How she is the only person who can bypass all my lock codes and get me to open up. Just like on the night we first met.

God, this is turning into such a clusterfuck.

Luckily, after she detached herself from me, we've maintained some semblance of personal space while out for the day. While she sunbathed, I swam in the ocean. While she cooled off in the pool, I continued to eat my weight in ceviche.

While this place is amazing, I do wish that they would serve some actual Dominican food. I get the whole *discover the world at our resort* vibe, but for fuck's sake, what's a guy gotta do to get some plátanos?

Just as I lie back to relax under the sun, Nikki starts climbing out of the pool like a goddamn Bond girl. I swear she's moving in slow motion as water cascades off her blond hair, into her mouthwatering cleavage, then finally into the holy land of her bikini bottoms.

I almost lost my shit earlier when I saw her being covered by the equivalent of three tortilla chips. Her top especially. It was working overtime to contain her breasts. I won't deny that I went a bit caveman when I threw a towel to cover her up. She probably thinks it's because I didn't want other men to see her, which is also true, but it was mostly for my sake and the semi I was rocking within thirty seconds of seeing her.

"The water feels amazing. You should go in," she says as she wrings out her hair with a towel. Within seconds, a cabana boy is taking the towel from her and offering her two new ones.

"I just ate. I'll go in a bit." I nod.

She smirks. "Such a boy scout. Waiting thirty minutes before going into the water to swim? Something tells me you don't break many rules, officer."

I groan. Why does everything she says sound so sexy? If only she knew the things I want to do to her are probably illegal in a few states. "No teasing, Nikki. Remember the truce. We're trying to be *nice* to one another."

She opens her mouth to respond, but we're interrupted by a petite blonde in a uniform that's different from the rest of the staff. "Hello there, my name is Anya." She turns to speak solely to me. "I work at the spa here at the resort. I noticed that your shoulders are reddening a bit, so I thought I'd bring over some sunscreen to prevent a burn," she says with a Swedish accent.

With my eyes hidden behind my sunglasses, I chance a look at Nikki, only to see her glaring daggers at our new little friend. *Interesting.*

"Thank you. I definitely need some." I smile graciously.

Anya perks up. "Great!" She pulls a lever on the lounger, laying it flat. "Just lie down on your chest and—"

"Thanks. I got it," Nikki says as she snags the sunscreen from Anya.

"Oh." Anya startles. "I don't mind. It is my job and all."

"Yeah, now that you mention it, I think I have a knot in my shoulder," I say as I move my neck from side to side, not able to hide my smile while I lie down.

"I can clear that right—"

"Oh, but I just can't wait to get my hands around your neck, *babe*."

Before poor Anya can catch up, Nikki is swinging a leg over me and straddling my lower back. "Oh yeah. You're tense, big boy. We might have to book us a couple's massage later in the week. Thanks for the sunscreen, Anita."

"It's Anya," she huffs but recovers quickly. "Okay, just call if you need anything." She bows her head and makes her exit.

"*Meow*. Didn't know you had claws, Nikki," I tease.

"Oh please. That was borderline sexual harassment if you ask me. Just be glad I was here to rescue you from her." She pats my back twice and shifts to move off me. My arm immediately twists up to keep her in place.

"I thought you couldn't wait to get your hands on me. Or do I need to call Anya back to take care of that knot on my shoulder?"

Nikki resettles on me. "Are you serious right now?"

"While you're back there, can you take care of the thorn in my side? Given that it's you."

She pinches my side. Hard. But all I can do is shake with laughter.

"Yeah, yeah. Laugh it up, big guy." She leans forward, her breasts pressing against my back as her lips come close to my ear. "But next time someone buys me a drink, I don't wanna hear a peep out of you."

I can hear the smile in her voice as I tense up and growl. She leans back up and uncaps the sunscreen bottle. "Whoopsies," she singsongs as a generous amount of cold sunscreen is squirted all over me.

"Jesus Christ, woman. Could you have at least warmed it up with your hands?"

"Oh hush. Just be grateful I don't let you sunbathe with a bunch of tiny penises drawn on your back with sunscreen," she says as she starts to work the cream into my skin. The moan that escapes my lips is not PG-13.

"There are children by the pool, Tony. Keep it together."

I stiffen at her use of my nickname. "I'm—ouch!"

"Oh, would you look at that? Took care of another thorn in your side." She laughs.

"Okay, that's enough. My turn."

"Wait, what? Eek!" She squeals as I spin under her while keeping her in place with one arm. She's now straddling my crotch, yet neither of us dares to make a move. While lying on my stomach, it was easier to keep from getting… excited. But now, I can tell the moment she can feel me at half-mast.

Her eyes widen, but she doesn't move. After a few moments of catching our breaths, we say at the same time.

"I'm gonna—"

"We should—"

"Yeah."

She scrambles off me as I sit up and then stand, readjusting myself. I sense the moment she's about to walk toward the pool, so I move to grab her elbow. "And where do you think you're going?" I raise a brow.

She avoids eye contact at all costs until I tug on her elbow again and her bashful eyes meet mine. Her cheeks are reddened by the sun and maybe a bit of embarrassment.

"Truth?" I nod. "I was going to dive straight into that cold water and act as if I didn't feel your size-fourteen package." She slaps a hand over her mouth, like she can't believe she said that out loud.

"That wasn't my full package, sweetheart." My smirk turns into a full-blown grin as her blush spreads to her neck and chest. Before I give it another thought, my hand reaches for the back of her neck, and I reel her in to my chest for a hug. It feels so natural to have her close, even if a little voice in the back of my head is telling me to tread lightly and ease off on the playful flirting.

"Uh, is this a hug or a headlock, because I can't really tell when I'm surrounded by your biceps," she says into my chest, her voice muffled.

I chuckle as I release her. And since I don't trust myself with her lying on the lounger, I grab the sunscreen off the chair and rub some into my hands.

"What are you doing?"

"Boop." I tap a generous amount of sunscreen onto her button nose.

"Did you just boop me?" she gasps.

"Yep. Consider yourself booped. Now hush and let me concentrate. You're going to look like a tomato if I don't apply this now."

She huffs with her hands on her hips but lets me go to work on her. I leave her face looking like she has white warrior paint on it, thoroughly enjoying myself.

"I don't even wanna know what I look like," she mutters.

I smile widely. "Turn around." She rolls her eyes, but I don't miss the small smile playing on her lips. I spread the remaining cream on her shoulders and accidentally lose myself in the process of rubbing it in. Only when she releases a moan that rivals my own earlier do I know it's time to call it quits.

With a swift smack on her ass, I announce that I'm done.

Her glare toward me has no heat behind it as she rummages through her tote bag to look for a mirror. Once she's fixed the mess I made, she stands up straight and pats my cheek twice a little harder than necessary. "Look at us. The picture-perfect example of adults holding up a truce. Who'da thunk it?" Her eyes shimmer with mischief until they refocus on something behind me. Or rather, *someone*.

I follow her gaze until I spot an older guy looking at her like she's his next meal. Now, I personally think he's got nothing on me, but he's still no chump.

This guy is leaning across the bar in a three-piece suit in ninety-degree weather, looking like the poster child—err, man —for wealth. Looking like he owns the place. Looking like he owns *her*.

The instant fire burning in my chest unexpectedly knocks the air out of my lungs just as I turn back to Nikki. She's staring at her feet, trying to hide the blush that's creeping up her neck.

Is this how it's going to be? Stupid me standing on the sideline yet again as another fool takes and parades Nikki in front of me?

I don't think so.

With new determination and a menacing smile, I put my hands on Nikki's hips as I walk her backward. Her eyes widen as she asks, "What are you doing?"

I lift her up into the air and wrap her legs around my waist as she instinctively grabs a hold of my shoulders. "Hold your breath, Nikki."

Before she can ask me why, I have us airborne and crashing into the deep end of the pool. She quickly comes up, gasping for air. "What the hell was that for?" She splashes water in my direction as she pitifully tries to tread water.

I can't help laughing as I grab her hand to pull her closer to me. I didn't expect her to fully koala latch on to me, but I guess the fear of drowning overrides her pride in this instance.

She hugs me close and leans into my ear. "As soon as my feet are on solid ground, you are a dead man, Antonio Manuel Nuñez." Oh shit. She just used my whole name.

"In my defense, you looked like you needed to cool off," I say as I keep walking us around the deep end, where she can't touch the floor or reach the edges of the pool. "Besides, I grew up with Amelia, so I know the rules. Your hair was already wet, so you can't stay mad at me." I have the decency to offer a sheepish smile.

Nikki raises an eyebrow, then bursts out laughing. Just when I think this woman is going to give me hell or hold a grudge, she does the exact opposite.

She releases her arms from my neck, and I find myself wanting to put them right back. She spreads them by her head and softly laughs as her upper body floats. My hands stay firmly on her legs, which she still has wrapped around me. Thank God she's clinging to my abs and not anywhere near my groin. The visual of water lapping her breasts two feet in front of me is already requiring an absurd amount of strength from me to keep my body in control.

She hums in contentment as she continues to float with her eyes closed, face tipped up toward the sky. There's not a stitch of makeup left on her face, and she's without a doubt the most beautiful woman I've ever laid eyes on.

She finally peeks one eye open while tilting her head toward me. "I think I like this version of you."

"And what version is that, Nikki?"

"The one that acts like he's no longer mad at the world… or me."

9

NIKKI

WRONG THING TO SAY.

Clearly, whatever spell Antonio and I were under for the past few hours has run out, and I'm back to being public enemy number one.

After he untangles my legs from their death grip on his body, he guides me over to the shallow end and leaves me there, but not before mumbling over his shoulder that I need to text him before I go back to our room since he'll be in the shower. The shower that's visible from 80 percent of the bungalow. A real voyeur's dream. Not ideal for a couple of people who don't even know how to be nice to each other.

God, this is so annoying. I can't believe I got my hopes up.

To be honest, I'm more upset at myself for thinking that Antonio and I could actually be in each other's company for long periods of time and have… fun? No, that's not true. I know that I could spend endless hours with him and never be bored, and *that's* a sobering thought. Especially since most of my relationships have been with men who were easy to forget. But not Antonio. *Never Antonio.*

A part of me wonders if it would do any good to come

clean and tell him the truth I've been holding on to for years. Just let it all out and see if it'll change anything. But that thought alone terrifies me. He already struggles with thinking the worst of me. What would happen if I confirmed the worst truth about myself?

That I'm a liar.

But why bother admitting something that he's probably never thought twice about? I mean, this is Antonio we're talking about. Playboy extraordinaire. Relationship repellent in human form. What good would it do to expose my soul to a man who couldn't care less even if he tried? It would only risk putting Amelia in a weird spot, especially while she's on the road to recovery and sleeping happily in Evan's arms. Then I'd potentially have to extricate myself from all future family gatherings. Because at the end of the day, the people I've spent almost a decade celebrating every holiday with are his family, not mine.

It seems obvious to me that the right move is to just keep my mouth shut and go along to get along. Nothing is at risk this way.

Yet why do I have this niggling urge to shout the truth from the rooftops?

I'm freshly showered with a towel wrapped tightly around my damp body. There's no real privacy in this mirrored-wall bathroom emporium. So the system that Antonio and I (though he just grunted, so I suppose it was mostly me) have worked out, is that one of us stays out on the patio area while the other showers. Afterward, I have to walk downstairs in a towel and dress in the massive walk-in closet. Shouldn't be a big deal, especially since we've been in bathing suits around each other all day. But when I caught sight of Antonio with a low-slung towel around his waist on his way to the closet, it almost sent me to an early grave.

Now that I've closed the door to the closet, I drop the towel and quickly put on my undies. I text Antonio the all-clear to move around the room just as I get another incoming call from my mother. I already declined two of her calls while sitting poolside. Today is not the day for us to chat. The second she gets wind of my fancy vacation, she'll incessantly pump me for information… or worse, an invitation. I press the red button and stay on task as I move around the closet.

Curiosity has finally gotten to me, so I decide to open the massive suitcase that was packed by personal shoppers. Once I finally have it open, I can't help but laugh. Both sides are neatly packed and tucked in with tissue paper, and a black envelope with my name in white calligraphy lies in the center. I shake my head before opening it.

Nikki,

We have taken Amelia's suggestions and curated looks for your tropical vacation. We hope that we have provided everything you need. Please use the undergarments in the ivory box when you wear the Oscar de la Renta gown intended for New Year's Eve. It completes the look and will keep you secured in your gown.

Happy New Year!

Maribel & The Bergdorf Goodman Team

What the hell?

I start pulling at tissue paper like a kid on Christmas morning. My mouth drops open at the piles of luxurious fabrics and patterns. I've never seen so much beautiful fashion in one place. I could weep!

I stay on task and pull out the ivory box and, surprise, surprise, more tissue paper. Once I finally get my hands on lacy material, I pull it out and freeze.

These are not your mama's undies. Oh no. This is some kind of nude lacy bodysuit corset type of situation, with a *very* deep v cut. It is one sexy number, and I'm turned on just looking at it in my hands. I quickly check the label and see that it's my size but look at the bra cup, then down to my boobs, and wonder how I'm supposed to squeeze these puppies into them. But that's an issue for future Nikki.

For now, I stay on task, and that means not peeking at the mysterious garment bag that houses the gown. If I go down that road, there is no stopping me from putting it on now and parading around the room in it. For tonight, I need to hurry up and get dressed so we can make it to the dinner reservations that Kelsey informed me of as I was leaving the pool.

I pull out a deep blue slip dress that has a swoop neckline. It's so buttery soft and perfect for my newly tanned skin.

I'm impressed that I was able to avoid burning on the first day, but that was probably thanks to Antonio's expert sunscreen application. I blow out a breath as I throw the dress on and think about how it feels like it was a lifetime ago that Antonio and I were playing nice and even getting handsy with one another. It must have been a fluke, some kind of twilight zone that we stepped into. Antonio just got out before I did. Because if it were up to me, we would have stayed in that place forever.

Antonio: Meet you at the restaurant.

I walk out of the bungalow, staring at the text Antonio sent me twenty minutes ago. He couldn't even wait for me to go to the restaurant together.

Whatever. Fine by me. I thrust my phone into my clutch a little more roughly than necessary just as Chris pulls up in front of me. "Good evening, Ms. Nikki! I'm the lucky guy driving you to your dinner reservation." He smiles.

"Thanks, Chris." His playfulness eases my dread about having dinner with Antonio and reminds me of what I've been wondering about all day. "Hey, you mind telling me how news gets around so fast here?"

He chuckles. "Ah, so you've noticed. Are you sure you want to know? It might lose its magical appeal if you know all our secrets."

"Hurry up and spill before I think I'm being spied on by big brother while I'm in the bathroom."

"Well, it's not like those provide any privacy to begin with…" I give him a troubling look. "I'm just messing with ya." He taps his ear where a clear wireless earpiece sits. "We use these like walkie talkies. It's how I told Kelsey you were funny, and how she told Anya that you and Mr. Tony weren't a couple." His eyes widen at his last statement, like he has revealed too much.

"Don't sweat it. We're not a couple. We're just… I don't even know what we are, to be honest."

He nods and smiles as we approach the entrance to the restaurant. "Well, Ms. Nikki, if love and a little bit of magic are what you're looking for, you've come to the right place."

IO

NIKKI
SEVEN YEARS AGO – NEW YEAR'S EVE

My logical brain can't comprehend it.

I'm head over heels for this man. A perfect stranger.

Had I met him in Vegas, I'm sure the night would have ended with an Elvis impersonator and wedding bells.

But this kind of thing never happens to me. I thought I had higher odds of ending up on the side of a milk carton than in the arms of the most gorgeous man I've ever laid eyes on. The even crazier part? I think he's just as far gone as I am.

We played a rapid-fire game of twenty questions, almost in an attempt to spot red flags, but each answer seemed to only make us fall deeper.

He's a morning person, and I'm a night owl. But he promises to bring me coffee and breakfast in bed after returning from the gym.

I prefer ordering in and he likes eating out. But I love every cuisine, so I offer to always let him pick the place to order from, as long as I get to try a bit of his meal.

We go back and forth for what seems like an eternity. Creating a world in which we fit, in which we stay molded to each other like we are in this exact moment.

Little did we know that as the minutes were counting down to the New Year, so were the last moments of magic between us.

"Crap! Five minutes till midnight. I should probably go find my friend," I tell Tony as we stand near the bathrooms on the main floor of the club.

He nods. "Yeah, I need to find my family too." He hesitates. "Or we could wait until after midnight so I can give you your New Year's kiss." He leans down and kisses me softly, like a lover who's done this thousands of times before.

I wrap my arms around his neck and still have to pop up to my tiptoes while in platform heels to reach him. "But you've already given me my best New Year's kiss ever. Nothing is ever going to top it." I give him a quick peck.

His hands on my hips keep me close to him. "Hmm, I don't know if that counts. It was before midnight, and that might mean it's bad luck. Better to be safe and do it again at midnight," he teases.

I love this.

I love this ease we have with one another. Something that I don't even have with people who are related to me.

I used to think I was broken. That my mother's bad luck in love had automatically spilled over to me, and I was doomed to repeat her mistakes.

But I'm not my mother, and her mistakes are not my own.

I can do this. I can have this new life in New York.

With my new career waiting for me.

With Amelia and her loving family that has accepted me as their own.

With Tony. And whatever it is that's blooming between us.

I sigh as Tony gives me a funny look. "What are you thinking about, Nicolette?"

"Just that anything is possible."

And in that exact moment, movement from my right catches my attention. I release Tony as a wobbly-legged Amelia makes her way out of the bathroom with two of her cousins flanking her.

"Amelia!"

"Amelia?"

Tony and I say at the same time.

Wait, what?

"How—"

"What—"

Amelia throws her arms around both of us. "Ah! My favorite people are here! I can't believe it. It's a Christmas miracle."

"It's New Year's Eve, Amelia." Her cousin chuckles.

She waves her comment away. "Yeah, yeah. Whatever."

Tony speaks before I get the chance. "Amelia, you know Nicolette? Or is this some drunk girl bathroom bonding situation? If so, I'm gonna need you to take your hands off—"

"Nicolette," Amelia mocks. "Who are you, the IRS?" She bends over, laughing while my love coma brain is trying to connect the dots. She straightens and locks our arms together, turning me to face Tony. "This, my lovely brother, is Nikki. My best friend who's moving to New York with me. Duh."

Brother.

No.

This can't be.

"Wait, no. Amelia, you said Antonio wasn't flying in until

tomorrow. So this isn't him. Antonio isn't in Miami. This isn't Antonio. This *can't* be Antonio," I say frantically as Tony stares at me.

He clears his throat. "I texted Evan that my flight got canceled, so he offered to fly me down on his jet, since he was flying out to California anyway."

Drunk Amelia speaks. "Uh, Miami is nowhere on the way to California, genius."

Tony rolls his eyes. "He was bummed he couldn't make it due to work, so he wanted to make sure I was here for you. He got pretty sappy about it. But that's beside the point."

"Wait, you guys know someone with a private jet?" I gasp.

"Nico—*Nikki*. Focus. Why didn't you give me your real name? Or mention Amelia?"

Amelia shrieks as the countdown begins from sixty seconds. "Oh goodie. You guys met already. Don't take offense, Tony. She gives that name to all the strangers she meets at the clubs."

"Oh, now you call him Tony. How convenient," I mutter.

Fifty seconds.

Tony keeps his questioning gaze on me as my face does a terrible job of coming to terms with this truth bomb. "You really didn't know who I was?" he asks as softly as he can over the rowdy crowd.

"No idea." I feel my eyes prickle with moisture.

Forty seconds.

"Oh, don't feel bad about it, Tony. It's not like any of us are gonna remember any of this tomorrow."

Oh no. Amelia, please shut up.

"What do you mean?" he asks, eyes on me. *Always on me.*

"We've been drinking since breakfast. Going drink for drink. This one is probably gonna black out any minute now." Amelia jerks her thumb in my direction.

Thirty seconds.

"What?" he growls.

"Oh, don't be such a party pooper. This is our last hurrah in Miami. Let us live a little. Plus, my little Nikki over here is gonna terrorize all the men of Manhattan. A couple of us call her *the Maneater*. 'Cause she'll love 'em and leave 'em. Let her have her fun with whatever poor guy falls into her trap."

Ouch.

Twenty seconds.

"Amelia, please shut up. You're experiencing full word vomit, and I need you to reel it in." I send a pleading look Tony's way, and I can tell he doesn't know what to think right now.

"Oh, I forgot to ask!" Amelia pipes up again. "Did you ever find a guy to have that New Year's kiss with? Or have you given up that mission?" She giggles.

My stomach bottoms out as I see all traces of my soft, beautiful Tony turn to stone.

Ten.

"I'm not drunk."

Nine.

"Pfft, *okay*. If you say so." Amelia snickers.

Eight.

"Explain," Tony grits out.

Seven.

"Am I missing something here?" Amelia looks between us.

Six.

"I can explain," I start.

Five.

"Oh, I'm gonna be sick!" Amelia runs off to the bathroom.

Four.

"Nikki."

Three.

"Antonio."

Two.

"Fuck."

One.

And as the clock struck midnight, it marked a new year and the beginning of my heartbreak.

II

ANTONIO
SEVEN YEARS AGO – NEW YEAR'S EVE

I couldn't sleep last night.

I went through our time together again and again, trying to spot what I missed. What warning signs were overlooked. I couldn't find one. I take consent very seriously, so the thought that I could've possibly made out with a woman while she wasn't conscious of her actions sent me into a tailspin.

I'm trying not to think about the worst-case scenario, but my brain can't help it. Once bitten, twice shy and all that.

I need to stop running worst-case scenarios and instead have an important conversation this morning.

I arrive at Amelia's apartment with a box of donuts that my cousin Vanessa quickly takes off my hands.

It's a small apartment, currently littered with a couple of air mattresses in the living room to accommodate my family.

The ladies are still in various states of waking, but they all look like they've seen better mornings. Vanessa is passing around a bottle of ibuprofen, and Amelia is groggily filling up glasses of water. I'm dreading discovering what state Nicolette is in. If it's anything like the women before me, I'm going to be shattered.

I'm still holding on to a sliver of hope that what we shared was real. That she felt it just as strongly as I did.

I stand by the breakfast nook so I'm not in the way, and that's when I see her.

She's coming in through the back patio, wearing workout leggings and a sports bra. Her skin glistens with sweat as she brushes her hair back and away from her eyes.

Did she just come back from a run? A workout? If so, that must mean she was telling the truth. No way could she have been as drunk as the other women and bounce back that quickly.

She lifts a water bottle to her lips but freezes when she sees me. I make my way over to her, and she nods toward the back patio door.

Once outside, I take her in. She's just as beautiful as she was last night. I actually think this version might be my favorite: rosy cheeks and sweat clinging to her clothes.

But then I notice her eyes. Her big, beautiful blue eyes. Rimmed red with a hint of purple below them. As if she, too, didn't sleep last night.

Her body is rigid, but her eyes plead with me. How has this woman already put me through the wringer? I haven't even known her for twelve hours.

I raise my hand to her cheek, but she stops me by gently holding my wrist. She offers me a forced smile. "Hey, Tony!" she says an octave too high to sound natural. "Look, I just wanted to apologize for last night."

Huh?

She slowly lowers my hand, then releases it. "Yeah. You see, the girls and I got a little wild last night, and I'm sorry if I embarrassed myself or did something silly with you."

What the fuck?

Something silly? Like falling in love?

"You didn't seem intoxicated to me, *Nicolette*."

She winces. "Yeah. I'm pretty good at holding my liquor. Guess it's one of the perks of still being in my early twenties."

My brain is still struggling to catch what she's trying to tell me, so I go the direct route. "We spent time together last night. You—we—"

"I don't remember," she interrupts, looking at the ground.

I go still. "Say that again for me."

She sucks in a breath and looks up at me, the war of emotions evident in her eyes. "I don't remember. Any of it. Last night is just one big blur. I'm sorry."

I don't hesitate. "Bullshit."

She flinches. "Tony, please."

I cup her face with both of my hands in time to catch a rogue tear and wipe it away with my thumb. "Talk to me, baby. What's changed? If you need time—"

"What's going on out here?" Amelia interrupts, shielding her eyes from the sunlight.

Nicolette steps out of my reach. "He was just helping me with an eyelash in my eye. Got it, thanks!"

"Then what's wrong with you, bro?" Amelia nods at me while coming to stand next to Nicolette.

I have no idea how this has gone sideways so fast. I'd be inclined to believe her if her eyes weren't giving her away. Those sad blue eyes, pulling me into the deep end.

Does Nikki have regrets? Is this about my sister? My head is swirling with questions. But before I make any rash decisions, I need a minute to think. I need to regroup.

I shake my head, keeping my eyes on Nicolette. "Change of plans. I'm flying back home today." Nicolette's eyes widen as Amelia gasps.

"Wait, what do you mean? You just got here! Plus, you're supposed to help us with the move."

"Don't worry about it. I'll hire a company and have everything packed and shipped for you."

"Tony, that's too much money for just a couple of—"

"Don't worry about it. I have things I need to settle." I take one step toward the women. "And when you guys fly up, we'll all hang out. And we'll all *talk*. I'm sure there'll be a lot to catch up on." I lean in and kiss Amelia on her head as I discreetly squeeze Nicolette's hand.

And without a backward glance, I leave the apartment, not knowing whether the piece of my heart I gave away last night will be flying back up to me soon.

12

NIKKI

SEVEN YEARS AGO- NEW YEAR'S DAY

MIAMI

I can't breathe.

Since the moment he turned away and left, my lungs have forgotten how to function.

I lied.

Why did I lie?

I knew it was wrong, but I panicked.

The run I went on did nothing to help my frayed nerves. Nor did it bring me the answers I was looking for.

I want him. Badly. But I don't know how it would work out in the long run.

Could I really start a new relationship, with my best friend's older brother no less, right before moving to New York City, to his neighborhood? A man I've only spent a couple of hours with?

On paper, this is a no-brainer. Cut my losses, lie, and chalk it up to the effects of the booziest night of the year. Maybe look back at last night, years from now, and laugh it off. Just a short evening spent with a stranger who was clearly no longer a stranger.

But why doesn't it feel like a no-brainer? Why does it feel like I chose wrong when deciding not to date my best friend's older brother?

And why can't I breathe?

13

ANTONIO
PRESENT

SAMANÁ, DOMINICAN REPUBLIC

"The one that acts like he's no longer mad at the world… or me."

That sentence struck me like a lightning bolt. Because she's wrong. I'm still mad. Actually, I'm quite livid. It's much safer to stay angry at Nikki than to allow myself to feel the only other emotion I've ever felt for her. It's easier to lay all the blame on her, as if I haven't had ample opportunity to ask her to chat and talk things over.

Nope. Instead, I'll keep myself in the painful purgatory that has now added physical touch and minimal clothing to the agenda while on this trip.

God, this is such a cruel joke.

Why her? Why can't I just move on and let it go? The hellcat has her claws in my frigid heart and refuses to let go.

I've never wanted someone so badly. I can't even stand being in the same bungalow as her while she's changing, because it's pure torture.

But I need to get a grip. I refuse to put myself out there for her again. If our night wasn't as memorable to her as it was to me, and trust me, it's imprinted in my soul, then I need to power through and keep the truce alive until this vacation is over.

And just as I finish giving myself the world's most pitiful pep talk, I see her strut into the restaurant, looking like a goddamn siren, calling to me. The hostess walks her over to my table, and I can't keep my eyes from roving over her entire body. The dress clings to her like a second skin, teasingly sinful with a tasteful amount of cleavage.

I stand before her hand touches her chair and pull it out for her. She arches a brow but doesn't say a word as she takes a seat and shimmies the chair forward. I may need to keep some semblance of distance between us, but my mother raised a gentleman.

A waiter appears immediately, giving her the same rundown he gave me when I arrived a while ago.

"So, Ms. Nikki. Which tasting menu are you interested in? Or shall I prepare a sample of land and sea?"

"I'll do the seafood." She nods pleasantly toward him.

"Perfect. I shall come back with an aperitif, and each dish will come with a drink pairing."

"Actually, I know you guys like to play booze matchmaker here, but can I get something strong? Preferably something with tequila to start. I'm sure I'm going to need it." She gives me a bland stare.

Looks like I'm not the only one who's snapped out of our happy bubble.

"Of course. As you wish. And for you, Mr. Tony? Would you like another IPA?"

I challenge her gaze as I respond. "How about you get me whatever she's having?" I tip my head in her direction, which she responds to with a classic eye roll.

"Very well. I will be back with those shortly." He bows and quietly steps away, leaving us both to our quiet standoff.

I know why I'm in a mood, but I'm not sure what could have made her so upset. I mean, sure, I could have waited for her to finish getting ready so we could make our way to the restaurant together, but I need any Nikki break I can get at this point in order to stay somewhat sane.

I decide to break the tension by playing nice. "That's a pretty dress."

She ignores me and stares at her nail beds, as if they're the most fascinating things she's ever seen.

I run a hand over my face. "Is this how we're gonna play it, then?"

She lays her arms on the table and leans forward, her eyes laser focused on me. "And this is why we can't have nice things, *Antonio*. I am not playing a game here. I thought we were genuinely having a good time being friendly to one another earlier. But clearly, I was unaware that your niceties ran on a timer. So I'm going to go ahead and bow out of whatever fake truce you had planned. I'd much rather go about ignoring each other than play into this weird Jekyll and Hyde act you got going on," she finishes with a fake smile.

Before I can respond, I see it. A flash of hurt in her eyes. A quick *blink and you miss it* type of moment. But I never miss anything when it comes to Nikki.

Fuck.

It was so much easier when I could avoid her or brush her off when I saw her in the city. But sitting across from her and seeing how my actions hurt her kills me.

So I decide to take the hurt away. It's not like I haven't carried it for the both of us these last seven years.

"Look, I'm sorry if I was a little… brash earlier. I'm still getting used to this." I point between us.

Her face remains impassive. I'm desperate here, and the

thought of not being able to reach Nikki is enough to push my ego aside. So I lead with the truth.

"I was triggered by something you said."

Concern immediately takes over her features, and she straightens in her seat. I inwardly curse myself for using that word with a therapist, but there's no turning back now.

"What did I say?" Her eyes bounce back and forth between my own.

"Something about me being mad at the world. For the record, I think I am."

She deflates at my confession and reaches over to touch the hand I have wrapped around my empty beer glass. "I'm so sorry. I didn't mean to make you feel exposed. We were just getting along so well, and then I was blabbing and I just—"

"It's fine." I cut her off. "I asked for a truce, then ran away at the first sign of you getting too close to the real me." I risk it and release my glass to hold her hand. She takes a quick intake of breath while looking at our joined hands. Then looks back at me with a million questions swirling in her eyes. "I want us to get along, so I'm going to try harder. I still might be an asshole, but at least I'll be an asshole who's trying."

She chuckles and squeezes my hand before pulling hers away. I have to stop myself before I accidentally reach for it back.

"Well, as long as you're able to recognize your asshole tendencies, then I think we can give it another go." She winks, and it hits me straight in my chest... and maybe also my penis. I can only focus on controlling one thing at a time when it comes to her, apparently.

And just like that, I'm in her good graces again. No grudges, no drawn-out fight. Just simple communication and a mutual goal of keeping the peace. I don't know how she does it.

I was so ready to keep her at arm's length in one moment, then find myself struggling to control my desire to pull her onto my lap in the next. It's maddening.

Our waiter comes back with our drinks.

"A toast." She tilts her drink toward me as I lift mine.

"To?"

"To you being an ass—"

"Really, Nikki?"

"I'm just kidding!" she teases. "To a fresh start. Right here, right now. A clean slate that will not be just a temporary truce, but the beginning of… dare I say friendship?" she asks shyly.

I smirk and clink her glass. "Baby steps, Nikki. Don't run off getting best friends tattoos just yet. We know how that ended for you last time," I joke.

She throws her head back and laughs without abandon, and it's the most precious sound in the world.

It's enough to shake me to my core and remind me of why I fell so hard for her in the first place. Powerful enough to pull me out of this vicious cycle I've kept us in.

Seven years.

Seven years of lying to myself. Seven years of missed opportunities to tell her how I feel. Seven years of suffering in silence. Because I've refused to let her know that she holds my heart hostage. And all it took was one night.

Seven fucking years.

And now she's here, sitting across from me, looking like a dream come true. During a one-week vacation. Spending her nights in *my bed.*

I'm such an idiot.

I'm a better man than this. I may not deserve her, but that doesn't mean I won't put up a fight for her.

My last bit of resolve snaps at the playful look she gives me while taking a sip of her drink.

And it's in that exact moment that I make the decision. I no longer want to sulk in the shadows. I want to dance in her light.

I'm going to make this right. I'm going to make her mine.

14

NIKKI

Dinner is surprisingly enjoyable after Antonio and I agree to start over.

The food is delicious, and the drinks are flowing, but what keeps my attention the entire time is Antonio's smile. I don't think I've seen him smile this much in the whole time I've known him. I was sure the scowl was permanent, at least around me. But it looks like he's actually going to give us a shot at civility, and I'd be lying if I said it didn't make me giddy.

"So what should we do tomorrow? Same as today?" he asks as he licks his dessert spoon. I swear my brain almost short circuits, but apparently, my two remaining brain cells have my back.

"We should go somewhere. On the main island."

"That could be fun. This place is a little too stifling for my liking. I'm afraid someone might ask if they can wipe my ass for me." He chuckles.

"I'm sure Anya wouldn't mind," I say to myself. Unfortunately, not low enough, because he goes into a coughing fit that ends in laughter.

Before he can call me out on it, I continue. "Leave it to me. I'll plan something fun for us tomorrow."

He raises a brow. "Should I be concerned? The last time I let a woman plan something for me, it landed me here with you," he teases.

"Well, then, looks like you're a lucky man," I tease right back.

"Oh, Nikki. Don't start something you can't finish," he says in a daring tone.

I can feel my skin flush, and I move my hand around my neck in a poor attempt to cover up my reaction.

Antonio smiles. "Relax. I know this is new between us, but what I just did was called a joke."

I take a generous sip of water because I clearly need to cool down. "Yes, obviously. Ha ha. I was just distracted by the thought of all the fun activities we're gonna do tomorrow."

Antonio swirls the drink in his hand and mouths the word "liar."

I'm instantly turned on and guilt ridden at the same time. He has no idea how much that word weighs on me, and he probably never will.

Since there is no bill to pay, I stand up abruptly, causing my chair to screech behind me. "Well, would you look at the time." I fake a yawn. "This was fun. Meet you back at the room."

I go to push my chair back in and look up just in time to see Antonio towering over me. "I'll go back with you." He extends an arm, indicating for me to walk ahead of him.

"Oh, you don't have to do that."

"Friends don't let friends walk back alone." He playfully bends his elbow for me to hold, and I think the alcohol must be hitting me all at once because the sight of his smile and his flexed bicep almost makes me faint.

In an attempt to avoid any further embarrassment, I take the offered arm and let him lead me out of the restaurant.

"Thank you, by the way," I say as we wait for a golf cart to bring us back to our bungalow.

"For what?"

"For complimenting my dress earlier." I look down at it and swipe at a few wrinkles that formed while I ate dinner.

He stares at me for a beat before saying, "I didn't mean it."

My face scrunches up in confusion. Before I can respond, he continues, "What I really wanted to say is that *you* looked beautiful in that dress. I complimented the dress when I actually wanted to compliment the woman wearing it."

His face is so sincere I could cry. I actually think I feel my tear ducts betraying me, so I look down and say a soft thank you just as the loud motor of a golf cart alerts us of its arrival.

We ride in silence as I let his words sink in. Antonio thinks I'm beautiful.

Not Tony, the man I became instantly infatuated with years ago. But rather, Antonio, the man I've been around for seven years.

We pull up to the villa and hop off the golf cart. Antonio makes it to the entrance before I do and opens the door for me. A girl could really get used to this kind of treatment.

But the second I walk into the bungalow, I'm reminded of the fun little fact I've been trying to keep parked all the way in the back of my mind all day.

One. Fucking. Bed.

Antonio and I will be sleeping together tonight.

Well, not really. I will probably be wide awake the entire night knowing that I'm in such close proximity to this man.

Romance novels really don't prepare you for this kind of stuff. The fact that we're just going to casually lie unconscious next to one another for about eight hours isn't sexy. It's anxiety inducing.

What happens if he crushes me in his sleep while rolling

over, or if I get an involuntary leg cramp and kick him in the shin? The possibilities are truly endless.

I feel Antonio's hand on my lower back, pushing me farther into the room. "Relax. I'll be on my best behavior. I promise." His eyes promise the opposite.

I gulp audibly. Okay, maybe this situation just got a little sexier.

After we've completed our nighttime routines, we stand on opposite sides of the bed with our arms folded over our chests, like the bed has personally offended us.

"Would you mind if we slept with the patio door open and the overhead fan on? The ocean breeze feels nice," I say.

He silently nods as he walks over to the patio door in a cotton T-shirt and gray sweatpants. Ugh, don't even get me started on the gray sweatpants.

I turn on the fan and shut off the air conditioning, then remove my cardigan as I return to my previous bed stare-off spot.

"Hold up." Antonio raises his hand. "You're not going to bed like that."

I look down at the bougie new sleep set I found in the Bergdorf Goodman suitcase. A silky pink camisole with matching sleep shorts. "What do you mean?" I'm taken aback by the return of moody Antonio.

He runs both hands through his hair, then props one on his hip as the other points at my chest. "You're not wearing a bra, Nikki," he says, his voice sounding hoarse.

I chuckle and roll my eyes. "Duh. Do you think girls sleep in bras? I gotta let the girls hang free when I sleep." I smile at his obvious discomfort.

He closes his eyes momentarily while taking a couple of

deep breaths. When they open, they carry a mischievous glint. "Okay, fair enough."

Before I realize what he meant by that, he's reaching behind his neck and pulling off his shirt in one swift swoop.

My jaw drops as he just shrugs and says, "Free the nipple."

I put my hand up to cover my eyes. "*What the hell?* Put your shirt back on. We can't sleep in the same bed with you being half naked!" I shriek.

He gives me a slow perusal from head to toe, as if to prove his point.

"Ugh, fine whatever. But we're gonna need a pillow barrier." I jump into action and set up all the pillows in a straight line down the middle.

Antonio moves around to the foot of the bed to check my work. "Well, that doesn't seem really fair now, does it? I'm more than twice your size. I think we're gonna have to redistribute the pillows." He moves around me and places the line of pillows on the edge of one side, leaving me barely an inch of space.

"Very funny. Stop being a little shit and get in bed."

"Bossy," he whispers loud enough for me to hear.

I get under the covers and rearrange the pillows again.

The second the mattress dips under his weight, the bed shrinks.

And when he places both hands behind his head casually while smiling at me, I realize just how dangerous this setup is.

"Sorry, but there are way too many pillows. I'm gonna have to get rid of a few of these." He grabs a pillow, but I stop him before he can remove it.

"Absolutely not." My voice comes out breathless, as if I've just run a marathon.

He challenges. "I run hot, so either we get rid of a few of these, or the next thing coming off are my sweatpants."

I have a pillow flying toward his face before he even finishes the sentence.

"The pants stay on, you little exhibitionist!"

He laughs as he removes another pillow. "Oh, you're one to talk. You're basically lying next to me in lingerie. What have I done to deserve such torture?" He pouts.

"Stop that." I point at his face.

"What?" he asks innocently.

"Stop trying to be cute and flirty. This is not the time for those kinds of antics. We're just going to sleep in this very comfortable bed, then wake up in the morning and do a bunch of friendly activities, okay, sir?"

"Wrong move calling me sir in bed." He smolders.

"Oh my fucking God!" I throw myself back against my pillow and cover my face with my hands. I can barely panic in peace as Antonio laughs uncontrollably.

I feel the bed shift just as he peels my hands away. "I'm sorry. I promise I'll be good now. But I'm actually being serious. With no air conditioning and all these pillows, I'm going to be up all night sweating. Which I have no problem doing under other circumstances, but I don't think that's on your agenda for the night." He winks and gives me that smile that makes his dimple pop out.

"I knew you were the absolute worst. But this is just next-level cruel, Tony."

In an instant, his smile drops, sobering us both immediately.

I don't understand why calling him Tony changes his demeanor. When we decided to have a clean slate, I thought that meant the Tony ban was lifted, but I guess not. Truthfully, it's a welcome reprieve from the sexual tension that was building up inside me, so I take the opportunity to get us back on track to go to sleep.

"Okay, fine. But this pillow stays." I smack a pillow right

between our lower bodies. A chastity pillow, if you will. I turn to shut off the light on my nightstand and cloak my side of the bed in darkness.

Antonio takes the hint and does the same. We lie in silence for a few minutes. I'm convinced he's fallen asleep until he speaks. "Just so you know, you can call me Tony now."

I smile so widely into my pillow.

"Okay. Good night, Tony."

"Good night, Nicolette."

15

Nikki
SEVEN YEARS AGO – DÍA DE LOS REYES MAGO

New York City

I changed my mind.

Tony haunts me. And I don't want the feeling to go away.

It's been less than a week, and Amelia and I are all settled into our cozy new apartment. The apartment that is located five blocks from Tony's.

Tonight, we're on our way to Amelia and Tony's parents' home. They also live nearby, and I can't wait to celebrate my first Three Kings Day with their family. I've already met Amelia's mom countless times when she visited Miami, and I love her like a second mother.

Sometimes I feel guilty for gravitating toward Anna more than I do my own mom. But the woman gives the best hugs that make you feel like you're wrapped in a love cocoon. Almost like how Tony made me feel the night we met.

Amelia and I enter the apartment and are immediately greeted by shouts and cheers. "¡Feliz Día de los Reyes, mi amor!" Amelia's dad, Ramón, says as he pulls her in for a bear hug.

"Welcome, Nikki, to your first holiday with us. Consider it the first of many, please." He kisses me on my cheek.

I can't stop smiling as I'm passed around the living room to receive similar greetings.

I sense him before I've even laid eyes on him. I hear the front door close and see Tony standing there with his eyes already on me.

God, he looks so good with a white button-down shirt stretched tight across his chest and dark jeans. I want to run to him. Apologize for being an absolute fool and maybe see if we could go out on a date. Something small, like coffee, of course. I don't care what the next steps are. I just want to do them with him.

I offer him a small smile and wave. I can hear the breath he releases all the way from where I stand, and he smiles back at me.

Okay. I got this. We can do this. I mouth, "Talk later?" and he nods. I smile into my drink and try to jump back into the conversation with Amelia's tías.

Three hours later, I've yet to speak with Tony. He's been sucked into a game of dominos while I've been sequestered in the kitchen. Not to cook, but to gossip. At first, I was interrogated by all the tías, who wanted to know everything about me. I almost offered them my social security number at one point. Then they started talking about how their husbands drive them crazy, followed by good ole neighborhood gossip. Toward the end, Tía Carmen offered to teach me how to make Dominican cake. Tía Lourdes promised to introduce me to a friend of hers who works at the same nonprofit I'll be interning for, and Anna has announced that she has formally adopted me as a daughter. Everyone laughed at her theatrical declaration while I had to force myself to not tear up at the act of being claimed, of being wanted.

I was even invited to their family cruise this coming summer. An actual family vacation. Something I've never experienced before. Mainly because you need a family to attend one of those.

Later, the cousin crew ladies swapped out tías and picked up on the gossip train.

I mostly laugh at all the silly comments made, especially because I have no clue who they're talking about.

But then Amelia's cousin Priscilla starts talking. "Amelia, don't be mad, but I got some tea on your lovely brother."

Amelia rolls her eyes. "Leave it alone, Priscilla."

I can't help myself. "Leave what alone?"

Priscilla smiles devilishly. "So, my buddy Mark, who bartends at the sports bar on Ninety-Sixth and Amsterdam, told me that he sees our little Antonio there all the time."

"He's not very little, and going to a bar is hardly salacious, Priscilla." Amelia pins her with a hard look.

"I was getting to it! So anyway, Mark says that without fail, Antonio picks up at least a girl or two each weekend. And rumor has it he's a one-night-only kind of guy. He's even run into a couple of former one-night stands at the bar, and he turns them down for round two. Can you believe that? I mean, I know he's still not over—"

My stomach drops. One night only?

Is that what we were supposed to be?

I mean, I knew a man who looked like Tony must get around, but it still isn't a nice feeling to hear it out loud. And who is he not over?

"Ew, Priscilla, can you please stop? I don't need to hear about my brother's sexcapades. And we really don't need to be mentioning his ex." She huffs. "Besides, he's made it no secret that he doesn't do relationships. Why do you think even Mom has stopped trying to get on his case about finding a nice girl and giving her grandkids? It sucks, and I hate his reasoning, but if this is what makes him happy, we should respect it," she scolds.

He doesn't do relationships? Even his mom, the woman who has started asking *me* when I'm going to give her "gringo grandbabies," has given up on her only son to meet someone and have a family?

This doesn't sound like the guy who was vowing to be the only man to claim my kisses from here on out.

Or was that just a part of his ruse? His way of reeling in the ladies for one night, only to reject them when they came running back for more?

I think I'm going to be sick.

"Excuse me. I need to use the bathroom."

I make a beeline for the guest room bathroom before Amelia can notice anything off about me.

I take a moment to collect myself.

Maybe Priscilla has it all wrong, or maybe it's not as bad as it sounds. Perhaps he's changed his stance on relationships and just hasn't told his family. Not exactly something you want to announce to a group of females you consider family.

Something in my gut tells me to trust him. To, at the very least, have the conversation with him and get the answers I need before making a rash decision.

With new determination, I head for the door but come to a halt when I hear angry male voices on the other side.

"Dad, do we really have to do this right now?"

"Yes, because you ignore my texts when I ask you," Amelia's father argues.

"Well, then maybe it's because I don't want to talk about it."

"Antonio, it's been over five years. I thought by now you would have secured a safer job. One where your mother doesn't have to worry about you at night. I thought maybe you'd lose interest in it, or at the very least move up the chain to a point where you can have a respectable desk job."

"Do I look like the kind of man who sits behind a desk for eight hours a day, Dad?"

"Listen, mijo, we didn't immigrate to this country to just do what we like. We came here to do what needs to be done. For your future, your family."

"Oh, not this again."

"No, not this again. That's more your mother's arena. But at the very least, can you practice more discretion? Priscilla was pumping information about your flings to your mother and the other women. I'm in no rush for you to settle down. The last thing you need right now is something to distract you from getting to your next step in life."

"Jesus Christ. I'm gonna kill Priscilla."

"Look, son. I'm not here to make you feel bad, but you have to understand my stance as a father. I need to push you to make sure you're living your full potential. I don't want you to look back on this time and see it as time wasted. You need to make moves now while you're in your youth. You must take advantage of the opportunities that we moved here for in the first place. I say it out of love so you can have a better life."

"I know, Dad."

"Okay, let's get back to the party, and maybe give Priscilla different gossip to spread so you don't give your mother any more gray hairs."

"Yeah, yeah. Let's get out of here."

I hear retreating footsteps as I lean my forehead on the bathroom door.

Information overload. I feel myself getting emotional, so I do what I do best. I make a mental list and look at the facts logically, without catastrophizing the situation.

1. Antonio is a playboy who has previously claimed he has no interest in relationships.
2. Antonio is going through some career shift, in which his father thinks a relationship could be a distraction. And I'm just about to jump into my career and probably spend my time in underserved communities rather than on date nights.
3. Antonio's family is Amelia's family. The same family that has taken me in as one of their own. The family that I never had growing up, since it was just my mom and me. The family I will be creating new memories with for years to come. *Not just one night.*

My stomach is in knots as I straighten and reach for the door. I know what I have to do, even if it's the last thing my heart wants. But I don't make decisions with my heart. Never have, and I know all too well how dangerous it would be to start now.

Because if there's anything I've learned from my mother, it's how not to make her same mistakes.

16

ANTONIO
PRESENT

She called me Tony.

In bed.

And she misinterpreted my reaction.

She thought I was upset. Meanwhile, I tried to recall a time I must have kicked a puppy in order to earn this kind of bad karma. To have the woman of my dreams in my bed. Dressed like *that*. Calling me Tony.

Wanna know what's even better? Being awoken at eight in the morning to a content Nikki draped all over me. Her head lying on my chest, while her legs were tangled with mine. Cockblocking pillow nowhere to be found.

A perfect fit.

I didn't dare move a muscle. I just let myself hold her in my arms while being enveloped in her sweet scent of cherries.

As soon as I felt her stir, I removed my arm from her waist. As much as it pained me to release her, I knew her reaction to being the one to break our pillow barrier would be well worth it.

Her eyelashes flutter as she slowly opens her eyes. She releases a sweet moan that adds to the strain in my boxers due to my morning wood. She nuzzles into me for a moment with a lazy smile on her face. I make sure to catalog every detail before she inevitably loses her shit.

And right on cue…

"Oh my—oh my fucking God!" she yells as she rolls off me. She doesn't stop rolling until she's pulled the sheets off my body, exposing the tent in my pants while simultaneously burritoing herself, and finally falling off the other side of the bed with a big thud.

She pops back up like an out of breath jack-in-the-box and points an incriminating finger my way. "I didn't… we didn't… that wasn't… oh my God, cover up your massive boner!" she screeches, her cheeks taking on a deep shade of pink.

I link my hands behind my head with a shit-eating grin. "First of all, don't shame me for basic human biology. That's my morning wood, so I wouldn't classify it as a sexual boner. Second of all, once you unburrito yourself, take a second to realize that you, Little Miss Nikki, were draped over me. I, along with my morning wood, was an innocent bystander. It's okay. Take a minute. I can wait for an apology." I smirk.

I'm scared mosquitos are going to find their way into Nikki's gaping mouth. "Um. I-I didn't mean…" She turns and starts to walk toward the open patio.

I jump out of bed, laughing, and catch her before she walks the plank into the ocean. "And where do you think you're going?"

"Bottom of the ocean. I don't think my mortification can reach me there." She nods and makes to turn again, but I pull her into my chest instead.

"Good morning, roomie," I say into her hair. Her goose

bumps don't go unnoticed, and my chest puffs a bit at her physical response. "I'll order breakfast, then hang out here while you use the bathroom. But don't take too long. You promised me a day full of fun," I mumble in her ear.

She shakes me off and holds on to the sheets like a shield. "Order carbs. And maybe a mimosa. Better yet, a pitcher. Just go over there while you do it. Okay, bye!" She scurries off to the second-floor bathroom and closes the door behind the toilet room. The only place up there that offers any privacy.

I quickly call over for breakfast, then head back out to the patio to lie on a lounger. Somehow, this morning, the view is looking a lot more beautiful.

17

NIKKI

I can't believe my traitorous subconscious mind did me so dirty.

I was sprawled over that man like a mewling kitten. And my own kitty was almost dry humping his glorious thigh. *Where the hell was my chastity pillow?*

I'm clearly going to need a better system tonight.

Especially since the usually clean-shaven Antonio is now rocking some hot scruff that would probably feel delicious between my—nope.

Not going there.

Instead, I try to focus on the warm breeze and the beautiful scenery around me.

I bury my embarrassment from this morning's wake-up call as I wait on the patio for Antonio to get ready. Or dare I say Tony?

Last night, I was smiling like a goof when given the green light to call him by the same name his friends do. A monumental step in our relationship, if I do say so myself. And today will be another one, because I've planned the best day for us.

"I'm ready when you are." Tony stands by the patio door in

navy swim trunks and a white linen button-down shirt. I think this is the first time I've seen him without a freshly shaven face, and yeah… it's doing things to me. It takes all my willpower not to bite my lip and fan my face at the sight of him.

"Yep, ready to go," I croak out. I walk past him, ignoring the way his gaze roams my body.

"Wait, don't you need a swimsuit for the day?"

"I'm already wearing a one-piece suit under my sundress. And I have everything else we need in my bag." I wave him over to leave the bungalow. Once we've closed up, we hop on a waiting golf cart that'll take us to the resort lobby.

"So what exactly are we doing today?" he asks.

"It's a surprise!" I dance in my seat.

He shakes his head and chuckles. "Oh man. I'm sure this will be a treat."

We make it to the lobby and find Frobish waiting for us. "Ms. Nikki, are you sure you want to go off site? I assure you that we can accommodate any excursions you may be interested in here on the resort grounds," he pleads.

"No can do, Frobby. We're off for the day. And we won't be back for dinner, so no need to wait around for us." I pat him on the shoulder. He looks at the spot I touched, as if I wiped a germy hand on him.

"Wait, we'll be gone all day? Don't I need to bring a dinner outfit?" Tony asks.

"Aww, look who's turned into quite the fashionista." I pinch his cheek playfully while he rolls his eyes. "The place we're eating at is very… casual. So what we're wearing now is fine," I say as I turn back to Frobish.

"Very well, then. The boat is waiting for you on the dock, ready to take you to your next location. Just text this number"—he hands me a business card—"and we'll have you picked up within thirty minutes." He nods as he points to the waiting speed boat at the end of the dock.

"Thanks, man." Tony pats the same spot I did, and poor Frobish looks like he's about to have a dry-cleaning crisis. "I really hope you know what you're doing by taking us off the property," he whispers into my ear.

I wave him off. "Come on, it's going to be so much fun. Will you just live a little with me, Tony?"

He looks at me for a moment. Like really looks at me. Then gifts me with a warm smile. "Yeah, I think I can, Nikki." He pulls me into his side for a hug and keeps his arm around me as we make our walk toward the boat.

"You've gotta be kidding me." Tony sighs with his muscular arms folded across his broad chest. "Do I look like the kind of man who wants to go swimming with dolphins?"

I bend over and laugh at the look of pure devastation on his face. I'm really not trying to torture the man, but sometimes it's just too easy. "Relax, we're not going to an unethical aquarium where they keep them in captivity. We're joining that catamaran tour that'll show us places along the coast where we're likely to spot them. Then we're free to jump in the water if we want to get a closer encounter with them."

"You know what else we can have close encounters with out there? Sharks." He huffs.

"I never took you for a wuss, Tony." He gives me a stern look. "Besides, I'm sure you'll punch any shark that comes near me," I joke.

He grunts. "Then stay close." He pulls me to his side again as we get in line to board the catamaran.

He's been doing that a lot ever since last night. I didn't anticipate Tony being so touchy-feely with me, but you'll hear no complaints from me.

None. Zero. Zilch.

"This is an all-day tour. We'll go along the coast, looking for dolphins and maybe do some swimming. Then they'll take us to a sandbar for a buffet lunch and drinks. On the way back, they drop us off at a cave entry where we can do some cave diving. Then, finally, we enter the restaurant side that's built into the cave for dinner. It sounds fancy, but trust me, it's not. It's plastic tables and chairs with the Presidente logo on everything." I smile triumphantly. After so much pompous pretense, I figured we'd both enjoy having a no-frills evening. And the look in Antonio's sweet eyes tells me I just might be right.

18

ANTONIO

Watching Nikki light up as she spots another pod of dolphins is the highlight of my trip so far. Her blond hair whips around wildly in the wind as she squeals and points to the aquatic creatures following our boat. Every time she sees anything exciting, she squeezes my forearm in an attempt to direct my attention to what she's discovered, but I'm perfectly content just staring at her.

We stayed on the catamaran while others jumped in the water. Turns out Nikki wasn't so adventurous once she saw the size of the dolphins zipping through the water at high speeds. "I'm fine watching them from here. Besides, I heard dolphins are super horny, and I don't want to get rammed by one of those big boys."

I spit out a bit of my water at her blunt statement, biting back every sexual rebuttal I have on the tip of my tongue. "Noted."

She eyes me curiously. "You know, you seem different today. Like you're actually letting yourself relax for once."

I ponder her words, just as her cell phone starts to ring in her bag. She pulls it out, and the name *Mommy Dearest* flashes on the screen.

Yikes.

She quickly silences it and puts it back in her bag.

"What's that all about?" I nod toward her phone. "I noticed you silenced a few calls yesterday by the pool too. You avoiding your mom or something?"

She rolls her eyes playfully. "Of course you would notice," she mumbles. "And yes, I'm ignoring her calls for now. I sent her a quick text yesterday letting her know I was out of town and had limited access to phone reception, but the woman just won't quit."

I'm trying not to judge her. Especially since I had such a great relationship with my mom, and the limited information I have tells me that Nikki and her mom aren't very close. Hence why she has spent almost every holiday throughout the years with Amelia and our family. But a part of me feels like I need to understand their dynamic a little bit better.

"Care to shed some light on what's going on with you and your mom?"

Her short laugh lacks humor. "I thought I was the therapist in this duo. You coming for my job, big guy?" She elbows my arm.

I shake my head but stay silent, hoping she'll give me something.

She holds my gaze for a minute, then concedes. "My mom and I have a… complicated relationship," she starts. "She had me when she was in her early twenties. She had dreams of becoming an actress or a model, and instead, she ended up as a young single mom working in real estate." She sighs heavily.

"Anyway, fast forward to now. She's more interested in keeping up with her looks and finding men with deep pockets. She's been married three times and is on the prowl for her fourth as we speak. I try not to critique her lifestyle too harshly since she made sure I had everything I needed when I was growing up. And I don't want to make it sound like she fully neglected me or anything. But let's just say that if my mom had a sitter available and the option to either take me to the movies or go on a date, the date would win that competition. Every time."

"I'm sorry. That must have been really tough, especially as a kid" is all I can manage. Internally, I'm raging that my poor Nikki always felt like the lesser option to her mom instead of a priority.

"It's fine. When we're around each other, we get along well. I've been able to move past it, and she even agreed to do family therapy with me when I was in college, although that was short lived. But it is what it is. I've learned to love her as the person she is and not the mom I wish her to be." She pauses, contemplating if she should continue.

I tuck a piece of her golden hair behind her ear, and she offers me a sad smile.

"After Amelia survived the kidnapping and the news went viral, my mom called me immediately to ask how she was doing. I was so relieved to have her show up for me in such a mom-type role in that moment. I really needed someone to talk to about what happened. Especially since Justin and I had broken up on the same day Amelia was taken." I stiffen at the mention of her ex but hold her hand to encourage her to carry on.

She takes a deep breath, as if bracing herself for what she's going to say next. "After we spoke about Amelia and how she was going to make a full recovery for a bit, Mom started asking questions about Evan."

Fuck. I know exactly where this is going. "Go on."

"Amelia and Evan were on the cover of every newspaper in the city after she met up with him at his holiday party in that full black gown, right before she was taken. My mom saw it once the news went viral and, of course, focused on the fact that Evan is a billionaire. She started asking questions about him. How often I see him. Whether he has a father or even a brother." Nikki shivers at the thought. "She started going on and on about me being in his 'inner circle' and asking if I could introduce her to any of his business associates, and I just —" Her voice cracks as her eyes start to water.

Without a second thought, I pull her into my lap as the catamaran starts steering us toward our next stop.

I tuck her head under my chin and wrap my arms around her. I don't miss how she immediately melts into me.

She takes a couple of deep breaths, and I do the same, blissfully drowning myself in her cherry scent. "For so long," she whispers into my chest, "I gave up on the idea of her being a regular mom. I got comfortable with the reality that I had to treat her more like a girlfriend. But in that moment, when I was so emotionally distraught about Amelia, and my mom kept droning on about her favorite subject—men with money—I kinda lost it for a bit. I told her not to call me for a while and maybe used some pretty colorful language to drive home the point. She's been calling me ever since. I texted her to let her know I'm fine, but the last thing I'm going to do is answer her call while I'm on the world's most expensive vacation. She'd blast me with a million questions about it, or even worse, ask for an invite. So yeah, I'm just ignoring her calls until I'm ready. And I'm not sure exactly when that's going to be."

I give her a quick squeeze. "Take all the time you need, Nikki. I'll be here for you in the meantime."

She untucks herself and stares up at me. "You really mean that?" she asks with enough vulnerability to crack my heart in two.

"I'd love to see you try to get rid of me at this point, corazón."

"Corazón?" She quirks a brow.

I shrug nonchalantly. "Just go with it."

And for the rest of the ride, she stays on my lap while wrapped in my arms, like it's the most natural thing she's ever done.

Like she's finally home.

19

NIKKI

WE ARRIVE AT THE SANDBAR, AND I PRACTICALLY JUMP OFF Tony's lap like he's on fire.

A girl can really get used to being held by that man, but I need to remind myself that he's just being friendly. Because we're just friends. Very new friends.

No matter how badly I secretly want more.

But nothing has changed. Although I don't think Amelia would ostracize me for dating her brother, he's still a man with no interest in a relationship that extends past a couple of rounds in bed. Trust me, I've kept tabs on the gossip throughout the years.

So I hurry to exit of the catamaran and let the nice captain help me jump down onto the sand. I look over my shoulder in time to see Tony scowling at where the captain's hands rest on my waist. I ignore him and scurry over to an older lady who seems to be in charge of the food stand. She's currently firing off a million commands in Spanish while simultaneously frying tostones. My mouth waters at the sight. Loud bachata music is playing, and there are a couple of teenage boys wiping down plastic tables while dancing. I lean over to get a better view of the food options, but before I can practice my limited Spanish, I sense Tony looming over me.

"Hola, buenos días, señora. Esto se ve muy rico. ¿Nos puedes preparar dos platos con un poco de todo?"

The older woman lights up at him, because of course. "Claro que sí mijo. Siéntate y te lo llevo a la mesa. Pregúnta por mí, Maria, si necesitas algo," she says as she points at the empty tables.

He leans down and places his hand on my lower back to lead us toward one of the tables. "I told her that everything looks good, and if she could prepare us two plates with a bit of everything and—"

"And Maria told us to go sit and she'll bring us the food. Yeah, I got all that."

Both of his brows rise in surprise. "I didn't know how much Spanish you understood."

"I was born and raised in Miami, and I've spent almost every holiday for seven years with your Dominican family. Never underestimate me." I flip my hair like the brat that I am.

He chuckles under his breath as he slides a wonky plastic chair out for me, dragging it across the sand. "Noted."

I sit and immediately sink a few extra inches, thanks to the sand shifting beneath me. "You know you don't have to pull a chair out for me every time, right?"

"I don't have to, but I want to," he says casually.

Just then, the teenage boys working for the food stand walk by us with trays overflowing with various drink options. I grab a rum and coke while Tony takes a Presidente beer. Seconds later, we're bombarded by a group of older ladies who look identical to Maria. They flood our table with enough food to feed a football team. So, essentially, the perfect portion size for Tony.

"Yaniqueque, arroz con habichuelas, pica pollo, mangú, queso frito, salami—"

"Tony, breathe. I've never seen you almost have a heart attack over Dominican food." I lean forward and grab a hold of his muscular forearm.

He shakes his head. "You don't understand. I'm in the homeland now. Fucking finally!" And without another word, Tony is dead to the world as he devours every morsel of food on his plate, plus seconds.

To be fair, the food is absolutely divine.

We've been eating well at the resort, but this food feels like it was made with love and nostalgia.

I can't stop giggling as I eat, because Tony won't stop talking about the food he just inhaled. It's like he wants to propose to it. He might even propose to Maria at this rate.

"¡Maria, te amo!" he yells over the music with his arms stretched toward the sky.

It's quite the sight, and everyone around us chuckles at his reaction, but I couldn't stop the mini swoon session my brain had when he said *te amo*.

I clearly need to cool down.

I whip my sundress off and readjust myself to make sure I'm not flashing anyone.

Once I found this one-piece swimsuit in my new luggage, I knew I needed to wear it immediately. With all the lacy cutouts, it looks more like bridal lingerie than a swimsuit, and I can't wait to send Amelia a picture of it.

I go to reach for a second drink and halt all movements the second I notice Tony's eyes on me.

Had he not just eaten his own weight in food, I would have confused that look for hunger.

He groans like he's in physical pain. "Nikki."

"You give yourself indigestion or something?" I ask with my hands on my hips.

"Can you do me a favor?"

I quirk a brow.

"I can't be this full *and* horny. Can you put your dress back on? Maybe a paper bag over your head while you're at it too?"

My jaw almost hits the sand.

"Are you—is that—are you joking with me or…"

He lowers his head to the plastic table and starts banging his head softly against it.

Did he really just say that? What the hell did they put in his food?

I walk over to him and smack the back of his head. "What has gotten into you?"

"Blame Maria. I'm in a food coma. I can't think straight. Give me a couple of minutes." He looks up at me. "Unless you want to stick around and see a second showing of my… biological reactions."

"Antonio Manuel Nuñez! You did not just get a boner over bistec and boobies!"

He releases a pained laugh. "I'll get it under control. You just need to go… somewhere else. Or would you be okay with me burying you in the sand?"

I still don't know whether he's joking or flat-out saying that he's attracted to me. So I do what any other frazzled woman would do in this moment. I grab another rum and coke—yes, I'm double-fisting—and hurry off toward the water. I find the perfect sitting position where the ocean water gently laps at my waist, then take a sip of my drink and try to relax.

From where I'm sitting, I can see Tony chatting with the cooking staff, probably thanking them for the millionth time for the perfect meal. He catches me staring at him, and instead of giving me his usual scowl, the man does the unimaginable.

He winks at me.

Fucking winks.

Had I not been in the water, the wetness between my legs might have been instantly noticeable. How does he do that?

Hold the ability to turn my insides into Jell-O by just giving me his attention?

I should really address that during my next therapy session, because these psychosomatic symptoms are not my norm when it comes to men.

But Tony is clearly like no other man. He's in a league of his own.

He picks up another Presidente beer as he makes his way toward me, but he stops abruptly. The music has changed from bachata to pop, and "Shower" by Becky G is now playing.

I remember singing this song repeatedly when it came out, and always jamming to it with Amelia, especially during family gatherings when the cousin crew was around. Yet imagine my surprise when Antonio locks eyes with me and starts dancing to it.

This mountain of a man, dancing to Becky G. And because he clearly does nothing half-assed, he starts singing the lyrics too. More like butchering the lyrics while singing off key, but he's giving the tour crew and me a show, nonetheless.

I bite on my plastic cup to try and stop myself from laughing uncontrollably, but it's pointless once he starts trying, and failing, to make his pectoral muscles bounce.

He pulls Maria into the dance, and she eagerly joins him. The dance turns into a mix of merengue and swing dancing, all while he keeps his smiling gaze on me.

I've never seen this side of Tony. This unbashful, playful side. I would have never fathomed seeing this man dancing with strangers with the biggest grin on his face. It makes me wonder what else he's capable of.

The song ends, and Tony bows to Maria, while she claps her outstretched hands in his direction.

He snatches a water bottle from the buffet table before he makes his way toward me. I couldn't swipe the grin off my face even if I tried, and to be honest, I'm not trying.

Tony settles in the spot next to me, exhaling loudly as the

cool water washes over his lower body. He takes a sip of his water before asking, "You like my little performance back there?"

I nod. "I never knew that was possible."

"What? You didn't know I had moves like that?" He tsks.

I shake my head. "No, I meant I never knew you'd be able to let loose like that. Putting on a show for everyone."

He shrugs. "I didn't do it for everyone. I did it for you."

"Huh?"

He leans a little closer. "You were upset on the boat. When you opened up about your mom. Figured I had to find a way to get this back and make it stay." His wet knuckles stroke my uplifted cheeks.

A breath gets stuck in my throat as Tony's gaze pierces straight into my soul. His touch on my skin leaves a trail of heat, even though his fingers should be cool to the touch.

His eyes drop to my lips, and my brain starts to panic. I know I would not be able to kiss this man right now and survive it. Especially not this version of Tony.

So I blurt the one thing that should have him backing off. "So, uh, why don't you do relationships?"

His lips twitch with amusement. *Not the reaction I was expecting.*

He drops his hand and tips his water in my direction. "Swap?" He nods at the drinks in my hands.

My shoulders sag a bit. "I know this looks bad, but I can handle my liquor, Tony. I can switch to water after dinner."

His lips flatten as he takes a few moments to respond. "I meant that if I'm going to tell you the story of why I didn't do relationships, I might need those more than you do."

Oh.

Wait. Did he just say that in past tense?

"Oh, um sure," I say instead of trying to get my hopes up.

He turns one of the cups and aligns it so that he drinks

from the spot that has my lipstick on it. I could burst into flames right here, right now.

"As you know, I was born here. And we lived here until I was five. That's when we moved to New York. Right before Amelia was born." I nod, and he continues. "I had lots of neighborhood friends on the island, and when we left, it was really hard for me. I was a kid who didn't know how to speak English and was now living in a foreign country with different customs. My parents saw how I struggled, and somehow managed to save enough money to have me spend summers back here, with my grandma." He smiles into the distance, as if recalling those memories.

"It wasn't every year, but I was able to come back for months at a time and spend summers with all my friends. One of my very best friends was a girl named Aracelys."

Fuck. I know that's his ex's name.

"We spent every summer together, and eventually, we fell in love. She was my first everything, and I was hers. We knew everything about each other." He clears his throat, pushing down on his emotions. "Anyway, we were together for a very long time. Ten summers at my grandma's house. I had dreams of moving her to the states and getting married. I knew marriage was in the cards for us, no question about it."

The confession causes a pinch in my stomach, so I try to drown it with a few gulps of water.

"Unfortunately, I didn't factor her *other* boyfriend into the equation."

Oh no.

He runs a wet hand through his short strands as he blows out a harsh breath. "During my last summer at my grandma's house, I arrived a weekend earlier than planned because I wanted to surprise my girlfriend. Too bad I was the one walking away with the surprise of my life when I got out of the cab just in time to see her French kiss a random man goodbye."

Ouch.

He takes another long sip of his drink.

"Tony, if this is too hard—"

He places a hand on my thigh and squeezes while keeping his eyes trained on the ocean water.

"She was my everything. I was planning my life around her. I had even talked to an immigration attorney to get a head start on helping her immigrate to the states." He chuckles darkly. "I was too young and naive. I thought that we'd figure life out, and eventually, things would fall into place. But I guess while I played house in my mind, she was working up the courage to break up with me. Might have been nicer if she had done it *before* she started dating a guy from her university…" He finishes one drink, then slides the other full drink into the empty cup. "I confronted her as soon as I got to her doorstep. She was shocked to see me, but a part of her actually seemed relieved. Like she no longer had to hold on to the secret that she was cheating and living a happy life… without me."

"Oh, Tony—"

"The sad part? I still wasn't ready to let her go. To let *us* go." He lets out a harsh breath. "Don't get me wrong, I was angry as hell, but I was still clinging to a sliver of hope. But after she was able to convince me to move away from the front door, where prying eyes would be spreading the gossip like wildfire, she sat me down and spilled her truth."

"Which was?" I ask tentatively.

"While I was fantasizing about a life in New York with her, she dreamed about a life in the Dominican Republic. She had her friends and family here, along with a clear career path. She never had dreams of immigrating. She loved this country deeply and never felt the urge to leave. And you know what? Not seeing that sooner? That's on me. Because I grew up hearing how fortunate I was to have parents that immigrated to the states and believed that I was one of the lucky ones. It never occurred to me that anyone would purposely stay back, that they would be happier here."

I put my hand over the one he has on my thigh and give it a little squeeze. He finally lifts his eyes to mine, and I still when I see that they're on the verge of tears.

"She told me she couldn't live her life waiting for our summers. Like her life was supposed to stay on hold until I made my yearly return." He nods repeatedly. "And I get it. We were young, barely twenty, managing a long-distance relationship before video chatting was even a thing. I can look back and understand how hard that must have been on her. But it doesn't take away the sting that none of that mattered to me. I would have continued in that relationship for as long as I could, even if summers were all I could have of her."

I see a tear slide down his cheek, and I'm in motion before he has a chance to wipe it away.

I settle into his lap sideways, just like on the boat, and pull his head into the crook of my neck. He settles there willingly, wrapping his arms around me. My hands go up to the back of his head, and I slowly start scratching the base of his neck. "I'm so sorry, Tony. I'm so, so sorry."

"That wasn't the worst part. Not even close. Once our talk was over, the one where she made it clear that we were broken up, I begged my parents to book me a flight home. But… we didn't have a lot of money. Just a flight here and back was a stretch for my parents' budget. So I had to spend the entire summer at my grandma's. Watching the woman I thought I would marry go on with her life and be happy with another man by her side. I saw her leave her house with *him* in dresses she used to wear for me. I saw him hand deliver roses to her front door when I knew she preferred lilies. I even had the unfortunate luck of running into them just about every time I left my grandmother's home. It was so bad that during my last month there, I hardly left the property." He squeezed me tighter. "All in all, I was a wreck. And by the time I finally got on my flight back to New York, I vowed I would never allow myself to hurt like that again."

I think I've been holding my breath the entire time he has been recalling his heartbreak. All this time, I had Tony pegged as someone with a hard exterior, denying access to anyone who dared approach. Never could I have imagined that someone made him feel like he had to be that way in order to protect his heart.

I feel my own eyes start to well, imagining a young and heartbroken Tony. My own guilt gnaws at me. I've also caused him pain and have yet to cop up to it. He notices my tears and closes his eyes. "Please, don't."

Since I'm in his arms, I can feel his rapid heartbeat against my chest. I concentrate on matching my breaths with his until our chests fall into a synchronized motion.

I feel him take a final deep breath, followed by the faintest of kisses on my neck. I have no time to react, because when he lifts his head, his eyes are filled with newfound determination. "She's the reason I haven't been back here since that summer, and why I closed myself off to relationships in the past. If I couldn't trust someone I had known and loved since I was a kid, how could I trust a stranger?" He scrapes his lips with his teeth and shakes his head. "But that's in the past. I'm finally ready to move forward." His arms squeeze around me.

"W-what does that mean?" I croak.

"I'm ready for more, Nikki." He leans closer as I hold my breath. My eyes fall closed. I only open them when I realize that Tony has placed a chaste kiss on my forehead.

"More?" I ask breathlessly as his eyes lock on my lips.

"¡Señoras y señores, el catamaran esta listo para irse a su

próximo destino!" Maria yells at us, the only two people left to board the catamaran.

Tony holds his hands out to help me stand. Once we've both straightened, he leans into my ear and whispers, "More."

As if he knows I don't have the capacity to respond, he steers us toward the awaiting crowd so we can join the rest of the tour crew, bypassing the captain as he helps me onto the boat himself.

20

ANTONIO

She's quiet.

Too quiet.

I laid it on thick back at the sandbar, and since I have no intention of going backward, I'm fine with giving her all the time she needs to catch up to what's happening between us.

Because something *will* happen. That I am sure of.

I see the way Nikki looks at me, and how her body responds to my touch. I also feel how she cares about me and didn't hesitate to jump into my arms twice today.

And we're just getting started.

The cave diving area was too crowded with tourists, so Nikki and I agreed to skip that part and enter the restaurant portion of the cave right away. As Nikki mentioned earlier, it's a pretty casual spot. Plenty of cheap mismatched tables and chairs gathered in front of a small stage and DJ area. The ceilings are higher than I expected, with low budget strobe lights flickering along with the daytime club music.

I've barely digested Maria's delicious food, but hell will freeze over before I pass up the opportunity for more

Dominican food. So we pull up to a table and order a couple of appetizers.

Nikki has forgone the dress she had on earlier, instead adding the world's tiniest cut off jean shorts to her outfit. I swear she planned her outfits for the day with mental warfare in mind, because being this close to her while keeping my hands to myself is pure torture.

She interrupts my thoughts by tapping my forehead. "Oh, look, it's back."

"What's back?"

"Your scowl. I knew it was only a matter of time." She tries to hide her smile behind her water bottle.

"I wasn't scowling." She gives me a bored look. "Okay, just a little. But it was toward your outfit, not you."

She scoffs. "Never pegged you for a caveman, Tony. Can't control your big boy emotions?"

My reply is cut off by Nikki's cell phone vibrating on the table. My sister's blinding smile stares back at me. I swipe to accept the video call and bring the phone to my face.

"Oh, no. He's offed her, Evan. And he stole her phone!" Amelia shrieks.

I can hear Evan chuckling in the background as I reach below the table and drag Nikki's chair closer to mine. "Here's your proof of life, sis. All's good over here. How are you feeling?"

"Nikki!" she screeches so loudly I have to click on the side of the phone multiple times to lower the volume. "How are you? Are you guys getting along? Is Tony being an ass? I just got off my pain meds today, so the brain fog has faded. I'm all here. Firing on all cylinders. Ready to go. Locked and loaded." She snaps her fingers repeatedly while her left eye twitches.

Evan comes into view. "Sorry, guys. She's already had a couple of espressos and is climbing the walls being stuck at home. She still needs to take it easy, and it's snowing over here, so she can't do much but drink caffeinated drinks and call every single family member." He smiles down at my sister. Damn, how did I ever miss the way he looks at her? Do I look at Nikki like that? My eyes land on her profile, and she continues to giggle at Amelia's antics.

"Amelia! I'm so glad you're feeling better! We're doing great over here. Tony even agreed to try to be less of an ass. Can you believe it?"

I drape my arm over her chair and pinch her arm out of the camera view. She squirms in her seat but keeps her attention on the phone screen. Amelia starts talking again, but Evan's looking right at me, and something tells me he noticed me teasing Nikki. The look on his face is calculating, and the last thing I need is to have Evan and Amelia meddling in our business before we even get down to business. So I quickly say our goodbyes and end the call, ignoring Amelia's disgruntled face.

"Hey! I wasn't done talking to her. I still haven't thanked her for all the cute outfits she ordered for me," Nikki pouts, making me want to kiss it off her until she's smiling again.

I allow my eyes to wander all over her body, like I've done dozens of times today. "Yeah, we'll have to send her a thank you note or something."

Nikki slaps my bicep. "Will you quit it? Who knew being your friend would come with all this flirtatious territory? I'm gonna need you to tone it down and put a lid on it."

Friend.

As if we could ever be just friends.

But I'll leave it for now and ask a question I've always wondered.

"Have you ever met your dad?"

Nikki almost spits out the sip of water she just took. "Well, that's a sharp left turn if I've ever seen one." She tries to joke, but the smile is wiped from her face once she realizes I'm actually curious. "Are we just going to get all the sob stories out of the way today? Is that the game plan? Or are we doing ayahuasca later to cleanse all of our demons?"

"You don't have to tell me if you don't want to. I know it was a lot to talk about your mom earlier, so if this—"

She waves me off. "It's not a big deal. I don't have daddy issues." She scoffs. "Now, mommy issues? That will keep us in these chairs for the remainder of this trip." She shakes her head. "But to answer your question, yes and no."

"How is it yes and no? Have you met him or not?"

"It's complicated."

"Then uncomplicate it." I huff.

"Okay, you brute. Simmer down."

"Sorry. Go on." I don't even try to hide my smile. I love when she calls me out on my shit.

She rolls her eyes. "Long story short, my parents were never married. They met in Miami and had this whirlwind romance. After six weeks, my dad gave my mom a spiel about having to leave Miami due to his new job, and that it'd be best if their romance ended. Enter plot twist." She points to herself. "Mom was already pregnant with me. But that wasn't enough to keep Dad around, so he left." She shrugs.

"Wow. What a piece of shit. I'm sorry, Nikki."

"Well, I should mention that he did pay my mom child support every month, and a little extra in case I was ever interested in sports or extracurricular activities. It's still shitty, but many people have it way worse. My mom and I were never strapped for cash, and he's always remained a present being in my life. Just never in person."

"So…" I start, not knowing what to ask next, but Nikki saves me the bother.

"I've had phone calls with him all my life. He's always sent me cards and gifts for my birthdays and Christmases. But once I became a preteen, I cut off all communication after pleading for years for him to come and visit me. He always fed me some bs about not being able to because of his job, so I just assumed he had a whole other family, and I was his dirty little secret." She offers a pained smile. "After college, and lots of therapy, I decided to reach out to him again. I figured if I could accept my mom for who she is, why not my dad? I know it's still a shit situation, but it's a better alternative than me having to walk around with all that anger in my soul."

"You're a much better person than me, Nikki. That's for sure." I pull her in for a side hug.

"Yeah, we all know you can hold a grudge… I mean, can be a grump." She quickly pulls away and continues before I can give her comment some thought. "But everything is good now. We even video chat, believe it or not. So I at least know what he looks like, even if his name is still a mystery." She immediately winces. "Forget I said that last part. Where is the food anyway? Do we have to get up and get it at a counter or is this—"

"You don't know your father's name?" I ask incredulously.

She plants her elbows on the table and drops her head into her hands. "Ugh, can we go back to not being friends? I blab too much around you. A woman can only handle so much embarrassment," she mumbles into her hands.

I slide my hand behind her neck and lift her head. The movement brings her close enough for us to feel each other's breaths on our lips. Her eyes widen for a moment, looking at my lips before she meets my eyes. She clears her throat and painfully adds some space between us. "M-my name." She clears her throat again. "I hate my name. I mean." She closes her eyes and shakes her head. "Okay, let me try that one more time without my brain short circuiting." She gives me a shy smile. "When my parents met, my mom fell head over heels in love. She thought he did too, but clearly, he didn't because he gave her a fake name."

My body stiffens immediately.

Nicolette.

The memories of the night we met hit me like a ton of bricks. The feeling of betrayal when my sister informed me that Nicolette was actually Nikki. *Her* Nikki. Putting into question every moment we'd shared together, every second since I'd fallen in love with her at first sight.

I shake away the knee-jerk reaction and blow out a breath.

I need to stop. This isn't the same thing. Technically, that is her real name, and I need to stop feeling personally slighted by her giving me that name when we first met. After all, we were strangers to one another. This isn't about me. It's about Nikki's absentee dad, and I need to keep the focus on her.

"What name did he give her?" I drape my arm over her chair, leaning in a smidge.

She groans before finally answering. "John McClane."

I'm not quick enough to stop the laugh that bubbles out of my chest, but out of respect for Nikki, I try to cover it up with a cough. Her face lets me know she's not buying it. "Yep. Clearly my mom hadn't seen, or hadn't paid attention to *Die Hard* movies, even though I was born in the early nineties." She rolls her eyes. "I only found out during my preteen years, because I was watching the movie with my mom on Christmas morning, and she goes, 'Hey, what a funny coincidence that he has the same name as your father.' That was another reason I had cut him out of my life. He let me walk around with McClane as my legal name when it was just a stupid alias. To this day, he swears that John is his real name, but he won't disclose his actual last name." She starts peeling the wrapper off her water bottle. "It sucks when the first man who's supposed to love you unconditionally won't even claim you with his last name."

Her pain cuts me deep, and in that moment, I realize I would do anything to take it away.

It's his loss for never claiming her with his last name. A second realization hits me then—I'd happily give her mine.

Fuck. Why did I go ahead and plant that seed in my head? I need to slow down. I don't want a repeat of the last time I got close to Nikki. The one that ended with her forgetting me the very next day. If I'm in this for the long game, I need to start acting rationally.

"But there's nothing I can do about it. So I just take what he gives me, sporadic video chats and texts, and move on with my life. And I know I must sound stupid, but there are times when I feel like he's with me. Not like a spirit or anything like that, but ever since we've started video chatting again, I feel his presence more prominently in my day-to-day life. And it's kind of soothing," she finishes.

I take a moment to think about everything Nikki has disclosed about her family today. I can't even imagine how alone she must have felt growing up. It's worlds different from my experience. I've been smothered with family my entire life, some of whom I'm not even related to by blood.

There's nothing I can say to change her past, but I know with every fiber of my being that I'll make it my mission to make the rest of her days better.

I clap my hands, bringing her attention back up to me. "Well then, now that we've gotten your villain origin story out of the way—"

Her whole face lights up with mock fury. "Excuse me!"

I sloppily place my index finger over her lips, almost to the point of picking her nose. "Hush, I'm speaking. As I was saying —" She swats my finger away while giggling. "You've planned an amazing day for us, but now I'm taking over. We have a couple hours to kill before this excursion is officially over, so how about we have a little fun?"

She fully turns toward me with a mischievous grin. "So what do you have in mind, Tony?"

Oh, wouldn't she love to know?

We've been going at it nonstop.

Cave diving, bachata dancing, and eating. Lots of eating.

Nikki's tried every fruity cocktail under the sun, and I'm pretty sure the bartender who keeps sending beers my way is my second cousin.

For the last hour, this restaurant has turned into a dance club packed with young college students taking advantage of the legal drinking age.

I've never felt older than right now, seeing young kids vying to win the club's dance off competition. The prize? A mama-juana shot.

But that doesn't mean I'm not grinning from ear to ear as I watch Nikki cackle at all the outrageous dance moves these rowdy kids are performing.

I don't know if it's the drinks, the atmosphere, or my poor impulse control that leads me to brush Nikki's hair out of her face with my hand, rest it on the back of her neck, then pull her close to me so I can whisper in her ear. "Have I told you how beautiful you look today?"

Nikki shivers, and I know it's not due to any cool weather in this balmy cave. She pulls back just enough to peer up at me. "Um, no. Is that supposed to be your new thing now?" She bites her bottom lip, and I feel a low growl deep in my chest.

"Yes, Nikki. It's gonna be my new thing now." I kiss her forehead and lean back in my chair.

Nikki takes a long pull of her drink, then faces me. "You know…"

The DJ interrupts her by announcing that they're looking for a final contestant for the dance competition. Her smile widens, and I'm saying no before she can ask.

"Oh, c'mon," she whines, "you gave such a good performance earlier! It's only fair that you show these kids what a real man is made of." She tries to bait me, but there are not enough beers on this island to make me do *that*.

"I already danced for you today, Nikki. But if you want to go up there, by all means. I'm sure you can request a Taylor Swift song that'll make the crowd go wild," I tease.

Her jaw drops. "Are you mocking me and my Swiftie lifestyle, Mr. Nuñez?"

My cock twitches in my swim shorts, but I ignore it and keep my focus on her. "What? Are you scared to go up there and show me what you got? Never thought I'd see the day where you'd back away from a challenge." And in that moment, I know I've got her.

She puts both hands on my left thigh and leans into me. "Oh, you think I won't do it? Or do you think you can bait me and have me twirl on the stage like a cute little pop princess?" She fights back with a maniacal grin.

Before I can respond, she stands and bends at the waist. She knows exactly what she's doing as she gives me the world's greatest view of her cleavage while she leans in close to my ear. "Just know, you asked for this." And with that, she takes off into the massive crowd of partygoers, toward the DJ.

I feel a bit unsettled at her ominous threat, and even more so when she keeps her eyes on me while requesting a song.

She moves to take center stage, and I'm already regretting this. I may have been able to manage spending the day with Nikki in that titillating outfit, but these young boys are probably pitching tents by the second as she waves at the crowd playfully.

The DJ cuts the music and announces in Spanish, "We got a cute little blondie who is ready to show off some moves. Make some noise for Ms. Nikki!"

Nikki's eyes connect with mine, and it feels like she's miles away from me. She blows me a kiss. I smile and wink at her, basking in her attention.

But that feeling is short-lived as the first beat of her chosen song starts to play.

In that moment, her earlier warning flashes in my mind.

Never underestimate a girl from Miami.

My smile drops and my ass is flying out of my chair before she even starts to move.

I keep my eyes trained on her as I start to plow through the crowd. I feel feral that she decided to do this just to taunt me.

Well played.

I'm still a few yards from the stage as the chorus of Daddy Yankee's "Gasolina" starts playing, driving the crowd wild.

And Nikki isn't playing fair. She's got all the reggaeton moves down as she dances to the song, looking like a goddamn music video vixen.

By the time I reach the front of the stage, I don't hesitate.

My arms wrap around the back of her knees, and in the next second, I'm throwing her over my shoulder.

She must have expected this reaction from me, because she doesn't fight me. Instead, her body shakes with laughter.

"Hey, Tony! On second thought, maybe I do have daddy issues!" She laughs.

I give her ass a hard smack. Her yelp is quickly covered up by more laughter.

Noted.

I take out my cell phone with my free hand and text the number to have a boat sent out to pick us up.

It's time to take my woman back to our room.

21

NIKKI

"Despiértate, corazón," Tony whispers in my ear.

I slowly blink and try to orient myself to my surroundings. I'm covered by a towel and wrapped in Tony's arms while sitting on his lap.

"You fell asleep on the ride over. We're docked now."

Oh, right. Guess dancing to Daddy Yankee really does take it out of a girl.

I yawn and stretch before attempting to stand. Tony takes that as his cue to carry me bridal style as he carefully steps off the boat and onto the dock.

I wrap both of my arms behind his neck as I say, "You don't have to carry me. I can walk, you know."

"I know I don't have to, but I want to." He smirks down at me. "By the way, you were humming to 'Gasolina' in your sleep."

I gasp. "I was not!"

His chest rumbles with laughter. "No, you weren't. But it's only fair I mess with you after that stunt you just pulled on me."

I shrug. "I have no idea what you're talking about. I was

just doing what you told me to do. Plus, I don't see why it would be a slight to you."

His hand carrying my leg gives me a quick pinch. I squeal, shimmying higher into his hold.

We hop on an awaiting golf cart and ride in companionable silence to our bungalow.

Once we arrive, Tony offers to let me use the bathroom first, and I don't hesitate to run upstairs to wash all of the sand and sea out of my hair. I let the warm water cascade over my body as a highlight reel of our day plays in my mind. I don't even realize I'm smiling until I turn in the shower and face the massive mirrored wall opposite me. Rich people must be very conceited to want to shower while staring at themselves, but now I'm glad I caught a glimpse of myself in this moment.

A moment of happiness.

Lost in my thoughts about Tony.

I shut off the water and wrap one towel in my hair and another around my body. I take the stairs down to the main floor. I almost miss the last steps as Tony walks in from the patio. He's dripping wet with a towel hanging dangerously low on his hips.

"I used the outdoor shower. Didn't want you to feel rushed up there."

I simply nod, since words would take too much effort at this time.

Tony and I are frozen in place with just a few flimsy towels standing in the way of us being completely naked. The look on Tony's face tells me that the same thought has just occurred to him too.

He shakes his head but doesn't hide his small smile. "Go ahead and change in the closet. I have my clothes out here." He points to his clothes folded on the bed.

Our bed.

"Yeah. Right. Sure. On it." I scurry past him, and only

once the closet door is closed behind me do I allow my brain the much-needed oxygen it was lacking in the past few minutes.

My face feels like it's on fire. One look at Antonio post-shower and all that ground we gained today as friends has vanished.

Because friends don't look at friends like that.

Friends don't picture each other naked.

And friends most certainly don't make you hornier than you've ever been in your entire life.

I pick out a black spaghetti-strapped cotton pajama dress. My skin is still hot from the sun, the shower, *and* the naked man in my room. I need a material that will at least let my skin breathe, even if I cannot.

I slowly open the closet door to make sure Tony is decent.

Or to not give away my presence if he's not.

He's already in bed and under the covers. His upper body is bare, and he's leaning against the headboard.

Once he sees me, he silently pulls the sheets down for me to get into bed. The simple gesture cracks the walls around my heart.

The instant my body touches the mattress, I feel my exhaustion hit.

Tony must notice, because he turns off the light on his nightstand while I place the thickest pillow I can find between us. Maybe this one will do the trick tonight.

Tony turns in time to eye the pillow as I shut off my light.

We say nothing as we both lie on our backs, looking up at the ceiling.

I'm not sure if we lie for seconds or minutes.

But the next thing I know, Tony is throwing the pillow onto the floor. I lift my head to say something, but my words die in my throat as one of his massive hands pulls me toward him and he spoons me.

"W-what are we... you—"

"It's late. Go to sleep, Nikki," he mumbles into my neck.

"Oh, okay," I whisper as my heart races. "Good night, Tony."

"Good night, corazón."

I must have drifted off quickly, because the last thing I recall is dreaming of Tony placing a tender kiss on my head.

~

Today must be Groundhog Day.

Because I wake up spread over Tony's body while he smirks down at me.

"Good morning, Koala. Or should I name you stage five clinger?" He taps my nose, his eyes crinkling with his smile.

I don't even make an immediate attempt to peel myself off him. I'll be damned if I let him see me waking up embarrassed two mornings in a row. "I'm used to my heated blanket. My body is seeking out warmth. What did you call it yesterday? Ah, right. It's biology." I shrug.

Tony throws his head back in laughter while also tightening his hold on me. It's only then that I realize that he's clinging to me just as much as I am to him.

And I like it… a lot.

Too much.

And I don't deserve it. At least not like this.

Yesterday, Tony opened up about his ex-girlfriend and how her deception shattered him. And here I am, holding on to the secret that ended us before we even had a chance to get started.

There is no nook or cranny in my subconscious mind where I can hide the plain fact that I want this.

I want Tony.

But I know better than any psychology textbook that there is no way for us to even explore dating as an option if our foundation is based on lies.

My lies.

The guilt is enough to have me shuffle off him without meeting his eyes. "I'm gonna use the bathroom real quick." I start making my way toward the stairs.

"Go ahead. I'll order some breakfast."

No. Space. I need space to think. I need space so I can fix this.

"Um, actually, I think I might have breakfast by the pool bar. I need time to, uh, journal. And meditate and stuff. By myself. Like alone." Real fucking smooth, Nikki.

I don't give him a chance to react before I run up the stairs and lock myself in the toilet room.

I need to make a plan. I need to make this right. Being scared and panicked is what got me into this guilt spiral in the first place.

I've got to come clean.

I've got to tell him the truth.

Guess it's only fitting that I do it tonight, on the seventh anniversary of the night that started it all.

New Year's Eve.

22

NIKKI

I'm sitting at the pool breakfast bar with pen, paper, and mimosa.

I mean serious business.

It's been seven years too long since I freaked out and lied to Tony, and tonight, I'm going to make it right. Regardless of the outcome between the two of us, he deserves the truth. And I deserve to release myself from this never-ending guilt trip.

I start writing talking points as if I'm about to do a TED Talk. I'm barely done with one line before I scratch it out and start again.

This goes on for twenty minutes.

In my periphery, I spot Tony sulking on his way to the glass enclosed gym. I'm sure my hot and cold act has him needing to blow off some much-needed steam.

I stop for a moment to take in the buzzing environment around the resort. All the staff members are running around, preparing for the New Year's Eve event tonight. There are flowers, decorations, and twinkling string lights everywhere. It's going to look magical.

Or it's going to look depressing if I can't get my head on right and fix this with Tony before the clock strikes midnight.

"Mind if I join you?" a deep, sophisticated voice asks behind me.

By the time I've turned in the voice's direction, the man behind it has already taken a seat next to me.

And not just any man. *The man.* The older gentleman who ordered a drink for me the first day I got here. Again, wearing a three-piece dark charcoal suit, with an expensive watch and cufflinks to match. I spot a small tattoo on his wrist before he pulls his cuff lower. *An ace of spades playing card.*

I may be here trying to figure out how to work things out with Tony, but I'd be blind if I didn't notice that this guy is very attractive now that I'm up close and personal. And by the way he's smirking, he's well aware.

"You're hot," my idiot brain spews out.

His eyebrows raise slightly. "Why, thank you. Nice to see that we can skip all the small talk."

I shake my head and point to his suit. "No, I meant you must be hot. Why are you wearing a suit in this heat and humidity? Did your airline lose your luggage or something?"

His eyes sparkle with amusement. "No one who can afford to come to this resort flies commercial. I made sure of that, Nikki."

"Wait. How do you—"

He places his index finger on his lips and silently shushes me. Then he whispers, "No one needs to know that the boss is in town, now do they?" He grins, blinding me with his perfect white teeth.

I gasp. "You—you're..."

"Just call me Mr. B." He winks.

Mr. B. Holy crap.

Mr. Barlowe. He's the mysterious owner of this island resort. And he knows who I am.

"Wait, so how do you know my name? Do you make it your business to know everyone who stays at your resort?"

"I make it my business to know everything about the woman who is currently holding all my attention. Which is why I know that your name is Nicolette, but you go by Nikki. You're thirty years old. Live in Manhattan. Currently single." He pauses for dramatic effect. "Should I go on?"

I gape at him. "The resort files all that information?"

He smiles wickedly. "No. But your Instagram is quite informative. Might want to make your profile private if you don't want strangers knowing your business."

Shit. I really need to be more careful with my online activity.

"I can't believe I put all my information out there. I should just delete the damn app at this rate."

He chuckles. "Or you can be like me and create a separate fake account. That way, no one knows who you are, and you can keep a pulse on everything happening online."

"Wait. *You* have a finsta? A fake Instagram account? Why?"

He appraises me, then softly says, "Sometimes I like to play in the shadows."

I feel a chill run down my spine. Something tells me I should excuse myself and leave this man alone. But clearly, I've never been one for self-preservation, so I push him instead. "Is that why no one knows who you are or the fact that you're here? At your own resort?"

"That's not important." He waves my question away. "I'd rather focus on the fact that my sources tell me that you were very much upset that you had to share a room with the man you arrived with, which leads me to believe that I, at the very least, have a shot at convincing you to stay in mine." He leans in closer. Way too close for comfort.

I'm too mindfucked to realize that a raging bull has joined the party, and he's none too pleased.

"I'm going to need you to back the fuck up from my girl," Tony barks from behind me. He's shirtless and dripping in sweat like he just jumped off a running treadmill.

My girl?

My *fucking* girl?

Mr. B. looks Tony up and down like he's the dirt beneath his shoe and smirks.

The move instantly makes me want to throw the rest of my mimosa in his face for taunting Tony like that, but he stands before I can react.

"Nikki, my offer stands. I'm sure I'll see you at the New Year's Eve party." He winks and saunters away without another look at Tony.

I sigh a breath of relief when he's gone, knowing that we didn't cause a scene. Or better yet, get kicked out for fighting with the owner of the resort. But that relief is short-lived once I meet Tony's searing gaze.

"What the fuck was that, Nikki?" he fumes.

I'm taken aback by his harsh tone. Definitely not the sweet and funny Tony I've quickly grown accustomed to.

"I'm going to need you to simmer down a bit and take a deep breath."

"Were you really flirting with that guy?" he yells and runs a hand over his face. "For fuck's sake, not again," he says mostly to himself.

"Again? What are you talking about?" I huff. "If you took that breath I suggested, I would be able to tell you that he came on to *me*," I point at myself, "not the other way around."

His pained gaze takes me aback. He moves quickly as he places one hand on the bar and another on my stool, effectively caging me in. "You drive me fucking insane, you know that?" he says, his eyes fixed on my lips.

We don't move a muscle as we breathe in each other's air.

That is, of course, until my idiotic brain spits out, "You called me your girl."

And just like that, the air around us shifts as he takes two big steps away from me. "I'm gonna go for a run around the island. I'll text you when I'm back in the room for a shower." And he takes off without waiting for my response.

"Back to texting each other?" I mumble to myself. "Fuck that."

I turn back in my seat with new determination.

I order a *morir soñando,* a non-alcoholic Dominican drink, to help keep me fueled. I need all my wits if I'm going to do this right.

I'm finally coming clean.

I'm laying all the cards on the table.

And all I can hope is that by the end of it, he'll still want to call me his girl.

23

ANTONIO

I need to catch a fucking break.

I'm still fuming at the memory of seeing that guy sleazing over Nikki by the bar. My brain didn't even conjure a single thought before I realized I was sprinting my ass toward them, dropping the heavy weights I was using in the dust.

And then I had to go ahead and add the cherry on top by calling her "my girl."

The anger and humiliation I felt were enough to make me steer clear of her for the rest of the day. When I saw her by the pool, I took off toward the beach. When I spotted her approaching me at lunch by the pool restaurant, I left my meal half eaten and ordered more food to be delivered to the bungalow.

I don't trust myself around her right now. So the space is very much necessary.

She holds the power to drive me mad, and I need to get my head on straight if I plan on leaving this island with Nikki firmly planted by my side.

My girl.

My Nicolette.

Mi corazón.

But a part of my mind can't help harping on today's date. Our morbid anniversary. Seven years ago, to the day, I fell in love with this woman at first sight, only for her to forget me the next day. As hard as I try, I can't help reliving the week that followed. When she left me, and my bleeding heart, on the dirty New York City sidewalk.

24

ANTONIO

SEVEN YEARS AGO – DÍA DE LOS REYES MAGO

I've been itching to talk to her all night. But I know if I make a move for her here, all the women's antenna's will be up. And the last thing I need is to rope Nicolette into some juicy chisme on her first night with my family. As if my stupid heart wasn't a goner for her already, seeing her fit perfectly with my loved ones just sealed the deal for me.

I see her grab her coat and take it as my cue to exit as well.

"Are you sure you don't want to spend the night here? We can share the guest room," Amelia suggests to Nicolette.

"No, it's all right. I have work in the morning, and it would be easier to just get ready for the day from our place." She puts on her coat.

"I'm actually leaving too." I quickly shrug on my coat before I get pulled into the Hispanic forty-five-minute goodbye cycle. "I'll walk you home. It's late."

Nicolette looks my way but doesn't meet my eyes. "No, that's okay. It's just a couple of blocks." She walks to move past me, but I step ahead and open the door for her. "No worries. It's on the way to my place."

She gives me a weak smile and yells goodbye to everyone. The choir of voices and music quiet down immediately after I close the door behind me.

"Tony, it's fine. You really don't have to walk me."

"I appreciate you putting up the act in there. It was a smart move in front of the gossip piranhas, but we're good now." I reach up to touch her arm, but she turns on her heel and starts descending the stairs to the lobby.

"Hey, wait!" I follow her down and catch up to her right in front of the building doors. "Hey, are you all right? I thought we were going to talk now."

She stares off toward the mailboxes lining the wall behind me. "Oh, that. Don't worry about it. It was nothing." She places her hand on the door handle to push it open, but I place my hand over hers.

"What do you mean *nothing*?"

My heart starts racing. Earlier in the night, she seemed excited to talk to me, just like she was the night I met her. This version, the one that's trying to brush me off, is making me panic.

She takes a deep breath and finally meets my gaze. "I was just going to apologize again. For New Year's Eve. For being overserved and probably embarrassing myself in your presence."

"Nicolette—"

"Please, call me Nikki. Everyone calls me Nikki."

But I don't want to be like everyone.

"Nikki, that night. A lot happened. A lot was said. And—"

"And I'm saying that I don't remember. I'm sorry, Tony. Truly," she says firmly.

Air rushes out of my lungs as I struggle to stand straight.

How did I not see this? How did I get it all wrong?

And this Nikki person. How could she be so cold compared to the funny and affectionate woman I met less than a week ago? Clearly, I should have known better. I should have never changed my stance on relationships for her. I should have known not to trust a woman again, especially after knowing her for just a few hours. Stupid me.

I finally gather my bearings in time to see the look of pity she sends my way. If this woman thinks she can just mess with people's feelings, she's got a rude awakening coming to her. And I'll personally see to it that she never gets the chance to get near my heart again.

"Hey, Nikki?"

"Yeah?"

"It's Antonio to you."

I push the door open and let her step out. I decide to follow her, to make sure she gets home safe, but walk a few steps behind until we reach her block. When she approaches the door to her building, she turns to speak to me, but I just change directions and start walking back toward my apartment.

And that was the last time I ever called her Nicolette.

25

NIKKI
PRESENT

He's avoiding me like the plague.

I've written and prepared my apology speech to him fifteen times, but each time I try to reach him, he bolts.

My stomach is a ball of nerves, so I skipped the fancy dinner tonight and instead spent an hour in the shower using every fancy product this resort has to offer.

By the time I'm standing in the closet, my body is scrubbed, shaved, and moisturized within an inch of its life. And since I was on a roll, I was able to do my hair and makeup in record time. Leaving my blond locks half down with soft beach waves and natural looking makeup on my eyes and cheeks, since the tan gods have allowed me to be sun kissed instead of burned. And because I couldn't resist, I finished off the look with a bold red lip.

I stare at the garment bag hanging before me. I've been so wrapped up in Tony that I haven't been tempted to take a peek inside. But tonight is the night, and if I'm going to confront him with the truth, it might as well be in a cute dress that I'm sure Amelia handpicked for me.

I have to bend low to pull the zipper all the way down. When I stand, I do a double take.

The closet light above me hits like a spotlight on my dress, and a million reflective beams ignite over the space. Before me, sitting in a hanging half-bodied mannequin, lies the most stunning silver shimmering dress. It has a death-defying neckline, which might not be so bold if it wasn't mere inches away from the high slit on the side.

The material staring back at me is practically calling me poor with the way it glitters. I run my fingers over it to confirm I'm not hallucinating, and sure enough, the fabric feels just as decadent as it looks.

I make quick work of first putting on that hot lacy nude lingerie that the Bergdorf Goodman team said I needed to wear under this dress. And hot damn, if Tony doesn't forgive me after my apology, I might just need to strip down to this and use it as reinforcement.

I step into the dress, then raise it carefully as I slip my arms into the bedazzled winged sleeves and adjust the top so it at least covers all the important parts. Once on, I realize that I'm going to need help with the zipper. I can probably call Kelsey to come over, since I'll need help strapping on my silver satin heels as well.

I give myself one final look in the mirror and smile at the memories this twinkling dress conjures. This is a much fancier and *much* more daring version of the dress I wore on the night I met Tony. The material fits snugly over my perked-up breasts and cinches at the waist before falling straight down to the floor. I quietly laugh at myself for feeling like I'm playing dress-up, standing barefoot in an unzipped dress, as if it's completely normal to look like someone casually poured extravagant silver jewels all over my body.

I've never felt as confident as I do in this exact moment, and I hope it's enough to carry me on my mission tonight.

I grab my heels and head out of the closet but come to a quick halt.

Tony is standing shirtless at the bottom of the stairs with a towel in his hands.

His former scruff, now turned into a neatly trimmed short, soft beard, holds me captive as I try to remember how to speak.

"Oh. Hi. I didn't know you were back," I stammer.

His eyes rake over me from top to bottom with an unreadable look.

"Uh, since you're here, do you mind helping me with my zipper? I can't reach, and I—" I stop talking when he stalks my way. For some reason, I'm losing my nerve around him, and I need to remind myself to breathe.

He comes to stand behind me and growls. "Nikki."

Shit. I forgot what I was wearing under this, so I'm sure he has a full view of the lingerie that ends in a slinky thong.

"Oh, I'm sorry. This is awkward. I shouldn't have—" I shut up the second I feel his hand on my neck, gently moving my hair to the side. His other hand keeps a firm grip on my waist. Then, slowly, and I mean excruciatingly slowly, he starts pulling up my zipper, centimeter by centimeter. I don't even realize I've started to pant until I hear him chuckle behind me and whisper, "Serves you right," under his breath.

When I'm finally zipped up, I dart toward the bed and lean against my nightstand. I need space to have this conversation before I start dry humping his leg like an overexcited chihuahua.

He points to the shoes in my hand. "And those?"

I lift them in the air. "Oh, these old things?" I say, breathier than I intended. "I'm just gonna hold them like an accessory. New trend alert." I fake laugh.

The corner of his lip twitches as he makes his way toward

me. Before I can ask what he's doing, he drops to one knee, then slides his hands up my leg until he reaches my thigh. "Let me." He doesn't wait for my response as he grabs a shoe and places my foot in it. He then works diligently to wrap the strap around my ankle and buckle it in place. "How's that feel?"

I clear my throat. "So good. I mean. Fine. It's fine."

He keeps a sexy smile on his face as he repeats the same task for my other foot. When he stands, he leans in close and lifts my chin with his index finger. "I'm gonna shower and get ready for the night. You should go ahead. I know you skipped dinner."

I open my mouth to protest, but he cuts me off. "Once I arrive, you and I are going to have a long overdue chat, *corazón*. And we're gonna settle some things once and for all. Understood?"

I nod in lieu of speaking since I can't guarantee a moan won't escape my lips.

"Good." He starts to make his way back toward the stairs but stops and turns back to me. "And Nikki, you look beautiful in that dress."

"Really?" I smile.

His eyes narrow slightly. "Actually, no. You look more than beautiful. You look like an absolute vision. Breathtakingly stunning. And straight-up sinful. So for my sake, and the safety of the other men on this island, make sure I don't find you dancing with someone else. I'm not above making a statement tonight."

My breath hitches. "And what statement would that be?"

He grins mischievously. "You'll see."

26

NIKKI

My skin feels like it's on fire.

I'm standing by the pool bar, waiting for a drink that I desperately need while replaying my last interaction with Tony.

I'm so aroused it's uncomfortable to walk with this lingerie that keeps riding up in the worst spots possible. And to top it off, I still haven't had my conversation with Tony, so I'm having major anxiety over how that's going to go down.

Horny and anxious. What a devastating combo.

I won't even let myself think about the way he touched me or the fact that he, too, wants to talk to me about something. I can only panic about one thing at a time, and right now, it's the apology of the century that hangs over my head.

My phone buzzes in my hands, and I laugh when I see the message from Amelia.

Amelia: Where are my pics, pendeja?

I angle my phone as far away from me as possible so I can get my dress in the photo and snap a quick selfie. I immediately get a response.

Amelia: YASSSS BITCH. I KNEW YOU WOULD LOOK LIKE A HOT BARBIE!!

Amelia: Post this one on insta right fucking now! And tag Maribel as the stylist!

Amelia: Omg you're gonna be setting off boners all night. You're def getting a NYE kiss tonight!! If not more *smirking emoji*

I try not to harp on the New Year's Eve kiss comment, but it's hard not to think back to the one I shared with Tony years ago.

I snap myself out of it and go ahead and post the picture to my social media with a disco ball as the caption. I was hoping to keep this trip in the dark from my mom and my ex, Justin, but my sense of gratitude toward Maribel and her team of stylists at Bergdorf Goodman override that thought.

Just as I slip my phone into my clutch, a familiar voice rumbles behind me. "That dress, and the woman wearing it, has the power to bring a man to his knees, Nikki."

I turn and face Mr. B., smirking at the memory of Tony on his knees earlier tonight while he put on my shoes for me. Mr. B. must think my reaction is for him, so he steps in closer.

"Have you given any thought to my offer? I can promise you a night you'll never forget." He smiles deviously.

I've already had one of those. Seven years ago. And tonight, I intend to let the right man finally know it. I go to move past him and stop as we stand side by side. "Thanks, but no thanks. I'm perfectly content with the current company I keep."

I move to step away, but his hand whips out to grab my wrist. "C'mon, Nikki. You can't possibly be better off with that guy. I heard his hardened New Yorker accent. What is he, a plumber or something? A woman like you deserves a lot more decadence than a man like him can offer."

I can feel the fury rising in my body, but before I can respond, a tiny voice interrupts us. "Excuse me, miss." I look down to find the little girl I spotted in the cabana the first day I arrived at this resort tugging on my free hand. "Can you help me find my mommy?" She pouts with sad puppy eyes.

That sentence has Mr. B. dropping my wrist instantly.

"Of course, sweetheart. Let's go find her." I take her hand in mine, then say lowly so only he can hear me. "And for the record, there's nothing you can offer me besides making yourself scarce. So if you don't mind…"

Before I'm out of earshot, he makes sure I hear, "Girls like you are a dime a dozen. Your loss for skipping out on a golden ticket, sweetheart. Enjoy riding off into the sunset on the subway." He scoffs as he turns away from me.

I shiver at the audacity of that man.

I'm so thankful I'm being pulled in the opposite direction by the little cutie who's attached herself to my arm. With a long breath out, I focus on my quest to reunite this kid with her family.

"Hey, what's your name, sweetie? I'm Nikki," I say as she continues to pull me with respectable force.

"My name is Moana!" She giggles.

We're now weaving between high cocktail tables and beelining it to a private table.

"Okay, Moana." I play along. "Slow down, there. Where did you last see your—"

"I did it! Can I have my ice cream now? Pretty please?"

Huh?

We're standing in front of a gorgeous woman. The same one I saw with "Moana" a few days ago. Looks like she knew exactly where her mother was.

"Moana, is this your mommy?"

She giggles infectiously. "No. My mommy is in Paris right now. This is my nanny, Isabella. But she told me I could have ice cream if I asked you to help me find my mommy. She said it was a tiny lie, so I won't get in trouble." She gives me a proud smile.

Isabella laughs. "Yes, that's right, go ahead and grab some ice cream off the desserts table, *Ariel*. But don't tell your father."

Ah, Disney princess names, I gather.

Moana/Ariel wastes no time bolting to her reward as I regard Isabella with a confused smile. She waves for me to join her at her table.

"Sorry about the theatrics. I saw that guy getting a little too close for comfort and read your body language. Then I *may* have bribed the kid with sweets to defuse the situation. I hope I didn't read the interaction wrong." She winces slightly.

I smile and raise my hand for the passing waiter, who's holding up a full tray of champagne. I swipe two glasses and offer one to my new friend. From where I'm sitting, I can see Mr. B. has already moved on to another blonde. Glad to know I'm off his radar.

"No, you didn't read it wrong. Thanks for the save. Nice to know that even at places like this, women can still look out for each other." We clink our glasses and drink.

She looks over my shoulder and grins. "Yes, I got your back, girl. Although I will say, if that man approaching is here to maul you, and you're not down, I'll gladly take your place."

I turn to look over my shoulder and literally lose my breath at the sight of Tony approaching.

He's wearing a tailored black suit, a white dress shirt, and shiny black shoes. But the final nail in my coffin? The bowtie he didn't bother tying. Instead, it's draped around his neck so it trails onto his shirt.

I don't care that I'm openly gawking at him.

This man must already know the effect he has on me. But seeing him in a suit makes me question how babies are made. Because I'm clearly carrying his twins as we speak.

Moana/Ariel returns to our table at the same time Tony reaches me. She gasps when she looks at him, and I can't hold back my chuckle. Antonio is a big guy, something that I some-times forget until we're standing side by side. But I imagine he looks like an absolute giant to this little girl.

"Excuse me, mister. Are you Maui?"

Without missing a beat, he says, "Yes. The demigod. Are you Moana, by any chance?" he asks with mock seriousness.

Triplets. That definitely popped another baby in me.

She screeches. "I was Moana earlier, and Ariel before that, but now I'm Cinderella since we're getting closer to midnight." She looks between Tony and me. "Are you her boyfriend? Because if you're not, you should be. You'd make a perfect Disney couple."

I take a long sip of my drink, letting Tony tackle that one. His eyes twinkle as he squats down to her level. "Can I tell you a secret?"

She nods her head enthusiastically. He cups a hand over his mouth and whispers something into her ear that has her eyes widening dramatically.

"Really?" she gasps.

He nods. "But it's a secret. So you can't tell her, okay?"

She immediately shoots out her pinky finger, and he laughs. "Glad to see you know the rules of being sworn to secrecy." He takes her pinky in his and nods.

"Okay, but you're gonna tell her eventually, right?" she implores.

He looks up at me while he answers. "Yeah, I think I will."

27

ANTONIO

After our pinky promise, our little Disney princess begged Nikki and me to get on the dance floor since, and I quote, "Every princess needs to dance with her prince at the ball. Duh, you dummy."

Nikki and I are dancing to something slow and sensual. Our eyes are locked on each other's, yet we don't dare speak or break the spell we've fallen under. We seem to be having a conversation without words, and it's safe to say we're both well aware that we're no longer acting as if we intend on being just friends. Not when her hands roam my chest on their way up to rest on the back of my neck so she can play with the little hairs that are starting to curl. Or when my hands move from her waist to her lower back, dangerously close to her ass, keeping her as close to me as possible.

But her eyes always give her away.

She's struggling, and I need her to know that she's safe with me. That she can let go.

"Nikki, mi corazón."

She releases me and holds one of my hands in both of hers. "Tony, we need to talk."

Well, fuck. Just the worst sentence to ever exist.

I nod and pull her off the dance floor and walk toward the beach for privacy. If she's going to obliterate my heart for the second time, the least I can do is find some privacy.

I notice Chris and Kelsey watching us as we make our way to a small gazebo on the sand. I shoot them a subtle glare, and they scurry off in different directions.

We take a seat on the bench, but as soon as I get comfortable, Nikki shoots up and starts pacing.

This can't be good.

"Okay, so. I've been preparing all day for this moment. I've been working out what I want to say." She wrings her hands, then chuckles nervously. "But could you believe that I can't even remember how to start this whole speech?" She continues to pace, making me nervous.

"Nikki, relax. I think I know what you're gonna say."

Sorry, Tony. But I'm not interested in a relationship with you.

She rubs her hand over her forehead. "Ha. I have a pretty good inkling that you have no clue what I'm about to say."

I sigh, "Nikki, it's fine. We don't have to pursue—"

"I lied." She takes a deep breath. "To you. I lied to you, Tony." Her lip quivers.

I stay still, confused about what she could be talking about. "Um. Okay. You want to give me a little more context here?"

She must not hear me, because she continues. "And I just want to say, before anything else is said, that I'm sorry. I'm so, so sorry. And I understand if you never forgive me, but I just need you to know that I've lived with the guilt and regret, and I am so terribly sorry." Her eyes begin to mist, and I'm on my feet, pulling her into my arms.

"Nikki, *mi amor*, you're not making sense," I mumble into her hair as her body shakes in my arms.

I'm scouring my brain for what she could have lied about

recently that would garner this kind of reaction, but I'm coming up short.

Until she says the two words I never thought I'd hear from her lips.

"I remember."

I don't even realize I've moved until I feel the ocean water softly crash over my ankles.

"Tony. I'm so sorry." I hear Nikki sniffle behind me.

I don't turn back to her as I speak. "Seven years, Nikki."

"I know," she whispers.

I turn to face her. "No. You don't know. For seven years, I've convinced myself that our night together never happened. That what I experienced with you must have been… couldn't have been…"

She's no longer in her heels as she steps into the water with me. "It was. It was everything. I felt everything. But—"

"But you lied. To my face. *Twice.*" The flashbacks start coming in fast and hard. My desperation for her to remember our night, along with my desire for her to finally make her way back to me.

She bows her head. "I know. Fuck. Yes, I know I lied, but… but…"

"What was it? Was I not good enough for you? You were only in it for the stupid New Year's kiss? Was I just some dumb guy you met at the club—"

"I was scared!" she yells.

I jerk back. "Scared? You were scared of me?" I point to my chest.

She shakes her head. "No, Tony. I could never be scared of you. But… but I was young and scared of us."

I pinch the bridge of my nose to stop myself from shouting

or running away. Because if this is the last conversation we ever have, I damn well will be walking away with all the answers I've been waiting for. "Explain," I say gruffly.

Nikki looks up at me and squares her shoulders. "Look, I don't expect you to understand. You come from a family full of people who love and support you. You have a community of strangers who, at some point, chose you and decided that they would be your family as well. I never had that. It was just me, my mom, and the ghost of my dad. Amelia is the closest thing I've ever had to a sister. And your family…" She gets choked up on the last word. "Your family… chose me. They took me in. They gave me what I never had as a child. And I was too scared… too afraid to risk it after only having spent one night with you."

I chuckle darkly. "So you chose my family over me. Is that it?"

Her features darken and her words start to pack a punch. "No, Tony. I looked at the situation from a sensible perspective. You were a man I'd only known for a few hours. A man, who, according to your family, was very anti-relationship. A man who didn't spend more than one night with a woman. And to top it all off, you were my best friend's older brother. And at the time, I couldn't trust my feelings for you. Because there was no way that I could have… that we could have…"

"What. We couldn't have what, Nikki?" I snarl.

She takes a tentative step toward me. "I didn't know if I was capable of falling in love." I suck in a breath as she continues. "I learned from my mother that nothing good can come from it. And that night with you. My brain couldn't compute. And logically, it wouldn't have made sense to tell myself that I… that we…"

"But I did, Nikki." I take one step closer to her, letting her feel the raging heat emanating from my body. "I fell in love with you that night. I don't know whether it took a minute or an hour." I run an aggravated hand through my hair. "Fuck, it's been seven years, and the wound still won't fucking heal."

She gasps as a tear runs down her face. "Tony."

I rub my face harshly. "And you wanna know the worst part? It's knowing that I would never feel that spark with anyone else. Being stuck on the sidelines as you happily moved on with guy after guy. Knowing that they got Nikki while I was stuck with the memory of Nicolette."

She advances on me, her hands softly placed on my chest. "I'm so sorry. My decision has haunted me for years. And as much as I want to say I would take it back, I don't know if I would." I tense under her touch, but she bunches my shirt in her hands to keep me in place. "I was a twenty-three-year-old girl in a new city, looking for a sliver of security." She lays her forehead on my chest and releases a breath, then whispers. "I just wanted to belong."

I just wanted to belong.

The sadness in her voice cuts me to my core.

I wait three breaths, then cradle her face in my hands, tilting her back so she can look at me. "You could have belonged to me." My thumbs slowly wipe away the tears that fall freely. Her eyes plead for my forgiveness, and something in me snaps.

"Fuck it. You've always belonged to me." I crush my lips to hers and swallow her surprised gasp.

Her sounds.

Her lips.

Her love.

It all belongs to me now.

I break the kiss too soon and meet her watery gaze. "Two questions, Nikki. And for the love of God, you better answer them honestly."

She nods frantically as she clings to the lapels of my suit.

"Do you want this? Do you want us? Because if I kiss you

again, that's what we'll be. An us. We can leave the past where it belongs, but I need to know what you want now. Do you want me?" I'm not able to remove the vulnerability in my voice.

Her face softens and she sighs. "Yes, Tony. I want us. Very badly. If you forgive me, I would very much like to start over."

I nod repeatedly, my heart beating a million times a minute in my chest. "Second question. If I make you mine tonight, will you promise to remember it tomorrow?"

She grins up at me, stands on her tiptoes, and whispers on my lips. "Do your worst."

Her words from seven years ago light my soul on fire.

I kiss her again, and this time, she wraps her arms around my neck and pulls me closer to her.

The world may as well have disappeared, but a loud popping noise breaks us apart. I look at my watch and notice that it's still not midnight. But the impressive fireworks show above us seems to have been timed with our kiss. We hear a frantic Frobish up by the pool deck yelling into his phone, asking who set off the firework show early. It's only when Nikki pulls my attention to Chris and Kelsey, who are waving and giving us enthusiastic thumbs-up from behind the DJ booth, that we realize we've had an audience this whole time. But luckily for Nikki, the real show will begin once I get her back to our room.

Right now.

28

ANTONIO

It's a miracle we made it to our room in one piece.

After we found a running golf cart with the keys in the ignition, I hopped in the driver's seat and pulled Nikki sideways onto my lap as I drove. I swear she intended for me to drive us into the ocean, because her lips were all over me, kissing me while whispering her apologies over and over again.

The sincerity in her eyes washed away every morsel of resentment in my heart.

I'm sure there will be more conversations to come, but right now, my only interest is worshipping her body.

Now if I could just rip this dress off her…

"Don't even think about it, caveman. Use the zipper." Apparently, she can read my mind now. She turns around, and I quickly unzip her out of her dress, letting it pool by her feet.

I get an unobstructed view of the lingerie she's been wearing all night and immediately go hard.

Nikki's delicate fingers get to work on my dress shirt buttons, but I'm too impatient for her diligence. I rip the shirt off me, sending pearly white buttons flying across the room.

Nikki leaps back with her mouth wide open. "I should call

you a brute for pulling that move, but that was actually pretty hot." She lunges toward me, and I catch her midair and kiss her deeply. Quickly wrapping her legs around my waist, I let her feel how ready I am for her.

She gasps. "Tony! Is that—"

I silence her concern with a searing kiss, then lean forward to whisper in her ear. "You can take it, baby."

Her eyes widen, and her breathing starts to quicken. I walk her toward the bed and drop her in the center of it. "Lie down."

She follows my orders but stays perched up on her elbows. "Don't want to miss the show." She smirks as her eyes trail all over my body.

I make quick work of taking off my wet shoes, socks, and pants. I also make sure to grab the condom from my wallet and throw it onto the bed before we get too carried away. Nikki eyes the square foil and bites her bottom lip.

I grip my erection through my black boxer briefs to help alleviate some of the pressure. "We don't have to go all the way tonight, Nikki. You let me know what you're comfortable with, and that's all we'll do. If we stop right now, I promise I'll die a happy man." I pause. "Cause of death will probably be blue balls, but I'll be happy nonetheless." I grin.

She raises a brow and slowly lets one of her hands trail down her body, making me want to rip off that lingerie, until she's covering her entrance. Eyes on me, she pops two hidden snaps of the bodysuit and reveals her bare pussy to me. "I love a consenting king, but if you don't get over here and fuck me, I think I'm the one who's gonna die of lady blue balls."

I move at lightning speed.

I pin her arms above her head and grind myself into her core, earning me a sweet little moan. "Tony."

I lick and suck my way down her body, flipping over her bra cups in the process and showing her pert nipples some much needed attention. I force myself to keep moving down her body before I get the urge to stop and fuck her tits.

I finally settle my head between her thighs and can see that she's glistening for me. "Is this all for me, mi amor?" I use two fingers to spread her arousal, and she hums in contentment.

"Tony. You don't have to do all of that. We could just—"

I flatten my tongue and lick her from entrance to clit. Her back bows off the bed, and she whimpers. "I'm sorry, you were saying?" I murmur.

She's panting, seemingly rendered speechless, with heavy-lidded eyes on me.

"I'm a big boy, Nikki. Let me eat in peace." I wink just as my lips descend on her pussy to feast.

She writhes beneath me, her hands clawing at my scalp while pushing me farther into her.

It doesn't take long for her to come undone, and I slowly lap up the evidence of her orgasm.

I crawl over her body, memorizing every inch of her as I find my way to her lips. "Look how sweet you taste, corazón." My tongue dances in her mouth in the same way I just brought her to climax, and she meets my kiss with the same vigor. "Now give me one more so I know you're ready for me."

I start to descend her body again, but she stops me. "No. Wait. Tony, I can't go again. That was… holy crap, that was amazing. I'm still catching my breath here."

"Lucky for you, you don't have to move a muscle. But this has to go."

She yelps as I tear her flimsy lingerie down the middle, releasing her breasts from their unfair confinement. "Much better." I kiss my way back down her center and make myself at home between her legs.

"Tony, let me take care of you. I've already—"

"Nikki, I'll have you on your knees soon enough. But right now, I'm asking you for one more. And then I'm going to fuck you so deep, there's no way you can claim not to remember our night together. So take your punishment like a good girl."

Her head hits the pillow as she chuckles. "Oh God. I just remembered your shoe size." Her laugh comes to a halt as soon as I push two fingers into her silky heat. She squeezes around me, and I have to concentrate so I don't blow in my underwear.

I work my fingers over her G-spot as my tongue teases her bundle of nerves.

Nikki screams my name as she comes for the second time. Her body falls limp against the bed after thrashing on my face.

I stand and lock eyes with her as I suck my fingers clean.

Nikki makes a pained noise in the back of her throat. "I've never been this turned on in my life. And I've already come twice." Her eyes track my movements as I remove my underwear and my erection springs out, pointing right toward her. "Is that a joke? There's no way, Tony. Like just, logistically!" She tilts her head to the side as she attempts to do some sex-induced calculations.

I smile as I pump my length twice and rip the condom wrapper open with my teeth. "Why don't you worry about letting me take care of you tonight, and I'll handle the rest."

I slide on the condom and climb onto the bed. I settle between her legs and coat myself with her lingering arousal, sliding myself over her oversensitive clit. "So what do you say, Nikki? Do you still want this?" She nods with lust in her eyes. My girl is ready to go again. "Use your words, corazón."

She licks her lips, then says, "*Sí, mi amor.*"

I slide into her with a roar.

My fingers keep a bruising grip on her hips as I try to feed her an inch per thrust.

"Oh, God. Tony!" Nikki pants beneath me.

"You're doing so good, baby. Almost there."

I lean forward on my forearms, careful not to put my weight on her, and drive all the way home.

She screams as she tightens around me.

I lower my right hand and pull on her nipple while I bite down softly on the skin beneath her ear.

"Tony, oh my God, I think I'm going to—"

I angle her legs higher and pump deeper. At this rate, her throat is going to be raw from screaming my name.

She pulses around my cock as she digs her nails into my back, and it tips me right over the edge with her. We come together and ride out our orgasms while clinging to one another.

After a few moments, Nikki takes a big gulp of air and says, "Jesus Christ. I've never come from penetration alone. That was... intense. Like, really, really, really good kind of intense. Like, we should do it again sometime intense."

I brush the sweaty strands of hair off her forehead and kiss her cheek. "Your wish is my command, pillow princess. Now let's go take a shower so I can see if my naughty dreams of seeing you wet and naked do you any justice."

She slaps my arm while laughing, then stops abruptly. "Wait, did you just call me a *pillow princess?*"

29

NIKKI

PILLOW PRINCESS? A FUCKING *PILLOW PRINCESS*?

Look, I understand that this man just rocked my world six ways from Sunday, but that doesn't mean I'm a pillow princess. I mean, he was doing that whole "I am man, hear me roar" bit, and I just let him run with it. Who was I to stop him from taking me to pleasure town *three freaking times*? But a pillow princess I am not. I may be the one walking with a limp up the stairs on the way to the bathroom, but I'll be damned if this man thinks he's the only one who can turn up in the bedroom.

Tony turns on the shower and keeps his hand under the running water until he's satisfied with the temperature. "How are you feeling? Are you sore?"

I huff and wave him off. "What? Of course not."

He crosses his arms over his chest. "Oh, so did you manage to sprain your ankle or something on the way up the stairs? You seem to be leaning all your weight on one foot."

Smartass.

I roll my eyes and walk past him. I pick up a hair clip and secure my hair before stepping into the hot shower.

The water feels so good over my sensitive body. I think I'm

still having aftershocks as the water cascades to where Tony was buried deep inside me.

I reach for the cherry scented body wash I always use, but Tony grabs it instead. "Let me," he whispers into my ear from behind me.

He squeezes a generous amount into his large hand and goes to work, applying it all over my body, all the way down to my toes. We're quiet as he slowly takes a self-guided tour of my body, only slowing when he's caressing my breasts or my pussy. I lean back into his chest, feeling his breath on my neck, his cock nudging my ass.

I can't believe how quickly my need to have him inside me is awakened, and before I know it, I'm reaching behind me and stroking his length as he plays with my nipples.

"Nikki…" He groans. "I don't have another condom on me. And I'm not letting you get on your knees on a tile floor."

What a gentleman.

I turn my head, and I see the lethal desire in his eyes. It must mirror my own, because one of his hands abandons a breast and runs down my body, surely to provide me with some relief, but I stop him. "Tony, I'm…" I bite my lip, not knowing how to voice what I want.

"What do you need, baby?"

"I-I'm on birth control. And I got tested recently, and I'm… you know… all clear. But we don't—"

"Are you asking me to fuck you bare, Nikki?" His voice turns gravelly.

"No… yes… but only if you're comfortable with it. It's just that I've never done it without… you know… a condom. And I trust you. But again, only if—"

Oof.

I'm in Tony's arms and pinned against the shower wall in an instant. My legs automatically wrap around his hips. He leans down so his eyes are level with mine. "I've never done this without one either. And I'm also all clear. I can even show you the results of my last test. They're in my email." He takes a fortifying breath, preparing himself for his next words. "But if we do this, Nikki, I hope you understand that I'm branding you from the inside. And there will be no going back. I don't care if I sound like a caveman, or if this comes off as macho." His caramel eyes go dark as his voice drops to a sinful whisper. "You do this to me." He thrusts his erection between my folds, and I almost come undone by the lack of a barrier. "You make me fucking feral. And if you let me fuck you raw, there is no place on earth you could hide from me where I wouldn't find you, corazón. Understood?"

Hide? Why on earth would I try to hide from this man? I made that mistake once. I'll never allow myself, or anyone else for that matter, to stand between us. Does he have no clue that I'm so far gone for him that I'm a lost cause? Does he not notice how my body and heart respond to his?

I don't even realize that my body has begun rocking against his length until he asks me one more time.

"Understood?"

His roughness has me ready to shout *yes*, but then I remember the one nickname he's given me that I don't love. *Pillow princess.* If we're gonna do this, we're doing it on my terms.

"Put me down." I smile teasingly.

Tony's brow furrows in confusion as he gently sets me on my feet.

I place my hand on his chest. "Now go sit your ass on that bench and let me ride you."

He throws his head back and releases a dark chuckle. "You think you can ride me, *pillow princess*?"

Oh, the fucker knows he's taunting me. Luckily for him, it's also turning me on. "Do I need to repeat myself, *mi amor*?"

Yeah, don't think I didn't notice him go wild the moment

he heard me speak Spanish in bed earlier. He may have memorized every inch of my body, but I'm a fast learner, and I know what turns him on.

He steps back from the overhead spray, hungry eyes on me as he sits on the bench that runs along the massive shower. I take a minute to admire his naked physique. Broad shoulders that lead down to his toned abs and thick, muscular thighs. And right between his legs lies his most formidable body part, with the power to wreak havoc on my body.

"You gonna stand there all day and stare, or are you gonna do something about it, *princess?*" He raises a brow while rubbing up and down his length.

I take slow, torturous steps toward him. He watches me like a predator, disbelieving that he could ever be my prey. *We'll see about that.*

As soon as I'm within arm's length, he strikes.

He pulls me onto his lap so I'm straddling him. "Enough toying around. Show me if you can really take it all." He holds on to his cock as I ease him inside me. We both gasp when we feel his head enter me bare. "Fuck, Nikki, you feel so fucking good. Don't stop," he grits, baring his teeth.

I keep my hands on his shoulders for balance as I slide all of him inside, groaning when he bottoms out. "Tony, don't move." I don't think he realized he was slowly thrusting into me.

"Shit, look at my fucking view." He moves his hands from my hips to my breasts. "I don't know if I'll ever be able to fuck you from behind. Because your tits have me hypnotized, baby. I need to see them at all times." He takes one nipple into his mouth, causing me to grind on him. "Yeah, that's it. Bounce on that cock."

I'm so turned on, and about to move, but then an idea strikes. "Hold on a sec."

Before he has a chance to react, I'm standing, and he's no longer inside me. "Wait! What are you—"

I turn around and slowly settle him back inside me so my back is to his chest.

"What are you doing?" His arms come around me, and he palms my breast. "I'm serious when I say I want to see you."

"If you want to look at me so badly, then why don't you look straight ahead, *princess*?"

His eyes shoot up, and his jaw drops. Only now does he realize what I've done. I've sat us right in front of the massive non-fogging mirrored wall that currently shows all of me. *All of us.* The moment I start moving, we can see the way I sink onto his cock and rise again.

"Nikki," he growls loudly behind me.

Pillow princess, my ass.

I bounce, grind, and swivel on his hardness. I lean back and accept all the dirty words spoken into my ear as his hands travel all over my body. His eyes stay trained on the mirror in front of us.

Right when I feel my orgasm start to build, he takes my hands and places one on each of his thighs. "Hold on."

"Wha—"

That's the only warning I get before his hands are back on my hips, and he starts to piston into me at an unforgiving pace, leading me to believe that what I was doing before was child's play.

I throw my head back and let myself get lost in the raw power of this man as he thrusts my body against his as if I weigh nothing.

His hands leave my hips, then one sneaks around my waist to rub firm circles on my clit. The other grips my breast firmly.

Our eyes lock on each other's in the mirror, then we fixate on where he's entering and massaging me. The visual is depraved. It's enough to send me flying over the edge. "Ahh, Tony! I'm—"

"Fuck, baby, I'm right there with you."

I feel myself clench around him like a vise, and my body lights up for the fourth time tonight.

"That's it. Let that pussy milk every last drop out of me."

If words can induce secondary orgasms, then this man successfully achieved that. My nails dig into his thighs so deeply that I won't be surprised if I draw blood.

Tony's continuous string of fucks fills the air as I collapse back on his chest, gasping for air in the steamy room. I feel his heart beat frantically behind me, and I can't stop the smug smile from taking over my face.

"Gloating? So soon? Where's the sportsmanship, Nikki?" He breathes heavily in my ear as we stare at our reflections.

I shrug a shoulder. "I have no idea what you're talking about. But I'm sure you'll never call me a pillow princess again."

His whole body shakes with laughter behind me. "Oh, on the contrary. If that's what I rile out of you, prepare for me to have it tatted over my heart."

I glare at him. "You wouldn't."

"No, I wouldn't. Besides, you've more than proven yourself to be a queen, not a princess."

"Oh, have I?" I stand slowly, hissing quietly at the sudden loss of him inside me. "Or maybe you just like it when I called *you* princess. That's when things really turned up a notch."

A playful smack lands on my ass, and I clench at the same time as I yelp. Tony's laugh goes silent. I turn my head just as his hand lands on my lower back. "Don't move."

"Why?" And then I feel it. Our releases seeping out of my body.

His hand adds a bit of pressure, so I bend at the waist. "Hands on your knees, Nikki." His voice is laced with authority. His change in demeanor turns me on, and I don't even realize I've clenched again.

"Fucking hell." I look back in time to see Antonio collect our releases with his fingers, and slowly push it back inside me. "You see this, Nikki? You see this mess we've made?" His sticky fingers run along my seam and my clit. "Look how much is dripping out of you. I can't even get it all. Do you see how wild you make me?"

I close my eyes as my breath quickens.

"Hey, Tony?"

"Yeah, baby?"

"We're not getting out of this shower anytime soon, are we?"

"Not a fucking chance."

30

ANTONIO

Fucking finally.

For the first time, I'm waking up with the knowledge that Nikki is my girl. For real this time.

It might have taken an eternity, but having her soft body pressed to my chest as I rest my hand on her stomach has me feeling all sorts of territorial. I've never been a cuddler. Hard thing to do when all you have are quick one-night stands. But being Nikki's big spoon is going to be an every-night occurrence. Especially when I get to breathe in her sweet cherry scent.

Everything about last night was perfect. After going for a few extra rounds, Nikki and I were a pile of loose limbs sprawled all over our bed, happily sated. I ordered every carb available on the island, per Nikki's request, and was pleasantly surprised when a couple of bottles of Gatorade were sent along with our food.

Thanks Chris and Kelsey.

I'd be lying if I said I wasn't worried that this could be too good to be true, but the look in Nikki's eyes when she kissed me good night was enough for me to leave the past where it belongs.

Now my only concern is waiting until my sweet girl finally decides to wake up.

"If that's your ding-a-ling poking my ass, I swear to God I'm going to snap it off clean after all the damage it caused my lady bits last night," she mumbles into her pillow.

Oh, well. So much for sweet.

"Good morning to you too, pillow prin—"

Nikki springs into action.

"Ouch! Okay, okay!" I laugh while Nikki desperately tries to pinch me.

"I thought I'd be waking up to sweet pillow talk, not the hammer of Thor trying to poke through my clothes!" She giggles.

I eye the massive white T-shirt that does nothing to hide her hard nipples. "Yeah, but for the record, that's my T-shirt. And second… Um…"

She snaps her fingers in front of my face. "Did you just get distracted by the boobies again?"

"Yeah." I take a moment to get a good look. "But they're great boobies." I try to make a move for them, but she swats my hand away.

"Cool it!" She bursts into laughter as we start wrestling each other. I let her come out on top, of course. Especially when she's literally on top of me, straddling my hips. And as much as my morning wood pleads for relief beneath her, it's the look on her face that has my complete attention.

The look of pure adoration. Aimed straight at me.

"Hi." She smiles while catching her breath.

"Hey, you." I tuck a strand of golden hair behind her ear.

"I like this. I like waking up next to you." She smiles shyly while tracing the tattoos on my chest. "And I know that we still have lots to talk about. And it's going to take some time for you to trust me…"

I cradle her head in my hands and guide her down until our lips meet. After a soft peck, I pull her back an inch so she can see the honesty in my eyes. "I trust you, Nikki. I know we're just getting started here, but I don't want you to feel like we're on uneven ground." I pause, then smile widely. "Unless it would make you feel better if you asked for my forgiveness by offering various sexual favors."

"Tony!" she screeches while slapping my biceps.

I grab her hands and slowly kiss each of her open palms. "I like hearing you call me Tony," I admit.

She grins. "I still can't believe I'm allowed to call you Tony after all this time."

"I don't care what you call me, as long as I get to call you mine."

Her quiet gasp is followed by a playful groan. "Fine! You win. One quickie to start the day, and then you're for sure keeping that thing away from me." She hops off me and starts making her way toward the stairs to the bathroom. "And only after I brush my teeth. I think you're cute, but I don't get down like that." She laughs.

I'm hot on her heels. "Thank God, cause your dragon breath was kickin'!"

"Tony!"

Yeah, I like hearing her call me Tony.

~

A quickie it was not.

But after we finally managed to leave the room, Nikki banished me to the gym to burn off whatever "demon energy" I have left while she took off to sunbathe by the pool. Apparently, tanning was the only activity she had the energy for. And if that fact didn't puff my chest with pride...

I spend most of the time at the gym stretching out my muscles. The last twelve hours have me on the verge of pulling a muscle. And I'll be damned if Nikki realizes how worn out she has me by day two.

I grab a water bottle and stand by the windows facing the pool area. It's been less than an hour, but I'm already missing Nikki.

Yep. Guess I'm a simp now.

I spot her easily. She's lying in one of the cabanas while reading. I really hope I gave some of her "book boyfriends" a run for their money.

Boyfriend. Hmm, we're going to have to discuss titles, because the one thing I do know is that I'm not abiding by today's warped dating rules. There will be no gray area. I belong to that woman as much as she belongs to me. And I'll provide no mercy if any man gets those facts twisted.

Which may be why my radar spots an older blond guy staring straight at Nikki. My hackles instantly go up, because he's not leering over her like that Mr. B. creep, but rather observing her like she's the missing piece of a puzzle.

It may be nothing. Rich people can be weird. But that doesn't mean I like it one bit. Which is how I find myself walking out of the gym and toward Nikki's cabana. I run into Chris and quickly give him a fist bump for providing those electrolytes in our time of need. And by the time I turn the corner, the weird older guy is gone, but the pit in my stomach remains. Something feels off, but I don't want to worry Nikki as I approach her.

"Hey, stranger. Mind putting on a shirt so the waitresses don't drop their drink trays?" Nikki teases while shading her eyes from the sun with her hand.

"Hmm, territorial already? I can get behind that." I crawl

over her body and give her a sensual kiss. "There, now everyone knows I've claimed you as mine."

"You know, sometimes you say shit that has the feminism flying out of my body at lightning speeds. Yet somehow, it works for me." She laughs while pulling me in for another kiss. "But I think I'm ready to head back to the room. I need a nice bath to recover from… you know." She blushes.

I stand and put my hand out for her to take. "How about we head back, and I'll prep a nice bath for you with all the fancy essential oils lined up on our bathroom sink and order some sweet and salty treats?"

"*Oh*, that sounds—"

"And then, I'll wrap you up nice and snug in a fluffy robe and set us up on the bed so we can watch a Julia Roberts movie. How does that sound?"

"Quadruplets," she whispers under her breath.

"Huh?"

"Oh nothing. That sounds perfect."

Nikki's finally settled on which movie she wants to watch as we arrive at our bungalow.

My Best Friend's Wedding was the winner.

I'm almost too distracted by her cuteness to notice that something is off.

The door to our cabana is cracked open, and the CCTV cameras that point at our room have been covered up with a spray.

The air has shifted, and I instantly transform into cop mode. "Nikki, stay out here," I whisper as I stand by the open door.

"Why?"

The plank under my foot creaks under my weight, and the older man from earlier darts out of our closet and heads for the back patio. My strides have me reaching him in a flash, and I have him pinned to a wall before he can make a jump for it into the shallow ocean water.

"Nikki! Call the front desk and have them alert security and the local authorities."

"Oh my God, Tony!" Nikki shrieks.

"Do it now, babe!" I keep my weight evenly distributed to keep him pinned.

"This isn't what it looks like, buddy," the man huffs.

"I'm not your *buddy*," I say menacingly into his ear.

"Check my back pocket. You'll have your answers there."

"I'm not checking anything until you're in handcuffs."

"Tony!" Nikki pleads.

"Nikki, why aren't you calling? Don't worry, I got him. He can't hurt you."

"She's not calling anyone, pal." He looks past me and straight at Nikki.

"Oh yeah? And why are you so sure, *pal*?"

"Tony, let him go."

"What? Nikki, are you okay?"

She ignores me and looks straight at the man struggling beneath my arms.

The shocker of the century happens when Nikki speaks up and says, "Hi, Dad."

31
NIKKI

"DAD? AS IN SCUMBAG, JOHN FUCKING MCCLANE?" TONY seethes.

"The one and only. But is it possible to have this conversation without popping my shoulder out of its socket?"

Tony eases off him but keeps a protective stance between us.

"What's in your back pocket that will magically give us answers as to why you flew to this island and broke into your own daughter's room?" Tony steps closer to my father, but I place a hand on his arm to stop him.

"Antonio, please." The use of his full name has him relaxing his posture and pulling me to his side.

"Why don't we talk outside on the patio? I'm sure we could all use some fresh air." Tony leads us out back and pulls me down to sit next to him on the couch while my father takes the chair opposite us.

My father.

I can't count how many times I've thought about meeting my dad in person. When I was a kid, I would imagine him swooping in and taking me to Disney World. As an adult, I hoped he would show up at any of my graduation ceremonies and take me out to dinner after to celebrate. And now? Now I just can't even compute whether the man sitting in front of me is real. So, of course, I do the most logical thing that my stunned brain can think of.

I lean over and poke him in the face. Twice.

Tony hauls me back toward him while my father smirks.

"Huh" is all my brain can come up with.

"I know, Nikki. It's probably hard to believe that I'm real, but it's really me." My dad smiles softly.

"This moment would be much more heartwarming if it didn't start with a breaking and entering. So can you fill us in on what the hell is happening, and why you decided to meet your daughter for the first time this way?" Tony asks.

My dad straightens in his chair. "I wanted to make sure she was safe." Tony opens his mouth to speak but clamps it shut when my father throws something onto his lap. "This is what's in my back pocket. And what's brought me here."

A badge. And not like the one Tony carries around in the city.

An FBI badge.

My eyes threaten to pop out of their sockets. I look down at the badge and back at my father repeatedly, as if watching a tennis match between the two.

"Wait, hold on. You—you're in the FBI? Is this thing real? Tony, bite it. Check if it's real gold."

"Nikki," they say in unison.

"Explain," Tony says in an ominous tone.

My dad exhales and leans his elbows on his thighs. "Last night, you posted a picture on your Instagram page."

"Are you really here to scold me on my social media usage? Because let me tell you, I've already gotten an earful from everyone around me."

He shakes his head. "That picture almost sent me to an

early grave, Nikki. Because in the background, as clear as day, I saw Adriano Bartoli. He was standing right behind you."

"Adri—"

"Bartoli? As in the Bartoli crime family? Here?" Antonio tenses next to me.

My dad gives a single nod.

I grab my phone as they have a silent discussion with their eyes. I pull up the photo and zoom in behind me, but I only come up with more questions than answers.

"This is Mr. B. Mr. Barlowe. The owner of this resort."

My dad shakes his head. "No, sweetie, that's Mr. Bartoli, and he's an extremely dangerous man. Especially when it comes to you."

"And why is that?" Tony interrupts.

"Because he's the reason it hasn't been safe for me to be in your life for all these years."

I feel all the blood drain from my face as I sink into Tony.

"Let me start from the beginning."

"When I met your mom, I was fresh out of the academy and waiting on my first assignment. As a rookie, I was expecting to put in some desk duty time. I could've never imagined that my first case would send me undercover and forever change the trajectory of my life." He pulls my hand into both of his. "You were made out of love, Nicolette, and I have so many regrets in life. Mainly accepting that case and leaving you and your mother behind. I was naïve and thought I could continue seeing your mother, but once I got debriefed on the men I would be engaging with, there was no way in hell I was putting your mom in the line of fire. And when she told me she was pregnant with you…" He shuts his eyes tightly, as if recalling a painful memory. "I vowed there and then that no harm would ever come to either of you because of my career aspirations. I kept myself unattached to anyone so there could never be anyone to go after if one of my jobs went sideways. And Adriano, he's the guy I've been after for over thirty years now. He and his family have brought the mob into the twenty-first century and swapped out sketchy warehouses for Fortune 500 companies. Embezzling and laundering more money than God himself could create. And although he and his men wear custom suits, they are still very much the thugs who tormented New York City in the eighties."

"Adriano Bartoli… he's my white whale. The person I've been collecting evidence on throughout my entire career so I can put him behind bars. So imagine my reaction when I see him less than three feet from my daughter. The same daughter I haven't allowed myself to meet in person for all these years. The one whose graduations and major life events I've had to witness from the back of crowded auditoriums."

It isn't until I feel a tear hit my bare thigh that I realize I'm crying. "You were at my graduations?" I whisper. My father just dropped a bomb on my lap, yet all my heart can latch on to is that nugget of information. That my dad tried, that he was there in any way he could be. That I was made out of love and not an inconvenience.

My dad smiles sadly. "I was there for your prom too. Had to make sure your date didn't think that just because your dad wasn't around, he could get handsy with you. Although I must say I wasn't impressed with you sneaking vodka into the venue." He gives me a fake scolding look.

Tony unwraps his arm from my shoulders and rests his hand on my knee. "So you flew down because you thought your cover was blown?"

"No. My undercover work is long behind me, and I was pulled before I ever got to work with Adriano. But in my line of work, there are no such things as coincidences, so I came down to see if there was something we may have missed. I was in your room checking for bugs or any other devices he may have had planted. He's known for being paranoid. I didn't know if you guys had interacted with him, so I wanted to make sure that you weren't on his radar."

"But you're a fed. You don't have any jurisdiction here," Tony points out.

"Well, then, I guess you can say I'm here as a father." He releases my hand. "Although that angry Russian at the front desk doesn't need to know that. He still let me cruise through here after I showed him my badge."

Tony pulls out his phone and starts typing ferociously. "I've heard enough. I'm booking us a flight out of here ASAP."

My dad waves him off. "No need. After I landed, a buddy of mine got a tip that he's been spotted in Miami as of this morning. He never stays put in one spot for long, and I'm surprised that he even risked coming here and having his presence linked to this resort, given that it's his main money laundering project. Trust me, if I thought for a second that Nikki was in danger, I would fly the plane out myself."

I rub my temples as I try to absorb the information overload. "So what now?"

"Now I fly back to Quantico and touch base with my team. Him coming here was a deviation from the norm, and it must mean something. We've been waiting for him to slip up and provide us with something to go off, and the key might be this place." He looks at Tony. "Besides, seems like you have your own personal bodyguard. Don't think I could come up with a better protective detail if I tried."

Tony grunts.

My dad sighs. "Look, clearly, I'm not winning any father-of-the-year award anytime soon, but I did what I thought was necessary to keep the women I love most safe. I can't imagine you would understand the pain of having to love someone from afar."

"I understand more than you know," Tony says while looking straight at me.

Love.

Oh God. Last night, he mentioned that he had fallen in love with me on the night we first met, but what about now?

My brain is mush, and the two men sitting with me are the ones to blame. Before I can shoot off any more questions, my father stands. "I've got to get back, but I'll keep you in the loop, Nikki." He pulls me up and wraps me in his arms.

At first, I stand frozen, realizing that my father is hugging me for the first time in my entire life. The physical touch is enough to snap whatever hold I had on my sanity. I hug him around his middle and don't even try to stop my sobs from breaking free. He tightens his hold around my shoulders as I fill his shirt with my tears, my body shuddering with the intensity of my cries. My father rubs my back silently as I unleash a life-time of grief. Once the tears have slowed, I back out of his arms, only to see that he too was crying. His face is flushed and his eyes are red-rimmed.

Before my vision threatens to blur again, Tony pulls me into his side while putting his hand out for my dad to shake. "I'll take good care of her, I promise."

"My daughter has never needed rescuing. She's had to be her own damn hero throughout her life. But it's nice to see that you've joined her along for the ride." They shake hands, and we walk my dad to the door, but not before he pulls me in for another tear-jerking hug.

Once he's gone, Tony is guiding me toward the stairs, then up to the shower. "Tony, I don't—"

"I just want to hold you, Nikki. Please let me take care of you," he says softly. I relent and nod silently.

Tony pulls us into the warm shower with our bathing suits

on. Once I'm under the soothing spray, I break down again. And as promised, Tony is there to take care of me.

I cry for the little girl who had to grow up thinking she was never wanted.

I cry for my mom, who lost the only man she's ever truly loved.

I cry for my father. Because he missed out on what could have been a beautiful life with us.

All these years, I stayed away from love, placing the blame for ruined lives on that emotion. And now I see that love wasn't at fault, but rather the lack of love. How different would my family's life have been if we could have loved on one another a little harder or communicated a little better?

What if.

What if.

What if.

I let the water wash away the pain and regret. Once I'm all pruned up and cried out, I look up at Tony. And there, on his face, written as clear as day, is the emotion I've been running away from my entire life.

This man loves me.

I tip my head back as a silent request for a kiss, which he gently provides. The look doesn't waver. The feeling doesn't fade. I hope when the moment is right, I'm able to tell this man what he deserves to know.

I love him too.

32

ANTONIO

My shoulder feels like it's being stabbed by a thousand tiny needles, but I'd rather cut off my arm than wake Nikki from her nap.

After our emotional shower, I made good on my promise of making her feel as cozy as possible and putting on a movie. But within five minutes, my girl was knocked out cold in my arms. I guess meeting your long-lost FBI agent dad will do that to you.

My mind is completely blown by the revelation, and if I'm being honest, it's bringing up feelings against my own employer.

I thought this time away would help cool my anger, but what it's done is show me how the badge can implode your life.

Don't get me wrong. I've always known the risks and have always worn the uniform with pride, but I'd be lying if I said my feelings haven't changed as I've gotten older. Especially as relationships between the police and people of color continue to be strained.

I joined the police academy with a longing to belong to an entity, a brotherhood, after what my ex-girlfriend had done to me. I needed to feel a sense of kinship with something that could claim me and keep me grounded. Although she hurt me deeply, she showed me what a person who feels connected to their roots looks like. And as an immigrant, I constantly struggle with feeling neither here nor there.

When I got back from that trip, I couldn't think straight. My mind could only focus on funneling all my energy into researching professions that felt less like a job and more like a community.

My father is a doctor and has always pushed for my sister and me to follow in his footsteps because it's a "safe" profession in terms of financial security. But my sister and I have never had the passion for it like he does. Yet I used the idea of saving lives as my starting point in my search.

When one of my neighbors, a former officer, joked about me putting my size to good use, it planted the seed in my mind. I started looking into the police academy, and the more I thought about it, the more it checked all my boxes. Community based, coworkers who were more like family, and a pension that even my dad couldn't argue with in terms of stability.

I excelled at the job and found that I may have joined because of my past, but I stayed because of the difference I felt I was making. Having kids in the community seeing me, a brown, Hispanic officer who speaks Spanish, as the person keeping them safe. The guy who turns on his siren as a joke just to announce that I want in on an impromptu basketball game in the park.

But things have changed.

I don't feel the same passion I once did. And the more I think about it, the more I realize it's probably normal to feel this way after doing the same job for over a decade.

But I'm stuck.

Being a cop isn't something you just casually walk away

from. I didn't take a blood oath, but sometimes it feels like I did. And whenever I have these thoughts, I feel like I'm letting my brothers in blue down. When I enrolled in the police academy, I felt like I had found a place where I belonged for the first time since immigrating to this country. A place where it didn't matter what I looked like or where I came from, because I carried the badge. Finding a brotherhood where someone who was once a stranger would lay their life on the line for you? That was something special. That was something that wouldn't be easy to abandon.

I'm sure if I spoke to Nikki about it, she would probably tap into my subconscious brain. Attribute it to my inner child or something like looking for a safe space to belong. Or point out that I, as an immigrant, bound myself to an agency that takes an oath to protect and serve its citizens, earning my right to be a part of something larger than myself.

Perhaps she'd point out that I got a master's in business because my parents expected me to have at least one degree after college, and I never truly picked a career based on my natural interests, but rather my lost sense of duty.

Regardless of what's buried deep in my psyche, what I know is that I have Nikki in my life now, which means I need to be the best version of myself. And I know I would never make the same mistakes her father made when it came to choosing his work over his love.

As if my thoughts stirred her awake, her lids start to flutter until she slowly peeks them open. Her vision is unfocused until she finally sets her sights on me, and the most beautiful smile emerges.

Her hand raises to caress my bearded cheek. Her eyes sparkle with renewed peace. I'm just about to comment on it when the best moment of my life happens.

"Hi. I think I love you."

33

NIKKI

"Shit, did I do that wrong? I did, didn't I? Just give me a sec to remove my eye boogers and I promise I can get it right," I say as Tony continues to stare at me, unblinking.

I shuffle out of his arms and sit cross-legged in front of him. I swipe at my eyes, then my entire face in case I drooled in my sleep.

Tony's stare is making me feel like I've grown a second head.

God, I'm so stupid. I read this whole thing wrong. He said he fell in love with me seven years ago. Not currently, right?

"If I said that I was just sleep talking, would you believe me and move on as if nothing happened?"

A slow grin starts to spread across Tony's face. "Not a chance, Nikki." He cups my face in his massive hands and stares cautiously into my eyes. "But I have to ask, are you sure? Because after the day you've had, I wouldn't blame you for being… overwhelmed."

I lied to Tony once, and it derailed our entire relationship. So regardless of whether he'll say those three little words back to me, I have to be honest with my feelings.

I cover his hands with my own and whisper my confession. "I've never been in love before. I've purposely avoided falling my whole life. That's how I know I'm sure."

Tony's eyes soften further. "Nikki." He kisses my forehead. "How is that possible?"

"I've always been in relationships, but I've never let anyone close enough to hold the power to break my heart. I promised myself I'd never be like my mother, coping with money or material things to fill the void of a broken heart. So I guess I picked men I knew I would be able to walk away from when the time came. I'd leave them before they ever got the chance to leave me." I shrug. "Just because I was against falling in love didn't mean I wanted to be alone. But funny enough, I was always lonely. Until… well, until you. And you… you fucking terrify me."

His thumbs stroke my cheeks softly. "Why?"

I lean in and faintly brush my lips against his as I speak. "Because you're everything I promised myself I never needed. And now that I have you, I'm petrified of losing you."

"Nikki," Tony whispers before sealing his lips over mine. He kisses me slowly until his hands wander and he hoists me onto his lap. He breaks the kiss and leans his forehead against mine. "I'm not going anywhere, Nikki. And clearly, I haven't been keeping up my caveman antics if you think otherwise." He smiles.

I purse my lips. "Yeah, but I know that kind of came out of nowhere, and usually people have a cute speech or something before they drop the *L* word. I literally woke up and mumbled it. I should have, at the very least, enunciated it better. I'm already failing at this. Maybe that's why I've never done this before. I shou—"

"It was perfect, Nikki. You want to know why?"

I nod hesitantly.

"Because I started loving you the moment I laid eyes on

you, and I've never stopped. So if you need a little speech or a dramatic moment from me to declare my love for you, I'll give it to you. But just in case you don't, let me make myself perfectly clear right here, right now. I love you, Nikki. And there is nothing that could tear me away from you. Ever. So please let me hear those three words from your pretty little lips once more to make sure I'm not dreaming."

My heart starts to beat wildly as my smile takes over my face. "I love you."

Tony's lips crash onto mine as he kisses me senseless. A first kiss of sorts. Between two people who are in love with one another.

I lean back to study his face, and just as I thought, that same look of adoration is there. Long gone are those scowls that were a permanent fixture. The memory alone makes me chuckle. "When you told me to say those three words, I almost said, 'Hi pillow princess.' It was so hard to stay in the moment and be a mature adult. The joke was almost too good to pass on, but I held firm."

A swift smack lands on my ass cheek, and my yelp turns into uncontrollable laughter.

"Don't make me redden that ass, *princess*."

"Don't threaten me with a good time, *love*."

"Fuckin' hell. You're gonna be leading me by the balls now, aren't you?"

"I pity that you ever thought I wasn't already."

"All right. Over my knee you go."

34

ANTONIO

The next few days flew by in a blur.

We decided to go off the island every day and visit Maria and her crew. Nikki was hell-bent on learning all of Maria's cooking secrets, and I was perfectly content being her food tester. Even if that meant Nikki picking up some extra Dominican slang words she could taunt me with.

We spent hours in the ocean and playing dominos with the locals. I peeled mangoes for Nikki as she made dancing TikTok videos with Maria's grandkids.

I was able to set up a tour to take us to La Romana, and I showed her all the places I used to visit as a kid. Nikki's jaw was on the floor the entire time we were at Altos de Chavón. I had to actually throw her over my shoulder when it was time to leave.

We lived in what Nikki called a "love bubble." Now that the cat's out of the bag, we've spent countless hours exchanging I love yous and making love.

I really have to thank Amelia for sending us down here. Not only did it alter my relationship with Nikki in the best way, but it allowed me to heal my relationship with my country.

After I broke up with my ex, I stayed away and never visited. I was plagued by the memories of the years I spent here visiting the woman who'd sent my life into a tailspin.

But now I've replaced the bad with the good. My memories are filled with afternoons spent eating what Maria's cooked up, dancing bachata with Nikki, and making love under the stars.

This is now the place where Nikki and I fell in love… for real this time. It is a place that holds my past and has given me the person who will be my future.

Today is the last full day of our vacation, so we've decided to take it easy and just lounge by the pool.

Nikki sighs, then rolls onto her side, facing me on the cabana bed. "I'm gonna miss this place." She starts tracing the tattoos that run down my forearm.

"Me too. We'll be back. To the Dominican Republic. Just not this resort." I chuckle at the idea of us ever returning to this place after imagining how much it must cost per night. Plus, I'm not a fan of the owner.

"Pinky promise?" Nikki lifts her hand with an outstretched pinky finger. I cock my eyebrow, and she giggles. "Hey, you did it for Ariel/Moana/Cinderella the other day, and I want in on the pinky promises too!"

I link my pinky with hers and smile. "I pinky promise that we'll be back."

Her eyes glimmer with joy, and I don't think I've ever felt luckier in my life.

Just as I'm about to pull her in for a kiss, the pinky-promise Disney princess herself runs up to our cabana. "You guys are pinky promising! Does that mean you told her?" Ariel/Moana —geez, we really need to learn her actual name—asks.

"Hey there, cutie! No, he actually hasn't told me. And I'm dying to know. What secret did he tell you that night?" Nikki asks eagerly.

The memory of what I whispered into the little girl's ear

comes flashing in, and before I can suppress it, I bark out a laugh that will be hard to reel in.

"Can I tell her? Pretty, pretty please?"

I nod my permission through my fit of laughter as Nikki eyes me, confused by my reaction.

The little girl steps into our cabana and proudly says, "When I asked if he was your boyfriend, he told me his secret. He said that one day, he was going to make you his princess, and that one day, he would tell you himself."

Nikki's face slowly turns crimson red. The innocence of what this child has said, compared to our pillow princess sexcapade, is surely flashing through her mind. She covers her face with her hands. "Oh my. That's, um. Very, uh, nice of…"

"Don't worry, Moana. I've already made her my princess." I grin.

Nikki slaps my arm and widens her eyes.

"Yay! She's your princess!" the little girl cheers. "But I'm not Moana anymore. I'm going home today, so I'm just me now." She smiles.

Nikki collects herself enough to ask, "What's your name? We must know who you really are."

"My name is—"

"Anna, it's time to go, mija!" a man yells.

Anna.

My mother's name. My guardian angel.

I hear Nikki's intake of breath. I tip my head up and send my mother a silent thank-you. I'm not one to believe in signs, but I'll happily take this one. Imagining her meddling from heaven with Nikki and me this whole time. When I look back at Nikki, her eyes shine with unshed tears, and I know she's thinking the same thing.

"Anna, leave these nice people alone. They're trying to enjoy their vacation. Sorry about my daughter. She loves chatting people up everywhere we go," her father says.

Wait, hold up.

"Mateo Martinez? *You're* Anna's dad?" I ask, stunned.

He chuckles graciously. "Yep, that's me." He tips his head in our direction.

"Um, is it rude to say that I'm a little lost here?" Nikki winces.

I groan internally. If Nikki is gonna be with a Dominican man, she's going to have to brush up on some baseball knowledge. "Mateo is the pitcher for the Monarchs. The new baseball team in New York. They took over the old Yankee stadium."

"Oh!" Nikki brightens. "I knew your face was familiar! You're plastered all over the subway!" She laughs.

"Yeah, gotta love seeing my face graffitied all over the city." He smiles good-naturedly. "Just taking a trip here with my little girl before spring training starts. It's about to get chaotic, so I'm taking advantage of some one-on-one time."

"Oh! I met your nanny, Isabella. We exchanged numbers. She's awesome!" Nikki exclaims.

"Yeah, but she's a family friend. Just helping out temporarily." He runs a hand through his hair. "I need to find a permanent nanny before the season starts—"

"Because you keep firing them, papi."

"Because they aren't good enough, mija." He sighs. "But we'll find someone. Don't worry about it." He pulls her ponytail playfully. "I'm sorry, I didn't get your names, even though I'm sure you know all of my daughter's aliases." He chuckles.

"I'm Tony, and this is my girlfriend, Nikki."

Nikki blushes at the title but otherwise goes along with it.

Success.

"Nice to meet you guys. If you ever want to come to a game, just text Isabella, and I'll set it up."

"Wow, thanks, man." I shake his hand. "By the way, I

heard about the team's owner passing away recently. I'm sorry for your loss."

He nods. "Thanks. I only met him once, but he did right by me during the signing negotiations. It's a loss, but the real shit-storm comes now."

"Papi, you said a bad word." Anna giggles.

"Sorry, mija." He rolls his eyes while laughing. "Anyway, the team was left to his billionaire grandson, who I hear is a real piece of work." He gives us a pointed look.

"Ouch," I say.

"Yeah. Even worse? I just know he's gonna butt heads with our general manager." He shakes his head.

"Why? Is he also a piece of work?" I ask.

"*She*. First female general manager in MLB history."

My eyebrows shoot up. "Wow. Impressive. Looks like she's gonna have to watch her back with this billionaire douche."

"Nah, my money's on her."

"Oh yeah? Why?"

He smirks. "She's Dominican."

I throw my head back in laughter. "Enough said."

"Anyway, it was great to meet you. We gotta fly out of here now." He waves at us as Anna lunges toward me. She whispers something in my ear that has my heart melting. When she leans back, she offers me her pinky.

Her father looks at us quizzically.

"It's their thing," Nikki provides.

I interlock our pinkies and make my second promise about Nikki to Anna.

"What was that all about?" Nikki asks Anna.

"Just another promise before I have to go home. Don't worry, it's a good one!" She hugs Nikki tightly, then runs to her father's side.

Nikki turns to me just as they make their way toward the lobby. "What did she say?" she asks eagerly.

I feign seriousness. "I take pinky promises very seriously, Nikki. I can't tell you. At least not yet."

She grumpily mumbles a few curse words under her breath. "Fine. I'll drop it. But only because you're really cute with kids."

I intertwine her hand with mine and bring it up to my lips. "Do you think you'll want kids one day?" I hope the *with me* was silent in my head.

She stares off toward the pool. "You know, in theory, I've always imagined myself with a kid or two. But I never saw myself being in a traditional family. I always thought I would adopt or do IVF by myself. And raise my kids with Amelia." She laughs softly. "But now…"

"But now?" I urge her on.

"I dunno." She shrugs. "I guess that's a conversation I'll have to have at a later date. With my *boyfriend*." She smiles smugly.

Hearing her say boyfriend makes the possessive beast awaken in me. I nip her hand playfully. "Damn right. Good to know that you got the memo."

She rolls her eyes. "Love, your caveman is showing."

"Aw, she even calls me *love* now," I tease.

"It rolls off the tongue easier than *barbarian*. It's only one syllable too."

She barely gets the sentence out before I've rolled on top of her, keeping my weight balanced on my forearms so I don't crush her. "Yeah, but I'm *your* barbarian. So get used to it." I plant a passionate kiss on her lips, but have to pull back much too quickly, given that we are in public.

She grips my biceps. She's about to say something when a tattoo on my inner left arm catches her attention. "Is that a—"

Here we go.

"Disco ball," I finish for her.

It's the one tattoo that seems out of place in my ink collection. Aside from my mother's angel wings on my neck, I have a massive tiger piece on my right thigh, coordinates of the cities where my family members and I were born on my chest, and about two dozen odd smaller designs that decorate my arms.

And then the disco ball.

I roll off her and sit up against the plush headboard of the cabana.

"I got this one seven years ago. The day after Día de los Reyes Magos. Three Kings Day."

My admission leaves Nikki stunned into silence, and her face looks paler than it should.

I sigh. "I got this because of you."

Nikki's jaw drops. "But… How? Why would you?"

"When I got it, I told myself it was a reminder of why I don't do relationships. Of why I shouldn't trust people. Maybe even spewed off some of that 'not all that glitters' crap." I shake my head. "But if I'm being honest with myself, with you… I got it because it reminded me of your dress. The one you wore when I first met you. It reminded me of the rooftop we sat on, the one littered with tiny disco balls all around us. The ones you specifically said you loved. I got it because I needed a piece of you, even if I never got to have you for myself."

A choked sob escapes Nikki's throat as she reaches for me. I pull her into my lap instinctively and wrap my arms around her tightly. "Tony. I don't know what to say. I'm such a fucking idiot. I'm so incredibly sorry I did this to us."

I shush her softly before placing a delicate kiss on her lips. "I didn't tell you with the intention of making you upset. I just wanted you to know the truth."

"But all this time." A tear trails down her cheek, and I make quick work of wiping it away. "I put you through so much unnecessary pain."

"We're not going backward, Nikki. And I promise you.

These past few days with you have made the past a distant memory. Now that I have you, the tattoo takes on a different meaning. It was just a placeholder for the real thing. This." I squeeze her tighter. "You in my arms. The look you give me first thing in the morning. The twinkle after you say I love you. All of it. You're my little disco—"

"Okay, hard stop if you're about to call me a disco ball." She sniffles.

I smile. "What can I say? I'm a corny caveman."

"And I'm one very lucky girl." She lifts my left arm to inspect the tattoo, then leans in to place a quick kiss right above it. The feeling sears through my skin more than the tattoo needle ever did. "And now I want to go back to the room and make up for lost time. And you're giving me a full tattoo tour." She smiles as she kisses me.

And in that moment, I know the exact tattoo that I need to get next.

35

Nikki

"Evan better put a ring on Amelia's finger, because I quite enjoy flying on his private jet," I say as I look out at the clear skies from my cushy window seat.

Tony grunts. "You might not have to wait too long for that."

I whip back to face him where he's sitting across from me. "*What?* He's proposing? Did he say when? Does he have the ring? Does he need my help?"

Tony runs a hand over his face. "At Christmas, Evan pulled Dad and me aside to ask for her hand in marriage. My dad was in tears before Evan got the full question out. Needless to say, he got his blessing. Mine too." Tears instantly start flowing from my eyes. "But I'm sorry, baby. I can't tell you any more information. I've been sworn to secrecy." He smiles warmly.

I wave him away. "Just make sure I'm not wearing white or any light colors that day. Deal?"

"Deal."

I take a deep breath and wipe my tears away. I can't believe my best friend is going to be a bride. A wife. She's going to be so happy, and I can't wait to be with her every step of the way.

"Do all women do this, or are you just that happy for Amelia?" he teases.

"She's like my sister. I'm planning her bridal brunch as we speak."

He groans. "Stop calling yourself her sister. That would make us… you know."

I roll my eyes and scoff. "Sorry. Amelia was first, and you know what they say; you never forget your first." I smile widely.

"Pfft. What am I? Chopped liver over here?"

"Don't worry, I got a saying for you too." I tap my chin dramatically. "Ah, yes. You never forget your worst."

"Excuse me?" He almost spits out his water, looking offended.

"You were my worst New Year's kiss." I put my hands up defensively. "My fault, to be fair. I tainted it with all my lying and whatnot. But we've clearly long since redeemed ourselves. Just look at us now!" I laugh.

The infamous scowl is back, and to be honest, I kinda missed it. "Consider yourself lucky that the seat belt sign is on," he warns.

I feel my body start to tingle, remembering a few days ago when he made good on his promise and bent me over his knees. I had to wear my swimsuit coverup the rest of the day to hide his handprints.

"Yeah, that's what I thought." He smirks as he takes another sip. I swear this man can read my mind.

"Pardon my reach." Cortney, our flight attendant, places a charcuterie board on the table that stands between us. "We have some meats and cheeses, freshly sourced from the Dominican Republic, on the board, along with some fruit and nuts." She places a cute bottle next to the board. "And this is Harissa Hot Honey. A sweet and spicy honey that goes well with just about everything. The brand is actually owned by a Dominican woman, Gloribelle Perez. She and Evan struck up a deal to have an endless supply of her honey on board once Amelia fell in love with it and the funny owner." She chuckles.

I'm digging in and drizzling the honey on everything before she even has the chance to place a few water bottles on the table.

"Do you know when you go back to work? The two-week suspension should be over in a few days, right?" I ask as I reach for a grape on the table between us.

Tony visibly tenses at my question. He waits until Cortney walks away before answering. "Yeah, not exactly sure about that." His grip on his water bottle tightens, making the bottle crackle. "I got an email this morning from my sergeant. I have a meeting with him and a couple of other higher-ups on Monday. Seems like they're still riding a high from the media circus Amelia's attack created. And by the looks of it, they're trying to spin it and make me look like the new NYPD poster boy."

"I don't get it. Why would they suspend you, only to then use you as positive PR?"

He sighs deeply, looking like he'd probably like to be having any conversation but this one. "When I didn't wait for backup and shot Amelia's kidnapper, it was a clear violation of proto-col. The shot was clean. Julian had a gun aimed at me. And he had a knife on Amelia. But the force panicked because they need to keep everything above board to avoid any police-related scandals." He places the mangled water bottle on the table. "Clearly, Amelia's relationship with a famous billionaire turned the series of events into a telenovela. Having her brother save her must be exactly the kind of heartwarming story morning talk shows salivate over. And now, I fear they might try to take advantage of my brown skin and use me as their shield for any racial accusations or deflections."

"You can't let them do that, love. You're not a media puppet. And the NYPD can't just use you for good press.

That's disgusting." My blood boils at the thought of anyone capitalizing on Tony, by weaponizing the color of his skin.

No sooner does the seat belt sign light flicker off than I'm shooting out of my seat, only giving Tony enough time to open his arms before I settle into his lap.

One of his massive arms curls around my waist as his free hand slides to my neck and his fingers gently dig into my hair. I lean down, and he places a soft kiss under my ear. "How do you do that?" he asks.

"Do what?"

"Make everything feel better."

My heart swells. I'm glad I'm already sitting, because that sentence would have easily buckled my knees.

My hands frame his face, and I pour every ounce of myself into our kiss. My promises to protect his heart. My desire to always have him near me. My hope for our future.

Which is why his pained words when we break apart shock me to my core.

"Please. Never leave me, Nikki. I won't survive it again," he whispers against my lips, avoiding eye contact.

I try to rear back, but he keeps me in place. "Why would you say that? I told you I love you, and I mean it." I tilt his face up so he's forced to meet my gaze. "Tell me what this is really about." My thumbs caress his cheeks.

The hits just keep on coming, because I did not anticipate what he says next. "I'm thinking of quitting the police department. I think my time there is done."

We're just about to land.

Over the last three hours, I've sat next to Tony as he spilled every emotion he's had about the police department for the last couple of years. How he walked away from his business degree to join the police academy. How his past relationship with his ex influenced his decision to join the force. The countless conversations he's had with his dad about not choosing "the right career path" and much more.

I can see defeat in his eyes, and I want to do everything in my power to fight for him.

"Okay, so I promised I wouldn't turn this into a therapy session, but—"

"Nikki," Tony starts.

"You're dating a therapist! I'm bound to throw a coping skill at you at some point."

"I don't need you trying to be my therapist. Just my girl-friend." He squeezes my hand.

"Why? Do you have something against therapy?" I challenge.

"Nope. I would just like to leave that to my *actual* therapist."

I grip his forearm with frightening strength. "You go to therapy? With, like, an actual therapist? And I mean someone with credentials. Not that guy who hangs by the bodega on 94th and Broadway."

He peels my hand off his forearm and intertwines our fingers instead. "Amelia and I go to the same therapist. Our mom set us up with her for grief counseling. After she passed, I continued seeing her. I don't have a set schedule for appoint-ments, but I make it a priority to see her at least once or twice a month."

A man who is self-aware and working on himself. I close my eyes and curse my past self for missing out on the national treasure that is Antonio Nuñez.

"Nikki."

I put up one finger. "Just a sec. Not done cursing myself out in my head. I'll be back with you shortly."

"Mi amor," he implores.

"Okay, fine. I'll respect your boundaries and let you have those conversations with your actual therapist. Just promise to speak to her before you make any final decision?"

He squeezes my hand. "Of course."

He moves in to kiss me, but I blurt out, "But can I ask one question? Then we can totally put a lid on this conversation, and you can take it to Kelly Olson, LMFT." Because of course I know my bestie's therapist's name.

He kisses my forehead. "Go ahead."

I take a moment to formulate my question properly, then ask, "If you had no outside influence, and the sole purpose was your daily happiness, what would be your dream job?"

Tony closes his eyes as his head hits the back of his seat. I think he might need time to come up with an answer, but instead he says, "You're gonna think it's ridiculous."

"Wait, you already know?" I ask, surprised.

He nods. "The income might not be very reliable—"

"Stop stalling. Spill."

He runs a hand back and forth over his jaw. His perfectly manicured beard almost distracts me. "I want to make beer." He pauses, waiting for my reaction. When I stay silent, he continues. "Own a brewery maybe. Create my own brand of IPAs and distribute locally. Or nationally. Who knows," he says shyly.

"That is… the most perfect job I could have ever imagined for you."

He eyes me as if he thinks I'm full of crap. "I'm serious! You're not your average beer drinker. You're more of a beer connoisseur. You're always feeding information on the craft beers you bring around your family, and you have an appreciation for the artistry."

He raises a single brow. "And how would you know what information I tell my family about beers?"

Busted.

I shrug nonchalantly. "I may have kept my distance, but I always paid attention when it came to you."

He moves in to kiss me, but I continue. "And you even have a business degree! So you could run your own operation. Whether that be as a brewery owner or creating your own brand of beer. Oh! And if you had a brewery, you could serve finger foods. Dominican tapas style. And then—"

Tony's lips crush down on my lips. He takes advantage of my surprised gasp and slips his tongue past mine. I don't even try to hold back the moan caused by the heat of this kiss. I attempt to crawl myself back onto his lap, but he stops me.

"Wait, why are we stopping? We were just getting to the good stuff," I pout.

He chuckles while rubbing his thumb over my bottom lip. "We've landed." I look around and confirm that we are, in fact, on the ground. He pulls my chin toward his lips and whispers, "But don't worry, I'm taking you back to my place, and I fully intend to finish what I've started."

36

NIKKI

WE SPENT THE ENTIRE WEEKEND HOLED UP IN HIS APARTMENT.

There was a small snowstorm, so it gave us a perfect excuse to stay in our little love bubble.

And without realizing it, we kept true to the silly promises we made on the night we first met. Every morning, Tony brought me breakfast in bed after he came back from his workout. Every night, we ordered takeout, and I let him pick the cuisine as long as I got to eat off his plate. We settled into an easy routine, but one that would soon come to an end.

"Are you sure you can't stay another night? We can hop in a cab to your apartment now and grab some of your work clothes." He pulls out the puppy dog eyes. As if this man needed any more pull over me.

He's sitting on the arm of his couch with his arms folded across his chest. I walk over and step into his open legs and wrap my arms around his neck. "Tomorrow is Monday, and I have to go to work. I need more than an outfit to prepare for a day full of meetings and clients. I need to go over my notes and get ready for my supervision sessions with my students. Which means I need to go home. To my apartment. Alone. Plus, you have that meeting to go to." I pepper his cheeks with kisses since my words are making him grumpy.

He wraps his arms around me and holds me flush to him. "I don't like the idea of you sleeping alone. Not a fan of sleeping by myself either."

My man is a new member of the cuddling fan club. And he gets extra cranky when I try to slip away at night. Lucky for me, he's the coziest big spoon a girl could ask for.

"We've been attached at the hip for over a week now. I would for sure have thought you'd get sick of me by now," I tease.

"When will you be back?" The touch of vulnerability in his voice takes me by surprise.

"Why? What's this really about?"

His grip on me tightens a fraction. "Just want to make sure you come back to me. That's all." He kisses my cheek, but I'm not buying it.

This man has offered me reassurance every step of the way, even when I struggled to believe I deserved it. And although many of our conversations have me feeling bare to him, I decide to lay on one more vulnerable truth about where my heart lies.

Because he's worth it.

"Do you remember the day you walked in on me talking to Amelia and Evan about my breakup with Justin?" He stiffens at the mention of my ex.

We've spoken briefly about him since Justin texted me yesterday, asking me to meet him for a chat to discuss his plans to move out. He's been in Florida with his family for the holidays, and we haven't gotten around to having a conversation about logistics since the breakup happened.

"Yeah. What about it?"

"If you had gotten there earlier, you would have heard why I broke up with him." I nudge his face toward me when I notice the tic in his jaw. "I didn't see a future with him. With anyone I've ever dated, for that matter. I've always been fiercely independent, and when I looked to my future, I could see all the well-laid plans I've worked toward vividly, but never the men who were currently in my life." I sigh.

"I played by the rules. Made sure the men ticked every box, went on the appropriate number of dates before becoming exclusive, and never took any risks that could lead to getting my heart broken."

"And what about me? What's the difference with me?" His voice cracks on the last word, giving away his fear of where this conversation is going.

I shake my head at the absurdity of the situation. This man, who, by all accounts, is larger than life, clings to me as if he hasn't already seared himself into my soul.

"The difference?" I chuckle quietly. "There are no boxes for you to tick. You have obliterated any sense of appropriate timelines for this relationship. I should have known when you told me you went ahead and fell in love with me at first sight." I smile. "And Tony? The men of my past? I couldn't see them, couldn't see a future with them in it. So if you're asking me what the difference with you is? It's this. I see you everywhere. You've embedded yourself in my bones. Not having you in my future would be like being forced to live life in black and white after you've shown me colors I never knew existed. Many years ago, I made a foolish mistake based on fear. I didn't want to lose the people I considered family. I wanted to set roots and create a new place to call home. But now? You are my family. You are my home. And that is the difference."

His head falls into the crook of my neck. "Nikki," he whispers. "I love you so fucking much. I promise to be the man you need me to be. Tell me what you need, and it's done."

"Well, you do look irresistible in a suit. Just wear one of

those, and I'll run my ass over to you no matter where I am or what I'm doing," I joke, attempting to bring levity to the room.

He lifts his head. "Is that so? I'll have to keep that in mind." His hand encircles my throat as he captures my lips with his, keeping me right where he wants me as he devours me whole. I feel the full force of his power in this kiss, yet his hand holds me gently, like I'm his most prized possession.

I clench my thighs together, attempting to relieve some of the tension building in my core. Tony notices, because he chuckles on my lips.

"What's so funny, big guy?"

He finally releases me and offers me a relaxed smile. "Oh, nothing. I could go ahead and take care of that for you." He nods at my lower half. "But then again, I'll let that be just another reason you run home to me." He smirks.

Jerk.

He moves toward his front door. "Come on. I'll walk you home. The cold air should help."

I chuck one of my gloves at him, which he dodges expertly.

"I survived many flying *chancletas*, Nikki. You're gonna have to try harder than that." He grins.

I huff and stomp my way toward the front door but can't keep the smile from emerging on my face.

I'm in love.

And that big hunk of man holding open my coat for me loves me right back.

Being in the spotlight of his gaze warms my skin more than the Dominican sun ever could. And I promise myself in that moment that I'll protect us at all costs.

After an inappropriate display of public affection, I say goodbye to Tony at my building's entrance. I still have the goofy smile on my face as I finish ascending the three flights of stairs to my apartment.

A smile that drops immediately as the reality of my not-so-distant past stands in front of my apartment door.

"Hey, Nikki. We need to talk."

"Hi, Justin."

37

ANTONIO

The meeting from hell did nothing to ease my rattled feelings about my future at the NYPD.

Luckily, I had the foresight to book an appointment with my therapist today. As I sit in the familiar office, surrounded by books and plants, I'm reminded of the first time I came here with my mom. It was one of the few things she asked of me before she passed.

Mental health still isn't mainstream in the Latinx community. Especially for men. Which is exactly why my mother wanted to make sure Amelia and I had access to grief counseling services before and after she was gone.

Truthfully, I went along with it because I would do anything my mother asked of me. But in reality, I'm glad she exposed me to therapy, because in a time like this, I'm glad I have this place to run to instead of the bottom of a bottle.

"Well, this is unusual. You usually book your appointments weeks in advance. I'm glad I had a light appointment day and was able to accommodate you on such short notice. It must mean there's something urgent you want to discuss," my therapist Kelly says.

I nod as I make myself comfortable on her oversized couch. Something I am immensely grateful for, given my size. "I had a meeting with my superiors today to talk about my suspension and my future at the NYPD."

"And how do you think it went?"

"Truthfully?" She nods. "I'm not sure." I rub a hand over my face. "They did a one eighty on me. First, they suspended me for not following orders and breaking protocol by going in without backup to save my sister from that lunatic. But now, I just came out of a meeting with my sergeant and a public relations person. They talked about making me 'the face of my community' and discussed when I can start media training." I shake my head. "Apparently, the story of my sister getting kidnapped by a deranged drug lord, only to be rescued by her police officer brother and billionaire boyfriend, didn't die over the holidays. Go figure," I say sarcastically.

Kelly takes notes but stays silent, allowing me the space to continue.

"So instead of me getting my detective badge this month, like I was promised, I was told that a 'better promotion' might be on the horizon if I'm a 'team player' and work with the department to 'explore options' that capitalize on the positive exposure this ordeal has brought to the force."

Kelly's face remains expressionless. "Meaning?"

I sigh and lean my forearms on my thighs. "Meaning that if I play along, you're looking at NYPD's newest media puppet. Most likely to be used to distract from the main issues the department has yet to address head-on. Like police brutality, profiling, and responding to calls that are clearly better handled by people trained in mental health crisis intervention."

"I'm tempted to ask you how that makes you feel, but I think that would be redundant. So instead, I'll ask you what you believe your next move should be."

And this is why I like talking to Kelly. She doesn't beat

around the bush, and she doesn't hide behind her wall of diplomas. She cuts to the chase, and while I'm busy spewing off my thoughts, she somehow always manages to meet me at the finish line with an epiphany I never saw coming.

"I don't know. My immediate reaction is… fuck that. I took an oath to serve and protect my community, not work the camera to make the whole police force look better." I can't hide the look of disgust that flashes across my face. "I refuse to let them use the color of my skin as a shield for those who only want to shake my hand in photo ops. It is not my responsibility to lessen the burden of those in power to do right by us. And I'll be damned if it's my face that's used to ease even a fraction of their dirty consciences."

Kelly waits a moment before asking, "Why am I sensing a *but?*"

I groan. "But… fuck! I don't know. I just know how powerful it could be for kids to see me, see my face as the person who is going to step in the line of fire and protect them. I know I can act as a bridge for the people in my community to trust me, if not the badge, to keep them safe. I know that hope can be a powerful thing. And if I'm the person who can help reinstate that in my community, why am I being selfish and not jumping at the chance to be that?"

I slump against the couch and lean my head back against the cushion. I stare at the ceiling, wishing it would give me the guidance I so desperately need. The kind of wisdom only my mother could provide.

"Tony, this isn't the first time you've sat in my office with mixed feelings about your profession. Even before your mother passed, you hinted at some unease in that area of your life. Which, may I say, is completely normal given the spotlight that you and your department are under."

She pauses, as if searching for the right way to phrase the question that's on the tip of her tongue. The look on her face is one I recognize immediately. It's the face she makes right before she takes me to the brink of a breakthrough.

"But I must ask, if only for clarification purposes." She places her pen down and graces me with her full attention. "Have you always felt that you've had to earn your existence by way of your career choices or by fulfilling the expectations of those around you?"

Silence.

Deafening silence fills the room.

Only when I see Kelly nudge the tissue box in my direction do I realize that tears are steadily running down my face.

"Fuck. Me." I groan as I angrily wipe the tears away.

This is only the second time I've cried in this office. The first was the session after my mom died.

Yet somehow, in this moment, I can't help but sense that I'm still in mourning. But for a completely different reason than my mother's passing.

I think, for the first time, I'm mourning myself. And the person I could have been if the choices I made were solely for me.

Why did I go to business school? My dad.

Why did I become a cop? My ex.

Why won't I walk away from my current job? My community.

When the tears finally subside, I speak. "You have to understand. I'm an immigrant in this country. Even though I came here when I was young, it doesn't take much to remind me that I'm an outsider, or that I was 'allowed' to stay here by becoming a naturalized citizen as a teen." I roughly wipe away another tear. "And if that isn't enough to influence my decisions, I also bore witness to my parents' struggles in this country. And their constant mantra of 'we're doing this for you and Amelia, so you'll have a better future. All of our sacrifices are so you can live a better life.'" I grunt. "But am I?" I raise my voice slightly. "Because when that constant line is drilled into you all of your life, the meaning starts to change. It feels like you're an investment. An investment in which your family expects a return on. Something that should come so easily because they already made all the sacrifices." I try to reel in my anger as I continue. "As much as I love my parents and I know they love me, there was always a thinly veiled threat against stepping out of line or trying to go for something, anything, that didn't have a guarantee at the finish line. I was always told to follow my dreams or to find a job I enjoyed, but always within the known parameters of acceptable jobs. Doctor, lawyer, teacher… I mean, I just listed the jobs of every person related to me. Even those not by blood." I shake my head, feeling duped that I didn't see this sooner. Didn't realize how programmed I was to abide by these invisible laws.

"I won't make the decision right now, but I know something has to change. I won't let this spill into the next phase of my life I'm about to embark on."

Kelly quirks a brow. "And what phase is that?"

For the first time during this session, a genuine smile takes over my face. "It's a long story, but after all this time, she told me she remembered."

"Nikki?" Kelly asks.

"Yep." I nod. "And… we're in love." I now smile widely.

Kelly looks at the watch on her wrist, not hiding the pleased look on her face. "My next appointment isn't for another hour."

That's all she needs to say to let me know that I've got the next hour to spill about the woman I've mentioned countless times in this room.

～

Even though I don't have a clear plan, I leave therapy feeling much lighter than I have in months, maybe years.

I leave the office and zip my coat up higher. January in the city is not as kind as January in the Dominican Republic. I'll tell you that.

I pull out my phone to send Nikki a text. Something that feels odd to do since we never texted before we left to spend the New Year in paradise. Just a random text here and there about logistics for Amelia's birthday party or directions to a family member's home.

When I look down at my screen, I'm delighted to see that I already have two messages from her waiting for me.

Nikki: How did your meeting go??

Nikki: Miss you so much! Can I stay over tonight? I can pick up dinner. xo.

I respond quickly.

Tony: Is that even a question? And don't even think about an overnight bag. I want to see that large suitcase Bergdorf packed for you filled with everything you need. Including all your work stuff. I refuse to sleep alone tonight... or any other night.

Nikki: Hi caveman.

Nikki: Was wondering when you would make an appearance.

Tony: Hi baby. Don't worry about dinner. I feel like cooking tonight.

Nikki: Ohhh I love having a stay at home boyfriend!

Tony: Watch it. I might make you pay for that.

Nikki: Always so bossy.

Tony: I'll show you bossy.

Nikki: Looking forward to it. See you at home ;)

Home. I love how she called me her home last night. And I promise to make my apartment feel like her home as well.

I take a detour toward Trader Joe's, and an hour later, my cart is overflowing with all the essentials, plus a couple of things I'm sure Nikki would like.

As I'm comparing which sauvignon blanc Nikki would prefer, I feel my phone buzz in my pocket.

Nikki: Hey, change of plans. Gonna stay home tonight instead.

The fuck she is.

I bypass texting and call her immediately.

"Hey," she whispers. "Just about to leave my office and head off to a meeting."

"You're coming over tonight."

She chuckles lightly. "You're really committing to this caveman bit, aren't you?"

"What's wrong? Why don't you want to come over?" I say, softer this time.

She sighs. "I know we said 'I love you' to one another, but I don't know if I'm ready to be *this* open with you." I hear the embarrassment in her tone.

"What is it, baby?"

"Uh. I uh, got my period just now," she says tentatively.

I ignore the irrational disappointment that comes out of

nowhere now that I know we didn't magically make a New Year's baby and instead focus on trying to figure out the issue at hand. "And?"

"And?" She pauses. "And I'm on my period. So I don't want to be *changing* and *managing* while at your place."

I shake my head, then put both bottles of wine in the cart. "I'm grocery shopping as we speak. I'll pick up anything you want. Do you need any tampons or pads? I can swing by the pharmacy after—"

"Tony!" she whisper-shouts. "You don't—I have everything I need. I just—" She huffs. "Look, I know we're speed rolling through societal timelines here, but I don't want to shatter whatever *allure* I have going on during this honeymoon phase. And today is day one of my period, which means I feel bloated and gross and maybe a little sensitive. So excuse me for wanting to spare you from boarding my hot mess express."

My smile is blinding. I never knew bliss could be bickering over mundane things while grocery shopping. But my girl trying to shield herself from me isn't gonna fly.

"Nikki, I need you to listen to me and listen to me carefully," I say sternly. "Are you in the mood for chocolate-covered marshmallows or chocolate-covered pretzels?" I eye the snacks to my right.

She groans. "Tony, stop mocking me."

"I'm dead serious, but I understand if you can't make decisions at a time like this, so I'll go with both." I toss both snacks into the cart and continue making my way along the aisles. "Now, moving on to dinner. What are you craving? I got enough food in this cart to feed us all week, so I can cook, or I can just make a couple veggie sides and order from whatever restaurant you desire."

Silence.

"Nikki, you still there?"

I hear her audibly exhale. "Yep. I'm here. Just trying to

figure out how I have my period when you say shit like that. Surely your words should be enough to knock me up. At this rate, I think I should be having quintuplets," she says rapidly.

I immediately envision her pregnant, her swollen belly growing our child. And if she thinks I was a caveman before, she has no idea the visual she just implanted in my brain. "Nikki," I say gruffly.

"Oh God, please don't tell me I just gave you a breeding kink. See? This is the kind of shit I spew off on day one. I can't be trusted. I'll just come over on—"

"*Nicolette.*" I slice through her words.

I faintly hear her whisper an "oh fuck."

"Either you're at my apartment, with a very large suitcase full of your belongings by six p.m., or I'm coming to your place to pick you up. Option two will make me upset. Upset enough to hide the chocolate-covered marshmallows in the cabinets over the fridge, where you can't reach."

She gasps audibly. "You wouldn't."

I grin. "I would."

I hear the smile in her voice as she speaks. "You drive a hard bargain, Mr. Nuñez. So, I guess you'll be seeing me tonight at six."

"Good girl."

"Ew, shut up! Don't say stuff like that in public!"

I laugh and get ready to end the call so I can drive the cart between the crowded grocery shoppers, but then Nikki speaks in a much more somber tone.

"Hey, and since I'll be over, there are a couple of things I want to talk about." She clears her throat. She likely realizes how ominous that sounds, because she immediately follows it up with "but it has nothing to do with you, or, like, us. I'm very, very happy. And I love you. And I definitely want those chocolate-covered marshmallows."

She must hear me sigh in relief, because she continues.

"I'm sorry if that sounded bad. It's just that I never want us to be in a place again where me holding back hurts us. So I'm just trying to talk to you as soon as things pop up, okay? We're moving fast, which is fine, but a lot of my life hasn't caught up. We need to talk about how to tell Amelia and—"

"It's okay, mi amor." I cut her off. I know we have lots to discuss. Mainly, how to break the news to my sister. I know Amelia loves us both, but she wouldn't appreciate us keeping her in the dark. "We can talk tonight when you're home. In my arms."

"Okay. Tonight," she says breathily. "I gotta head off to that meeting now."

"Call or text if you need anything."

"I will. And Tony?"

"Yeah?"

"I love you so much."

"I love you more."

I hang up and make my way back down toward the produce. But not before I snag an extra bag of chocolate-covered marshmallows for my girl.

38

NIKKI

I'M IN LOVE WITH MY DREAM MAN.

I just hope I'm not fucking things up by telling him about my conversation with Justin last night. Or even worse, what I agreed to.

Tony arranged for an Uber to pick me up at my apartment and is already waiting at his building's front door to greet me and take my luggage from the trunk.

"Hola, mi amor," he whispers over my lips.

Gah, I swear my knees go weak every time he speaks to me in Spanish.

I quickly peck his lips and escape from under his arms, because if I go full Jell-O in the middle of the street in this freezing weather, Tony might have two heavy pieces of cargo to carry into his building.

Tony laughs behind me as we make our way to his apartment. We remove our boots and shed our extra outer layers at record speed until Tony is left wearing a tight black T-shirt with gray sweatpants while I'm in comfortable leggings and an oversized blue sweater. Tony is ready a second before me, giving him just enough time to open his arms and prepare for my typical hug attack.

I always dreamed of climbing the man like a tree, but leave it to me to cling to him like a koala the instant he's within reach.

He's peppering my face with kisses, and I beam under his loving affection.

"How was your meeting today? Are you going back to work soon?"

He kisses that spot under my ear that makes me shiver. "I don't want to talk about it tonight." He sighs. "I'm still processing it all. But as soon as I get a better grasp on it, I'll tell you all about it. I promise." He kisses my nose.

I don't like being left on a cliff-hanger, but I understand the importance of respecting boundaries, so I leave it be.

"I missed you so much today," I say between kisses.

"I missed you more." He cradles my face in his large hands, and I melt.

"Ugh, are we that gross couple already? The ones I love to make fun of on social media behind their backs?"

"Whatever, sure. Just let me hold you for one more minute before you abandon me for the living room." His arms slide around my waist and keep me close.

"Why? What's in the—"

Holy mother of period gods.

I try to slide out of Tony's arms, but he squeezes me tighter while laughing above me.

He finally takes pity on me and lets me go, and I make a beeline for the couch. On the coffee table is an array of sweet and salty snacks laid out on a tray. And yes, I immediately spot the chocolate-covered marshmallows. There are two empty glasses next to a decanted bottle of white wine in an ice bucket. On the TV, a movie is paused on Julia Roberts's face, but the movie is easily decipherable by the still image lighting up the screen. *Runaway Bride.*

The couch is covered in a new dark gray throw blanket that wasn't here yesterday, and Tony picks it up and hands it to me. "This is a heated blanket. The remote is right here." He places it in my hand. "I wasn't sure if you'd want this or a heating pad, so I got both. I can get the heating pad ready in the microwave if that works better for you." He starts making his way back toward the kitchen and lifts a small teddy bear. "Thought this one was cute. It's also infused with lavender or something. Don't know what it helps with, but figured it was worth the upcharge. Plus, you said you might feel a little sensitive, and I couldn't shake the image of you cuddling this bear on your stomach." He smiles shyly.

And I… well. I do the most rational thing a woman in my position would do.

I cry. No, not cry. I start sobbing.

Before my ass hits the couch, Tony has swooped me up into his arms and sat me on his lap. "Are you okay? Did I… did I do something to upset you? Or is this, you know… the you being sensitive bit?"

I manage to laugh through the sobs. "Second option."

Tony rubs my back. "Ah, I see."

I snuggle into his neck while trying to get a handle on my emotions. "You didn't have to do all of this. This is too much. It's too… I don't even know what to say. Why are you so good to me?"

Tony lifts my chin with his forefinger, then gently wipes my tears away with his thumb. "I've waited what feels like a lifetime to be a boyfriend again. To be a partner. Never in my wildest dreams did I think it could be with you. And now that I have the chance, you better get used to me going all-out." He tucks a rogue stand of hair behind my ear. "You still have no clue how far gone I am for you, do you?" He chuckles. "I even spent an hour talking about you to my therapist today."

I sit up straight on his lap and place a hand on his chest. "Hold on, your therapist knows about me? You spoke to her… about me? Am I hearing that correctly, or am I love drunk in this moment?"

He pulls me in for a kiss. "We can talk about all this later. First, let me wine and dine you. Then we can discuss anything you want, mi amor."

I stiffen at the reminder of what I need to tell him.

He notices and rubs my back. "I promise, corazón. You have nothing to worry about. You can tell me anything."

"Fuck no. Not a chance. Over my dead body, Nikki."

Oh well, so much for having nothing to worry about.

39

NIKKI

"START AGAIN. FROM THE BEGINNING." TONY HUFFS AS HE paces back and forth.

After dinner and a couple of glasses of wine, I finally got the courage to broach the subject of Justin with Tony, and needless to say, my caveman isn't happy.

"Love, I've already told you all there is to know. Please sit with me?" I reach my hand out.

He looks at it for a moment, then finally concedes by taking it and placing a soft kiss on my open palm.

I take it as an opening to explain once more. "Look, when Justin showed up last night, he came in peace. There were no ulterior motives, and he didn't seem upset at all."

"Red flag number one. A man who loses you shouldn't be able to function in society so quickly after a breakup. Trust me, I should know."

I squeeze his hand in mine and carry on. "It's just a simple favor. It's the least I can do after ending our relationship so suddenly. A decision that triggered the loss of his living arrangement, may I add."

Tony rolls his eyes. "Overstayed his welcome, if you ask me."

I sigh. "Look, when I visited his family for Thanksgiving, your sister called me while we were touring a church. The same church his parents got married in. So when I answered your sister's FaceTime request, and she immediately started rambling about her wild night of sex with Evan—"

"Nope. Hard stop. How are you making this worse, Nikki?" He shuts his eyes tightly.

I grimace. "Ah, right. Sorry. Anyway, after that inappropriate conversation at the church, I felt like I had to redeem myself with them. So when they mentioned that they would be spending their fortieth wedding anniversary here in the city, I jumped at the chance to book a nice restaurant for their celebration. Everything is all set, and I don't have to do anything, but—"

"But Justin just happened to forget to mention to his parents that you guys are broken up? How convenient."

With my free hand, I caress his beard, and I don't miss how he leans into my touch slightly. For such a big guy, he really is a mush.

"I know. But it was right before Christmas, so I can see how he didn't want his holiday to turn into an inquisition about the breakup."

"And after?" he challenges.

"Well, after, he said that he knew the dinner was coming up, and since I planned it and all, he didn't want to ruin it by telling his parents, who are celebrating a big anniversary, that the girlfriend who planned it also happened to dump him before the holidays." I wince, knowing that the argument is weak at best.

"Nikki, you booked a reservation and asked the restaurant to add their gratuitous anniversary décor and menus. Hardly a reason to make your presence mandatory." He levels his glare at me.

And for the first time since we've been intimate, I feel like I'm facing the old Antonio. I desperately hope that I'm not hurting us by agreeing to this small favor.

My eyes plead with him as I say, "Two hours. Three, tops." I hold my hand up as he opens his mouth to speak. "I know it's not my responsibility to show up for an ex-boyfriend. And trust me, if the tables were turned, I would probably be going batshit if you suggested doing the same for an old flame."

"Then why, Nikki? Why must you do this? Why do you need to be there for him?" he asks, his voice sounding pained.

I take a deep breath and look down at my lap. "Because I feel guilty," I start. "What I did to him is what I've always feared. Giving yourself to a person, only to set off a domino effect of losing multiple things in the process." I sigh. "He lost a relationship, an apartment, our routines, our friend group, which includes Amelia…" I finally get the courage to look up at him, only to find him clenching his jaw. Might as well keep going at this rate. "And I also feel guilty, because he will never be you."

His gaze snaps to mine. "What do you mean?"

I shake my head. "Don't you see? I feel guilty because I'm happy. Stupidly happy. And even though there is a code you must abide by that means you have to hate every single one of my exes, I feel guilty because no matter how hard they tried, no matter how hard I faked it, none of them could ever hold a candle to you. All their efforts were in vain, because at the end of the day, I always belonged to you. Even if my boneheaded self didn't realize it at the time."

He pulls me onto his lap and ravishes me with his kiss. Within moments, I'm breathless and cursing the period gods for picking today of all days to grace me with their presence.

Tony pulls back far enough to look me in the eye. "Two

hours. *Maximum.* And don't you dare try to push it, Nikki. Because I damn well don't mind making a scene and dragging you out by your chair if you're a minute late walking out those restaurant doors."

I smile up at him as he continues. "I have more stipulations. You make it crystal clear that this is the one and only time you will bail him out with his parents. And while you're at it, let him know that you already have someone else you come home to, because *this*, Nikki, is your home, for as long as you want it to be."

"You're my home." I kiss him softly.

"Damn right. And you're *mine*." His chest rumbles with contained frustration.

Now that I got that major obstacle out of the way, I'm feeling *plenty* generous. Just because I refuse to let him go anywhere below the belt tonight doesn't mean I don't want him any less. Especially in those gray fucking sweatpants.

Tony must be able to hear my train of thought, because he catches on to the way my hand drifts south of his chest.

He unfurls a predatory smile and leans back on the couch. "But just in case you need a reminder, why don't you go ahead and get on your knees and show me, mi amor."

You don't have to tell me twice.

Men. Such simple creatures.

Tony may still be uncomfortable with the idea of me having dinner with Justin and his family, but given the tune he's whistling in the kitchen, I think we're going to be just fine.

The blow job definitely lessened the blow. Pun intended.

But now it's time to talk about the other most important person in our lives. Amelia.

Amelia has been trying to touch base with me to catch up

since we returned to New York. But every time I call or video chat, she has a different family member around fussing over her. She may be off the hard pain meds, but she is still recovering. She just started walking up steps slowly this week. And Evan has been watching over her like a hawk. Hardly the environment for me to drop the bomb that not only am I dating her brother, but we're in love and in it for the long haul.

A part of me wants to believe that she'll be happy for us, but a small part of me is terrified of her reacting poorly to the news. I never want to do anything to jeopardize our friendship and would hate for her to think that I'm carelessly keeping this secret from her.

But I just need to find the right moment to come clean to her and hope that she'll be just as happy for us as we are for her and Evan.

"What's wrong? Are you thinking about Amelia again?" Tony sits next to me on the couch.

I pout. "How'd you know?"

Tony rubs a thumb across my bottom lip. "You only pout over the ones you love."

"I just don't like feeling like we're a secret. She's my best friend, and I feel sick keeping this from her. Especially since you're the best thing that has ever happened to me."

"If you keep saying things like that, I'm going to break the *no-fly zone* rule you've implemented for this week." He presses a bruising kiss to my lips. When we finally come up for air, he says, "There's no use in worrying yourself sick. At this rate, we should probably tell her after—uh, I mean—"

My eyes widen. "After what? Is the engagement happening any day now? Oh God, it is, isn't it? We need to get our nails done so hers are ready for the moment it happens. I also need to gently recommend the right outfit for the occasion. What kind of timeline am I working with here?"

He rolls his eyes and shakes his head. "I'm not gonna be able to keep this from you any longer, am I?"

I cross my arms over my chest. "Nope. So spill."

"It's happening in about two weeks. Maybe less."

I shriek.

"Simmer down." He chuckles. "He's doing it at our mom's one-year celebration of life party. So we might as well wait until that passes before saying anything. Wouldn't want to be the center of family gossip and take away from her moment."

I lean in and kiss him on the cheek. "You're such a loving and thoughtful brother. Amelia is so lucky to have you."

He wraps an arm around me. "And now you have me too. So let's just lie low for the next couple of weeks. We'll find a way to tell Amelia after she's engaged. I'm sure she won't even care once she sees the ring Evan plans on getting her."

I open my mouth to demand more information. Obviously, I need pictures. But he silences me by placing his forefinger on my lips. "That's enough chatter for tonight. Let's wrap up out here so I can hold you in bed. I still don't forgive you for making me sleep alone last night." He kisses my exposed collarbone.

"Did you miss being the big spoon, love?" I tease.

He nips my neck with his teeth, causing me to giggle. "Yes, I did. I vote for never spending another night apart. It's over-rated, in my opinion."

"Is this your subtle way of asking me to move in with you?" I ask jokingly.

Tony leans back, assessing me with gentle eyes before he speaks. "My home is wherever you are. The apartments we lease? Those are just the places where we keep our stuff. But wherever you go, I go. Simple as that."

And in that moment, I know that I may be able to move anywhere in the world, but with Tony, I have found my forever home.

40

ANTONIO

As soon as Nikki heads off to work, I shoot Evan a text to meet me for lunch.

He's taken time off to take care of my sister during her time of healing, so I know he should be available.

We meet up at our favorite Chinese restaurant on the Upper West Side. We've never been the kind of friends who dabble in small talk, so Evan jumps right into it.

"Anything you want to tell me about your time away with Nikki?" He gives me a knowing smirk.

I knew he would be quick to catch on to us, but I promised Nikki we would wait until after their engagement to talk about it, so I need to keep it vague. "I'm not here to talk about Nikki. I'm here to talk about some stuff that has been going on in my work life."

Evan immediately straightens and gives me his full attention. All playfulness vanishes from his features, overtaken by the billionaire businessman.

I give him the rundown of everything that has been going on in my work life since Amelia's kidnapping. I've purposely kept Evan in the dark, since he's had enough going on with being Amelia's full-time caretaker and, unbeknownst to her, soon-to-be fiancé.

Evan listens diligently as I recount my meeting with my superiors and my therapy session, along with all the revelations that came out of it. I even mention my dreams of owning a brewery and creating my own IPAs.

I've had a day to let it all sink in, and the more I think about it, the more my decision solidifies.

"So you're quitting the force," Evan states, rather than asks.

I blow out a breath and nod. "It's not going to be easy. It's become a part of my identity. But I can no longer deny the opportunity to take a chance on myself and pursue something that truly drives me to get out of bed every morning. Something that I'm passionate about. And if there ever was a time to take the leap, it's now."

Evan looks out the quaint restaurant window and rubs his jaw while nodding. He looks back at me in time to say, "All right, I'm in."

Perplexed, I ask, "What do you mean you're 'in'?"

He gives me that front-page smile newspapers love to print. "It means I'll back you throughout this process. It's going to be a pricey endeavor. And I'm here to help as much or as little as you need. There are going to be investors, mainly me, since I don't want you getting screwed around. Then there's the real estate agent I need to get you in contact with. He's great at looking for commercial property. My guy who got me the cabin in the Berkshires highly recommends him. Then the attorneys for—"

"Whoa. Slow down there, man. I think we're getting a bit ahead of ourselves. Besides, I'm doing this on my own. I don't need your money."

Evan laughs. The fucker *laughs* at me.

If he wasn't my best friend, I would be tempted to smash his head against his chicken fried rice.

I lie. I'm still tempted.

Evan wipes his mouth with a napkin before placing it back on his lap once more. "Tony, I may have been that weird computer nerd when our friendship started, but now I'm a businessman... who is still a computer nerd, but still a businessman, nonetheless. And what I have learned in business is that time is money, so let me be efficient with our time here."

I roll my eyes and brace myself for his spiel.

"I know you're as hardheaded as a tank, but I'm going to help you fulfill your dreams of owning a brewery, and you're going to let me. Because long ago, when I was a scrawny kid in college with a dream, you believed in me. You worked all summer to save five thousand dollars, and in my time of need, you gave it all to me, no questions asked."

"You paid me back," I mumble.

Evan waves me away. "Not the point. The point is that you helped me first. You were technically my first ever investor. And now, look at how having someone believe in me, someone invest in me, changed my life. I'd like to believe that you didn't do it out of pity." He pauses.

"Of course I didn't. I did it because you were my friend."

Evan smiles widely. The fucker let me walk right into that one.

"Precisely. And over a decade later, we're still best friends. And soon we'll be brothers-in-law. So believe me when I say that there is nothing I would be more honored to do than to support you this time around and help you fulfill the dream you've kept on the back burner of your mind for all these years."

I groan and run a hand roughly through my short hair. "I don't know..."

Evan shrugs. "If anything, I owe you for not killing me when you found out I was dating your sister. Think of it as taking money from the man who dared to sleep with her behind your back." He smirks.

"Are you trying to propose to my sister with a black eye?" I growl.

He laughs. "There he is. And don't worry. I'm aware that my investment just doubled because of that joke." He lifts his beer bottle in my direction. "To the family business. And whatever went down in the Dominican Republic with you and Nikki."

I can't stop the hard laugh that escapes from my chest.

This fucker. Just what I needed. Evan's onto us. And investing in my dream.

Family business.

That wasn't the plan.

I was ready to go at this alone. By myself.

So why can't I stop smiling while I sip my beer?

41

NIKKI

IF TONY IS HOME, THEN FORWARD MY ADDRESS TO CLOUD NINE.

A part of me can't believe I held back from falling in love all of these years, yet the other part is glad that I waited for Tony.

It's finally Friday and I'm flying through my morning tasks at the office. I don't even realize it's lunchtime until I get a call from my dad.

We usually text throughout the week, and FaceTime on weekends, so having a midday call from him is odd.

"Hey, Dad, everything okay?"

"Hey, kiddo, just calling because I'm in town and in your part of the city. And I was wondering if, uh… I could take my daughter to lunch."

I stumble at the thought. Lunch with your dad must seem like such a mundane activity. But for someone like me, who was always starved for any sliver of interaction with my father, this is monumental. "Yes, of course! I'm ready now if you are. Where do you want to meet?"

"How about the lobby of your work building? I'm already here." He laughs.

"Wait, how do you…? Oh right. Of course you would know my work address."

"I swear I googled it like any other law-abiding citizen. I didn't need the FBI database to find your office at the university where you work," he scolds playfully.

"All right, on my way down!"

I don't know when hugging my dad will stop being weird. Or when sitting in front of him will feel natural. Because we're just about done with our lunch, and I still haven't settled into our conversation.

"Nikki, is something wrong?"

"No." I shake my head. "I think it's just gonna take a little time for me to, you know, get used to you being real and whatnot." I chuckle awkwardly.

He sighs. "Yeah, I know. I've got a lot of making up to do. And truthfully, I don't deserve all the grace you're giving me. But I'm too selfish to let you know it, because spending this time with you will forever be the highlight of my life."

Tears start forming in my eyes. And if I let my hormones run wild, I'll be sobbing in public in two seconds flat. So I try to change the subject quickly.

"Whatever happened to that Mr. Bartoli guy? Still living large?"

My dad's shoulders slump. "Yeah. The guy is untouchable. I think it's time I walk away from the case. I've been holding out on retiring, all because I wanted to see this through. I wanted to make my sacrifices worth it in the end. Although I can already tell you that they weren't. Any day spent away from you and your mother was an eternal loss on my end, and I'll have to live with that for the rest of my days."

I hold his hand across the table. I wonder if he would be open to talking to mom. I'm sure there's some closure that needs to happen there. But I hold off on suggesting it, since I'm not speaking to her at the moment.

Then, out of nowhere, a thought comes to me.

"Do the Bartoli families own casinos, by any chance?"

My dad raises a brow. "No. Why?"

I shrug and take a sip of my water before answering. "Oh, no reason. I just remember seeing a tattoo on his wrist and thought it was because he was big into cards or gambling."

My father goes stock still. "Adriano doesn't have any tattoos, Nikki."

My lips twitch. "Yes, he does. It's a small one, but I saw it. A little ace of spades playing card on his left wrist. Small enough for his watch band to cover it."

My dad's voice takes on an authoritative tone. "Are you absolutely sure about this? An *ace* of spades? How did you get that close to him to see it? Is there anything else you can recollect during your time around him? I need you to take a minute and think for me."

"Whoa, wow. Calm down there, Dad. He was mostly being a big flirt with me. The only thing noteworthy was the tattoo." I pause. Then widen my eyes when I think I remember something worthwhile. "His *finsta!*"

"Is that English?" my father asks, clearly confused.

"No. While talking to him, I mentioned that I should get off social media, and he countered with telling me I should just open a fake Instagram account so that I can still stay in the loop with what's going on online without people knowing it's me."

My father is out of his chair and fishing bills out of his wallet before I get my full sentence out.

"I gotta run into the office here in Manhattan and brief the technical analyst on what you've just told me."

He plants a big kiss on my cheek. "But I didn't really tell you anything, did I?"

He's about to head for the door but decides to lean into my ear before leaving and whispers, "All the criminal activity runs through one main corporation. It's the only solid evidence we have on the Bartoli empire, but we've never been able to link it to Adriano until now."

"Huh? Why?"

My dad smiles widely as he says, "That corporation is called Ace Enterprises. And I believe my daughter has just cracked this case wide open."

My head is still spinning from today's lunch when it's time to close up and head home for the day.

My phone buzzes in my hand, and I smile at the name on my screen.

Tony: Get your fine ass home.

I laugh at the audacity of this man. Although I can't deny the zing that runs up my spine any time I think of Tony's reaction to me being a brat. So naturally, I fight him on every little thing to rile him up.

Nikki: What for? Anything interesting waiting for me?

His response is immediate.

Tony: Stop being a brat. If you make me leave the warmth of this apartment to bring you home, be prepared for me to teach you a lesson.

Ha! He knows me too well.

Nikki: Promises, promises.

Tony: Only pinky promises for my girl.

Damn it. I was so ready to keep this defiant act up all night. But all this man had to do was mention our pinky promises, and I'm putty in his hands.

Nikki: Ok you win. Coming home to you now!

Tony: There's my girl. Have lots to catch you up on.

Tony: Just sent you an uber, it's too cold for you to take the train. See you in ten, corazón.

Tony: Love you.

Nikki: Thanks for the uber love!

Nikki: Te amo.

Tony: Fuck, Nikki. Tell the driver to hurry up so you can say that to me in person.

We spend all of Saturday morning in bed. Tony didn't even bother going to the gym today.

Last night, he spilled everything that happened at his work meeting and then in his therapy session. To say it was an emotional night is an understatement. But before the night ended, I helped him draft his resignation letter. For a moment, I worried he might be making a mistake. But then I heard all about his plans to start looking into the brewery business and how Evan plans on helping him. I couldn't keep track of how many smiles appeared on his face every time he talked about a different aspect he was interested in learning about within this new industry. It was like a new light has been lit within him, and I was the most fortunate person on the planet to be allowed to bear witness to it.

When we finally went to bed, we made love for hours. It was passionate and thrilling as always, but it also felt like more. Tony'd had his heart cracked open for the past couple of weeks after being thrown curveballs with his job and his love life. And last night, I was seeing a new version of him come alive, all while being connected and intertwined with our bodies.

And if that's the closest I'll ever get to heaven, then I'll consider myself lucky.

This morning, as I lie with my head on his chest, I absent-mindedly trace the disco ball on his inner bicep while I run through a list of things I want to research to help Tony pick the best spot for his brewery.

Anything in the city will be extremely costly, so I'll start my search in Brooklyn. Then, I'll move on to—

"Jesus, woman, I can hear the search engine of your mind going a hundred miles per hour. I know I'm the unemployed one of the duo right now, but must I teach you how to relax? I was sure I put enough work in last night." I look up in time to see the smug look on his face.

I smack his chest as I laugh. "I'm probably gonna walk funny all day thanks to last night." I work my way up and snuggle into the crook of his neck. Should have known after I lifted my flimsy sex ban. "But it was totally worth it." I sigh.

His hand rubs up and down my bare back as he speaks. "Then tell me what's on your mind." He kisses my temple.

"I'm just making a mental checklist."

"Of what?"

"Of all the things I have to do to help you set up your brewery."

He hums, saying my name softly. "Nikki. You don't have to do a single thing. This is my dream. I need to work on it."

I lean back so I can look him in his eyes. "Exactly. Which now makes it mine to support. You made my dream come true the night you kissed me on the beach and told me I belonged to you. It's only fair I help you achieve your dream now."

Tony closes his eyes while he leans his head back on the propped pillows behind him. "Fuck, Nikki. You can't just say shit like that."

"Why not?"

"Because you're sore right now…" He looks down at me, his eyes molten with hunger. "But I guess that just means I'll be having my breakfast now."

42

NIKKI

Monday morning came much too quickly for my liking.

Leaving the warmth of the apartment to go to work on such a cold and dreary day should be criminal. Yet my morning commute isn't too bad, especially since Tony always tags along to walk or train it to work with me. We pick up breakfast and coffees along the way, so every morning feels like a date.

Today, he is off to Evan's office, since they will be going over brewery business. I'm so excited to see him going after his dreams. Especially because he is in his midthirties, pursuing a second career in life. It's such a testament to his resilience, and I couldn't be prouder to be by his side as he strives to bring his vision to life.

We brainstormed all weekend, thinking about concepts and ideas for a bar menu, the décor, and the different types of beers he could offer.

I even braved the kitchen, and in my first attempt, made some decent *arroz con guandules*. The way Maria taught me how to make it on our last day visiting her sandbar restaurant. I still think there is some room for improvement, but by the way Tony was scraping the bottom of the pot for the *con con*, I think I did all right.

Incorporating Dominican snacks will be essential for Tony, and I immediately started researching other breweries in the area to see how they managed the food aspect of the business.

I never knew this type of love existed. The kind that makes you care so deeply for another human that you will pour all of yourself into making their goals come to life. This is the part of life I always felt was missing. Belonging to a team, a family. And belonging to Tony doesn't mean I'm his possession, but rather the person he does life with.

This weekend showed us how well we work side by side. Pushing each other lovingly toward our common goal.

Along with the way things are progressing with my relationship with my dad, I'm starting to feel at peace with everyone around me.

Everyone, that is, except the person who is trying to video chat me on my lunch break as I sit in my office.

My mother.

I have yet to answer any of her calls, but something about the way life is moving in my favor has me swiping across the screen and accepting the call.

"Nikki! I didn't expect you to accept, but I'm so glad you did! How are you, darling?" She smiles nervously.

I sigh. "Hi, Mom, I'm fine. What's up?"

Now, I know I'm more mature than asking my mother "what's up?" after ignoring her for nearly a month, but there must be something said about mothers and daughters and their innate ability to revert to the dynamics of the teenage years when there is trouble.

"Nikki, I haven't heard from you in weeks. I was concerned and I just… I wanted to apologize."

My eyebrows almost hit my hairline upon hearing her words. I don't think I've ever heard anything more than a flippant "sorry, dear" from my mother.

"Look, I would love to have this conversation in person, but since you weren't answering my calls, and we live in different states, I didn't want to chance boarding a flight for you to just turn me away," she says bashfully.

"Mom, you know I would never turn you away," I chide.

She tilts her head. "Are you sure? Because it's been radio silent from your end, and even though I know exactly how I messed up on that call with you last month, I would have still liked the opportunity to apologize for my mistake." She exhales heavily when I stay quiet.

It's hard for me to think back on that traumatizing moment, where I found my best friend's apartment ransacked after she was kidnapped, only to have my mom ask me, hours later, if I could introduce her to her billionaire boyfriend.

"My actions were inexcusable, Nikki. I don't know where my cables got crossed in my head or how I allowed myself to speak those words. I probably have a few ideas, but that's not what this call is about. It's about me apologizing to you and hoping that with time and action, we can move on." She tenses at the end of her sentence, fear of rejection clear on her face.

"What do you mean by action?" I ask.

She smiles. "I knew you would pick up on that. After the holidays, I started seeing a therapist. On my own. I know we've done the therapy thing before, but I think before I can be a better mother to you, I need to figure out how to be a better human to myself."

"You're seeing a therapist?" I'm barely able to contain my surprise.

She nods. "When you stopped answering my calls, I realized how lonely my world is. You are the only family I have left, and like everyone else in my life, I managed to push you away too." She shakes her head. "But we can talk about my issues another time. I'm sure you're busy at work right now. I just wanted the chance to apologize and let you know that I will try my very best to do better, to be better."

Unfortunately, I can't blame these tears on my period.

"Thank you, Mom," I say between tears. "It means so much to me to hear you say that. And please don't think that you've pushed me away. It was just a hard time, and I needed space after everything was said and done."

We both dry our tears and laugh at the sight on our screens.

"I've also written you a letter. Aside from the apology you deserve, my therapist and I worked on something that I would like you to read. In your own time." She sighs. "I'm not doing this so you pity me. And it's not an excuse for my actions, but I do think it's time that I let you in and show you parts of me that I've kept hidden from you." She hesitates. "It's a saved email draft. So you say the word, and I'll send it," she says anxiously.

As a mental health counselor, I know how hard it is to put your feelings into words and share them with others. I'm proud of my mom for taking this step. But as her daughter, I'm still wary of this rapid turnaround.

"Sure, Mom, you can send it. I might not read it right away, but I would love to have it and read it when I'm ready."

Our relationship won't be fixed in a day. Hell, it may even take the rest of our lives to get it back on track. But knowing that my mother is taking the appropriate steps to be a better version of herself softens my heart. I don't know if being in love has turned me into a mush, but I'll gladly accept her olive branch for the time being.

I look at the time on my desktop and realize I have thirty

minutes left before my next meeting. I know we have lots to discuss, but I figure now is a good time to break the ice.

"By the way, Mom, guess who I finally met while on vacation."

43

ANTONIO

Every woman I love is in this room, and they're all sobbing.

Evan just proposed to Amelia at my dad's apartment, and I swear they're going to burst the windows with their screams and cheers.

I, on the other hand, am enjoying making Nikki squirm by standing too close to her or accidentally brushing past her on multiple occasions. She knows she can't do much to fend me off, because that would be like blood in the water for these chisme sharks. My tías y cousins, non-blood related, can spot any inkling of gossip. So I know Nikki is walking on eggshells, trying to keep her cool.

Luckily for her, all the attention is on the newly engaged couple, as it should be. I watch Amelia pull Nikki in for a hug, and I can physically feel my heart bursting with love. Nikki beams at Amelia, wiping away her tears, as she gushes over her new engagement ring. She rapidly tells her to get ready, because she is already in wedding planning mode for her. Seeing Nikki stand by Amelia makes me look forward to the day when Nikki wears my ring on her finger and carries my last name.

I smile at the thought. The only thing better in this scene would be having my mother by their side. But I know she's here with us today.

I know she sent Nikki back to me.

Nikki steps aside to give the other partygoers access to the bride-to-be and decides to start making the rounds, offering to top everyone's glass of champagne.

I watch as she moves around my family's home with ease. My hands twitches to touch her and pull her to me. And I can't wait for the engagement excitement to die down in the coming days so we can tell Amelia about us and finally be out in the open with my family.

The only cloud overshadowing the joyous occasion is the fact that tomorrow, Nikki is having that dinner with her ex and his parents.

This is the only time I wish that Nikki didn't have such a pure heart, because the thought of her anywhere near a man who has touched her, made love to her, sends me into a goddamn tailspin.

Even though I trust Nikki to my core, I don't trust her ex. And I can't just stay home and watch the seconds tick by.

So I'll support Nikki's decision, and I won't stand in her way. But I never promised to play fair.

44

NIKKI

Why the fuck am I doing this?

It's a little too late to be having these thoughts, given that I'm standing in front of the restaurant where I'll be having dinner with Justin and his parents.

While getting ready, I decided to go with minimal makeup. I chose a simple little black wrap dress that hits right above the knee, and my black heels are ones I wear to work often. After giving myself a satisfied look in the mirror, I threw my blond tresses into a high ponytail and left the apartment before I decided to second-guess my decision for the billionth time today. I'm hoping my overall look screams "uninterested," yet before I left the house, Tony's gaze quietly ate me up, as if I were leaving the house in lingerie.

For a man who I have lovingly dubbed "caveman," he's been pretty calm about tonight. He had just stepped out of the shower when I was ready to leave, and he gave me a chaste kiss on the lips before I put on my peacoat and left the apartment. I was a little disappointed, to be honest. I was expecting him to ravish me, give me a hickey, or perform some type of ritual to claim me as his before I left. But all I got was a kiss and a "have fun tonight, mi amor."

Rude, if you ask me.

I take one final deep breath before I freeze my tits out here, then enter the restaurant. I'm immediately greeted by low ambient lighting and light jazz music. I picked this restaurant months ago for its classy and old-school vibe. Now I kinda wish I had picked a place with louder music so I could drown out of my thoughts of dread.

The hostess smiles politely at me as I make my way toward her, but I'm intercepted by Justin, who seems to have been waiting for me by the entry doors.

He's dressed better than I've ever seen him dress in our entire relationship. A tailored blue suit, crisp white button-down shirt, and shiny black shoes. And his dark blond hair is freshly cut and styled. I know this is an anniversary dinner for his parents, but for some reason, he looks more like a groom than a restaurant patron.

"Nikki, you look stunning," he says as he leans in to give me a kiss on the cheek. That action alone has my stomach churning. It feels wrong to have his lips on me when all of me belongs to the man waiting at home.

If I'm going to do this, I'm going to need some ground rules with Justin. Mainly, a hands-off policy.

"Hey, Justin. Can we just go over a few things before—"

"Nikki, so glad to see you, honey! We missed you at Christmas. How is your friend Amelia doing?" Justin's mother, Deb, barrels toward me with open arms.

I awkwardly return her hug and do the same with Justin's dad, Carl, who is standing beside us with a proud look on his face.

After we've all said hello, we're ushered to our table in the middle of the restaurant. This place is on the smaller side, so all the other tables are within arm's reach of each other.

Justin pulls my chair out for me, and we all settle into our table.

Now that I'm here, sitting across from Justin's parents, I recognize that I probably should have just turned him down when I had the chance. Because they're beaming with excitement, and I feel plagued with guilt. The same funny feeling that got me into this mess in the first place.

Note to self: when you break up with someone, you are entitled to turn down any dinner invitations, especially ones that include their parents.

I'm going to need copious amounts of wine if I'm going to get through the night. I eagerly flag down a waiter so he can start us off with a round of drinks.

"She'll have a glass of Chardonnay." Justin nods toward me while speaking with the waiter.

I hear a record scratch go off in my brain. This is not the time to mess with my drink of choice.

"Actually, a glass of sauvignon blanc. A heavy pour, please. If your glasses have that little line that indicates where the wine should come up to, just double it. Charge me whatever it costs, thanks." I salute the waiter when he gives me a knowing smile.

I look around the table and see questioning faces. I know I agreed to come to this shindig, but there was nothing in the agreement about being a demure pretend girlfriend. I'm riding this dinner out my way.

"So, forty years! Wow. Such an accomplishment. Tell us your secret," I say as I plan to keep the attention solely on the celebrating couple tonight.

Deb and Carl share a loving look before Deb answers for them. "There's no real secret. Obviously, communication and patience, but the biggest thing is not giving up on one another, especially when things get tough."

I can't calm my nerves or stop my head from nodding like a bobblehead. If she only knew how her words are making me squirm, especially since I dumped her son, who currently has an arm draped over the back of my chair. My body naturally tries to create space, but at this rate, I'm pretty sure my boobs are fully resting on the table, and poor Carl is having a hard time being seated across from me.

My new best friend, our waiter, Bobby, arrives with our drinks. I almost laugh at how well he followed my instructions, given the fact that my glass of wine is almost filled to the brim, and the other three glasses have a more appropriate pour.

I immediately bring the glass to my lips and only need to tilt it slightly to take a few sips. I'm so focused on not spilling a single drop that I fail to notice the rest of the table staring at me while holding up their glasses, waiting in silence for me to catch up so they can toast.

For a millisecond, I contemplate spitting some of my wine back into the glass but vote against it. "Oh, right. My bad. Let's toast to forty years! Yippee…" I softly clink my glass against their unmoving ones while I lock eyes with Bobby and give him the universal hand gesture for "keep these coming." I have a feeling that this is gonna be a long night.

I'm holding on by a thread by the time we're done with appetizers.

Justin finally got the hint to move his arm from my chair, and I was able to move my breasts off the table just in time to make space for the calamari.

I'm peppering Deb and Carl with questions to avoid having to answer any of my own, but I'm running out of things to talk about.

Carl is in the middle of explaining what vegetables they grow on their farm when I see my newly engaged best friend stroll into the restaurant, closely followed by her fiancé. They haven't spotted me yet, and I'm about to raise my hand to get their attention, when a suit-clad Tony saunters in behind them with his hands in his pockets and a sexy smirk on his face. His eyes immediately land on me, and he gives me a quick wink before anyone notices.

What are they doing here? And why the hell is Tony wearing a suit? He knows what the visual of him in a suit does to me. So he must know how badly I want to abandon this table and make a chair out of his lap.

Oh, he totally did this on purpose.

No wonder he was so relaxed about me coming here tonight. Because he would be here as well.

Well played.

Amelia finally spots me and has to do a double take when she sees the company I'm in. She knows Justin and I are broken up, and that I have no desire to reconcile, so it must be taking all the decorum she possesses to not mouth "what the fuck" to me.

They step up to our table, and I'm instantly on my feet. "Oh, uh, hi guys. W-what are you doing here?" I scratch my neck nervously, hoping to God that I'm not breaking out in hives as I speak.

Amelia eyes the table suspiciously as she hugs me, then says, "Tony invited us out for a little post-engagement dinner. What are *you* doing here?" I don't miss the accusation in her tone. She wants facts, and she wants them now.

Unfortunately, Deb answers for me. "Justin and Nikki invited us to dinner to celebrate our forty-year wedding anniversary. Who knows, maybe they'll come back here in forty years and celebrate theirs." She gives a knowing look to Justin as he coughs into his fist.

I don't miss the clench in Tony's jaw, and it is taking all my restraint to not jump into his arms.

Evan bites down on a smile he's trying to contain, but he's

not fooling me. He moves in to give me a hug, and whispers low enough so only I can hear. "Oh, this is gonna be fun."

I give him a quizzical look, and he just shakes his head while looking at the floor. And since I've greeted two out of the three people, I wiggle farther away from my chair to hug Tony. I don't know why I thought this would be a good idea, given the fact that he growls two words into my ear. "Eres mía." *You're mine.*

Two words in Spanish, and I can already feel the slickness between my thighs.

I release Tony when Evan clears his throat, and a part of me wonders if Tony told him about us, even though he promised not to.

"Well, then, we'll head over to our table and leave all you love birds to it," Evan chirps.

I involuntarily send a glare his way, and his smile only broadens.

Fuck, if he was suspicious before, that definitely gave him the confirmation he needed.

I sink back into my seat like a man bracing himself for the electric chair. And because the restaurant is tiny, the hostess ends up seating the fun trio right across from us. Naturally, Tony takes the seat that faces me.

I have a feeling that this is about to turn into a shit show.

45

NIKKI

I'm surprised I haven't burst into flames with the looks Tony is sending my way.

I've barely touched my main dish, which is a travesty in itself, since it's a delicious-looking lobster ravioli.

Ever since Tony arrived, I've gone from chatterbox to mime. I don't know how much longer I'll be able to carry on this ruse, especially when the man I love sits six feet away from me, along with my best friend, who is in the dark about this entire situation.

I'm so lost in my thoughts that I don't realize I've been asked a question until Justin squeezes my hand on the table. My eyes go straight to Tony, and I see him gripping his glass filled with dark amber liquid so tightly I'm sure it'll burst any second now. The fact that he's drinking hard liquor instead of beer is enough of an indication that this whole night is about to go to hell in a handbasket.

I'm too overwhelmed… and mortified. And okay, maybe a little horny too, from looking at Tony's muscles flex under his suit jacket.

I release myself from Justin's grasp and excuse myself to

use the bathroom. I don't necessarily need to use it, but I will definitely welcome the small reprieve it will offer. There are two gender-neutral single person bathrooms, and I push open the first one. I don't bother locking the door since I only intend to wash my hands. And maybe curse myself out in the full-length mirror that sits across from the sink.

Before the door has had a chance to slowly close on itself, a larger-than-life Tony storms through the door, making quick work of closing and locking it behind him.

"What do you think you're doing? Someone might see us!" I shriek.

Tony stalks toward me like a man who has all the time in the world. "Are you not *my* girlfriend? I'm pretty sure I'm allowed a word with the woman I love, no?"

I put my hands up in surrender. "Look, you won't get a fight out of me. You were right, and this was stupid of me to do. I'm floundering out there, and I really should have thought about this scenario before I went ahead and told Justin I would—"

Tony has me pinned with his hips against the wall by the sink. "Don't say his name. You're with me right now. The only words allowed out of your pretty little lips are *Tony*, *yes*, *ohmygod*, and *harder*."

"Why?" I ask breathlessly.

In one swift motion, Tony has me facing the sink. The momentum forces me to brace myself against the counter. He lifts the right side of my dress, and in the following second, I feel the hard smack on my ass cheek. "That wasn't one of your approved words, Nikki," he says in my ear, kissing my neck while his large hand massages my reddening behind.

"Tony." I moan.

"Good girl, you got it now. Safe word is *mía*. Something you should never forget you are." *Mine.*

He moves his hand from my ass and slides it into my

panties, finding the evidence of what he does to me. He hisses in my ear. "*Dime corazón*, is this all for me?" His fingers gently slide up and down my folds, collecting my arousal.

"Yes," I whimper.

"You're doing so well, baby, but we've got tables full of guests waiting, so we're gonna have to make this quick." I stop myself from speaking, since none of the approved words would help me get a better explanation.

But when he starts sliding my black silk panties down my legs, I get my answer. He pockets them, then turns me around. I'm lifted into the air as if I weigh nothing as he sets me on the counter. "Open up for me, baby."

With deft fingers, he works his impressive erection out of his pants as I wiggle my dress up higher around my waist. In the next breath, we make eye contact in the mirrors. He's facing the smaller one above the sink, while I face the full-size one behind him, making this the kinkiest house of mirrors I've ever experienced.

"Just like old times" is the only warning I get from Tony before he enters me in one brutal thrust, burying himself all the way to the hilt. "Ohmygod, Tony!" I yell.

"That's right, baby, say my name. Louder, so the whole restaurant knows who you belong to." He grunts as he sets a punishing pace.

"Tony!" I gasp as he rubs his thumb on my clit without easing his thrusts over that sweet spot that drives me wild.

"You're taking me so well, mi amor," he says through gritted teeth.

I'm such a goner. I no longer care that we're having sex in a public restroom. I no longer care that my ex and his family might hear my screams from across the hallway. And I'm sure as hell not thinking about my best friend, who would be mortified to find us in a compromising position.

No, all I care about is the man who has the innate ability to set my body on fire with a single touch and how he is currently wielding his power to coax an orgasm out of me in under five minutes.

"Harder!" My nails claw along his neck as he plows into me.

It only takes one tug of the bow holding my wrap dress in place to have my bra exposed. Tony impatiently flips the lacy cup over and wraps his mouth over my hardened nipple. He licks, tugs, and scrapes my nipple with his teeth, driving me wild, making me buck under him.

"Your pussy keeps sucking me in, Nikki. I know you're about to come, corazón." He swivels his hips and manages to thrust even deeper.

"Tony, ohmygod, ohmygod, yes, yes, yes!" are the last words on my lips as my orgasm explodes through me. The sight of us fucking in the mirror has me clenching him like a vise as my orgasm barrels through me.

"Fuck, Nikki, you look so pretty when you come on my cock. Fucking. Hell. Baby." He wraps my ponytail in his hand and tugs my head back, allowing him access to my neck, then bites down on my shoulder as he comes inside me. He's still pumping into me when I feel our releases dripping onto the bathroom counter.

That can't be sanitary.

Our heavy breaths fill the silence as Tony leisurely drops soft kisses over my neck and jaw, finally arriving at my lips and consuming me whole.

I'm still riding high off my orgasm. It takes me a minute to come back to earth and realize that I have to go back to my table after being fucked senseless by the love of my life.

"Tony, what are we gonna do? We can't go out there like this!" The mirrors that served as some kind of sexy voyeurism tool are now reflecting the image of a woman who survived a mauling and barely lived to tell the tale.

Tony slides out of me slowly and cleans us up silently and efficiently. He tucks himself back into his pants and appraises me from head to toe with his hands in his pockets as I stick my wobbly foot into a heel that must have fallen off while we were going at it. "You look properly fucked to me. Isn't that always the goal, baby?"

I send a scathing glare that must give off angry kitten vibes, because he chuckles as he undoes my ponytail, running his strong fingers through my thick strands.

A soft moan escapes my lips.

"Nikki, if you're not trying to go for round two, I suggest you keep those noises for when we get back home. For my ears only." He steps back and rights my dress, making sure the knot is tightly in place.

I put my hand out for my final but most essential piece of clothing.

"What?" Tony feigns confusion.

"My panties, *por favor*." I huff.

He takes them out of his pocket and dangles them on his forefinger. "Oh, these panties?" He holds them up high when I attempt to snatch them out of his hand.

"Real mature, using your mammoth size for evil."

He laughs as he turns toward the full-length mirror. My jaw drops as I watch him tuck my thong into his suit jacket and adjust it as a pocket square. "Perfect. I can still smell you like this."

"You're going to send me back out there without panties? Are you insane?"

He spins quickly and reaches me in one step. "And what if I told you that I was? That you've driven me mad by sitting pretty next to your ex all night while I kept your beloved *caveman* under wraps and well behaved... well, sort of, until you tempted me by breaking away to this bathroom. So yes, *mi amor*. I am sending you back to your table without panties. So you can sit next to your ex, and he can smell my come leaking out of you. So he, too, can be driven to the point of madness like I have tonight. And maybe then he will finally understand that you no longer belong to him, because you—"

"You are mine." I mock his deep, velvety voice.

"Do you think this is funny, *Nicolette?*"

"Oh shit, government name has been dropped." I try to stifle a giggle. He looks like he's about to bend me over and spank me again, and as much as the thought makes me tingle all over, we don't have the time for that. I put my hands on the lapels of his suit and work them up until they're intertwined behind his neck. "No, I don't think it's funny. I'm just laughing because I was sure you would Hulk smash our table and send our dinners flying when Justin touched my hand."

He grunts. "Thought about it." He looks down at me, and his eyes soften. "But I wouldn't want you in the blast zone." He kisses my forehead.

"Okay, guess we should get back out there. I'm sure they've cleared my table by now. Just dessert, and then I should be good to go. Should we leave separately?"

He shakes his head. "Absolutely not. Once you're done with dinner, you're joining our table, and we're telling Amelia and Evan about us. I won't wait a minute longer to claim you publicly."

I sharpen my gaze. "You didn't tell Evan about us? Because I'm pretty sure he suspects, if he doesn't already know."

Tony exhales heavily. "That bastard is like a bloodhound. I didn't tell him anything, but I know he suspects."

I nod. "Okay, then let's get out of here and get this over with."

"Um, Nikki?" I hear the smile in Tony's voice as I look down and make sure my outfit is properly in place.

"Yeah?" I look up to him.

"I missed a spot." He points to the trail of his release reaching the side of my knee.

"You sure I can't get those panties back?"

"Not a chance."

46

ANTONIO

"What took you so long?" Amelia asks as I take my seat, facing Nikki.

"Sorry, ran into an old friend from business school by the bathrooms." The lie rolls easily off my tongue.

Amelia seems unconvinced, but I'm too busy watching Nikki squirm in her seat. I'm wondering what excuse she gave for her change in appearance. Her hair is now down, and she no longer wears that luscious pink lipstick I made sure to kiss off her.

"Is it a full moon or something tonight? Because everything feels… off. I need to get Nikki away from that table and figure out what the hell she's doing with Justin and his family. Because something is up with my bestie. Actually, things have been off ever since you guys came back from vacation." Amelia narrows her eyes at me while Evan bites down on his bottom lip. Asshole.

"What are you looking at me like that for?" I mumble into my whiskey glass.

"Did you do something to my best friend?"

I fell in love with her.

"Did you make her cry?"

My name in ecstasy.

"Did you break her heart?"

Never, it's my most prized possession to protect.

Wait, what?

"Break her heart? What are you talking about, Amelia?" I ask.

She points a finger dangerously close to my face. "Don't play coy with me! Anyone with half a brain can tell that you two have always had something simmering beneath the surface. Why else would you guys constantly be at each other's throats and bickering like an old married couple?"

I'm unable to call upon the muscles needed to pick my jaw up from the ground. Is it true? Has Amelia always sensed there was more between Nikki and me? Have we really wasted all this time? Because if so, I'm about to bash my head against this table.

Amelia leans back and crosses her arms across her chest, revealing a triumphant smile. "I'm right, aren't I?"

Before I get a chance to answer, I hear Nikki gasp and loudly say, "You guys knew we were broken up?" She stares at Justin's parents in disbelief. This restaurant is small enough that Amelia's chair backs up to Justin's parents, and she has rotated her body completely so she is facing Nikki in silent, yet confused solidarity.

Justin's mother pats Nikki's hand across the table. "Just a small break. Not a breakup. Couples do it all the time. Once Justin explained the situation over Christmas, we knew what needed to happen, so that's why we're here tonight." She nods toward a nervous-looking Justin.

"Nikki," he starts. "I know that I was asking a lot of you by expecting you to move to Florida to live on my family farm with me. Especially as my girlfriend. I feel stupid that I didn't see it before. That a woman like you needs more of a commitment before she uproots her life and moves to a different state for a man." He nods toward a waiter, who's waiting in the shadows, and I watch as a sparkler is lit on a dessert plate.

"Oh no. Please tell me this isn't what I think it is," Amelia says loud enough for Justin's mom to look back and shoot a glare at her.

"What's happening?" I ask my sister, my brain too slow to catch up.

Justin moving out of his chair and down on one knee answers my question for me.

Looks like I'm going to have to Hulk smash a table after all.

I move to stand, but Evan shakes his head. "She's got this, man. Let her handle it."

The look on my face must be murderous, because he has the decency to look sheepish and say, "Just give her a minute before I have to pull up the getaway car." Yet he stays planted in his seat.

The dessert dish carrying the sparkler and a small velvet box is placed in front of Nikki. Justin grabs the ring box and opens it. "This is my mother's ring. It was my grandmother's before her. It's actually been in the family for almost eighty years. A true family heirloom."

The look of panic on Nikki's face tears through my soul, and I'm about to rescue her from this whole ordeal when she does the unthinkable.

She starts… laughing.

And not a normal or silly laugh, but a high-pitched laugh that would put banshees to shame. She has to stand and hold on to the edge of the table to keep herself from falling over. If my desire to rip Justin's head off clean for thinking of putting a ring on my woman's finger wasn't roaring in my ears, I probably would've joined in with a chuckle.

"Oh God, I think she's snapped. We can't let her get close to any sharp cutlery," Amelia whisper-shouts.

Nikki straightens and has to put a hand on her stomach to center herself. Then she wipes the tears that escaped during her laughing fit. "Justin, get up. We're not getting engaged," she says as casually as reading the dinner menu.

For a moment, I pity the waiter standing by with a bottle of champagne. His face says he would rather be anywhere but in the middle of this chaos. Only then do I notice that the whole restaurant is waiting with bated breath. The manager looks like he's about to break up this debacle, but Evan subtly waves his black American Express card, and the manager makes himself scarce.

Justin stands and holds Nikki's hand. "Nikki, I know this may seem sudden, but I know we can make it work. We've put in the time, we've lived together, and we have never had a real argument. We just hit a speed bump in our relationship, and this is me making sure we get back on track, because we are better together, babe."

"And you came to all those conclusions without consulting me? And figured I would just go along with your plan? Come on, Justin. Let's be honest with ourselves here."

"I have been honest with you, Nikki!" he spits. "Why are you being this way?" He takes note of the onlookers, embarrassment evident on his face.

Nikki pulls her hand out of his grasp and says, "Why am I being this way? Justin, you just ambushed me with a proposal after you bamboozled me into joining this farce of a dinner for your 'parents' sake.'" She uses air quotes on that last bit. "You lied to get me here, and now you expect me to fall in line and just what? Marry you and make it all better? Does that sound about right to you?"

He takes a deep breath. "Look, I could have gone about

this differently. My parents and I may have gotten carried away, but the sentiment is still the same. I want us to work through whatever issues you think we have so we can continue building a future together. I know if you give me another shot, we can make this work."

Nikki rubs her temples and sighs.

"Justin, that sounds lovely and all, but you made one large miscalculation."

Justin stiffens. "And what's that?"

"I'm in love with someone else."

"*What?*" Justin, Deb, Carl, and Amelia yell in unison. I look over to see that Evan's started to record this shit show.

"What? How? That's impossible. We *just* broke up." Justin assesses her with new eyes and scowls. "Is this why you reek of *man?* Were you with him before you even came to dinner with us?" he seethes.

"During." My voice booms through the small dining area, and all eyes land on me. "She was with *me* during."

"Oh no." I faintly hear Amelia whisper the words, but I'm too focused on Nikki, who has resorted to taking a few—no, many—gulps of her wine.

"And if you're done stomping your feet and throwing a temper tantrum, your time with her has officially expired." I stand to my full height.

Not wanting to lose face, Justin opens his mouth to argue, but I cut him off before he can get a word out.

"It wouldn't be wise to make me repeat myself." Justin's parents must make the right assessment and decide to cut their losses. They're standing and shuffling to grab their coats and Justin. He stands his ground for a moment but wisely decides to pocket the ring and walk out of the restaurant without a backward glance at Nikki.

My patience has run out. In two swift steps I'm cradling

Nikki's head into my chest. She tenses in my arms, and I realize that she must be worried about Amelia.

I keep her in my arms as I turn around to face my sister.

Amelia's standing as well, a scowl on her face, arms crossed over her chest, and her high-heeled boot tapping the ground. Evan stays seated behind her with a satisfied smirk on his face.

"Are you guys fucking kidding me? You're in love?" Amelia shouts.

I can feel Nikki start to tremble in my arms, and I'm just about to tell my sister to watch her mouth when talking to my future wife when Amelia throws her hands in the air. "Do you guys even know what this means? I only bet that you banged on your vacation. I know firsthand how close quarters can lead to panties dropping. But Evan bet that you two would come back madly in love!" Now I'm gonna have to get knocked up soon because you guys exchanged those three little words!" She faces her fiancé. "Wait no, you must have known. You cheated. This doesn't count if you have insider information!"

What the fuck?

"A bet? What the hell are you talking about?" I pause. "You know what, I actually don't want to know." Clearly my sister and best friend making bets that involve me having sex are not subject matters I want to be clued in on.

Amelia notices Nikki's pale complexion and immediately drops the hard-ass act. "Oh my God, Nikki. What's wrong? Are you okay?" She rushes to Nikki's side.

Nikki shakes her head. "Do you hate me? I'm sorry we didn't tell you sooner. We were waiting for the right moment, after Evan proposed and—"

"Nikki, why are you shaking? Everything's fine. I mean, I think it is, right? Is my brother treating you right? Because all I know is that he boned you in public while out to dinner with us, which doesn't bode well for my vote of confidence." She scrunches her nose in disgust.

I roll my eyes. "Nikki was worried that us dating might put a wedge in your friendship. Put my woman out of her misery already. Please and tell her it's fine." I silently pray that it's fine.

Amelia's eyes widen. "Whoa there, caveman. Throwing around 'my woman' already?" She shakes her head and focuses on a terrified Nikki. "Are you kidding me? If anything, my brother is the one who needs to be walking on eggshells around me. If he so much as causes one tear to escape from your pretty little eyes, he's dead to me. Cut out from the family, cousin crew included." She throws me what I assume is supposed to be a deadly glare.

Nikki hunches over. "Amelia, are you sure? I never want anything to jeopardize our friendship. You're my person, and I never want you to feel like I'm infiltrating your family or anything like that."

Amelia looks genuinely insulted by that for a second. Then says, "Nikki, you are my soul sister. Your happiness is my own. If my brother makes you happy, I'm over the moon about it and… and oh my God, we could actually become sisters-in-law if my dingus brother doesn't mess things up with you!" She squeals. Her mind is already running a hundred miles an hour.

I wrap my arms around Nikki's waist from behind and say, "She will be. One day soon." I feel the shiver that runs up Nikki's spine and finally acknowledge my shmuck of a friend. "Gonna need the name of your jeweler… and a friends and family discount." I laugh as Nikki slaps my arms.

Amelia steps closer to us. "I never thought I'd see the day. My brother, in a committed relationship." She puts her hands on top of mine, which are on top of Nikki's. "And to have found that love with my best friend? My person? Now I think I'm the lucky one here." And right on cue, the girls burst into tears. I release Nikki so they can hug.

"You can stop recording now, Evan," I scold.

"Not a chance. Can't wait to play this at your wedding. I'm kind of known for my romantic videos." He winks at me.

I roll my eyes, recalling how he proposed to my sister yesterday by compiling childhood home videos of them. Not gonna lie, it was cute as hell. Although I might have him beat, with the appointment I have planned for two weeks from now.

47

NIKKI

VALENTINE'S DAY

IT'S BEEN A WILD TWO WEEKS SINCE I HAD MY VERY PUBLIC AND very dramatic showdown with Justin and his parents.

And since Evan, Amelia, and Tony have recently been in the media, the whole story has blown up and even gone TikTok viral, whatever that means.

We've decided to keep a low profile and stay holed up in Tony's apartment for the time being, since Tony has officially cut ties with the NYPD. He gave his two weeks' notice, but since he was already on a paid suspension, his resignation was effective immediately. And surprisingly, he was still able to walk away on good terms. They put out a PR statement wishing Tony well in his future endeavors.

But the hiding ends today. Because today is Valentine's Day, and I'm pulling out all the stops. I'm going to make today so sweet it'll give Tony a toothache. If he's giving his all to win boyfriend of the year, then I need to step it up for the most commercialized day to celebrate love.

If someone would have told me that I'd be giddy to celebrate the cheesiest holiday about the one emotion I spent most of my life running from, I would have had them committed on a seventy-two-hour psychiatric hold.

Yet here I am, wrapped up in Tony's arms, dreaming about my romantic plan for the day.

That is, until my phone starts ringing at the ass crack of dawn.

Tony leans over me and looks down at the screen. "It's your dad. You should answer it."

I wipe sleep from my eyes as I take the phone and swipe to answer. Before speaking, I can see that it's five in the morning. "Dad? Is everything okay?"

"Nikki." I hear my dad's voice break and bolt up in bed. "We did it, honey."

"We did what, Dad? Are you hurt? In a hospital? Tony and I—"

I hear a ping, alerting me to a text message on my phone.

"Look at the picture, Nikki." My dad exhales harshly.

I put my phone on speaker and go to my text messages. I open the picture but have to rub my eyes once more to make sure my mind isn't playing tricks on me.

It's Adriano Bartoli. In handcuffs.

Being led out of a building in nothing but a robe and slippers embroidered with the Barlowe hotel logo. My dad, in an FBI jacket, holds Adriano's right bicep as a SWAT agent holds his left. A sea of officers and flashing lights flank them.

"We did it, Nikki. All thanks to you."

Is my dad crying?

I shake my head, unable to form words. Tony takes the phone to get a better look at the picture and smiles. "Congrats, John. It was a long time coming. Can't imagine how you feel."

I sit still, shell-shocked, as tears silently stream down my cheeks.

"You know"—my dad clears his throat a few times, attempting to fortify his voice—"I'm not naïve. I'm sure his son is already making moves and calling the shots to take over the multitude of illegal businesses we probably don't even know about. But it still feels like justice was finally served." He pauses for a moment. "I've always thought about this moment. Catching my white whale. Closing my last case with the one that started my career." He sniffles. "Yet it doesn't compare… doesn't even hold a candle to the moment I got to hug my daughter for the first time."

A loud cry escapes my throat, and Tony pulls me in close.

"I'm sorry, Nikki. You have no idea how much I wish I had done things differently. And I look forward to slowly earning a small place in your life." He releases a humorless laugh. "But I gotta say, the fact that you, rather than one of a multitude of people working this case for decades, gave us the breadcrumbs to nail the guy for life… now that's some poetic justice."

I quiet my sobs long enough to take my phone back. "So what was the evidence that got him arrested?"

"After we allocated more team members to comb through Ace Enterprises, we started looking for his fake Instagram account and found it. Our hackers were able to pin down the geolocations of where the photos were taken. Then we compared the dates large amounts of money were moved around to various countries over at Ace, to the dates and locations of his Instagram photos, almost like a travel diary. A lot of it seemed circumstantial at first, but then the idiot took a picture of a champagne bottle with the Sydney Opera House in the background. In the photo, we could clearly see his tattoo and documents on the table. Documents that, with some FBI technology, we pulled account numbers from. Hook, line, and sinker."

Tony chuckles next to me. "Al Capone was taken out by the IRS. Adriano Bartoli was taken down by Instagram. Unbelievable."

I smile. "Why Australia? I noticed that all his staff

members were from different countries, and it always struck me as odd that hardly any Dominicans worked at the resort."

"We've got a few working theories. He probably knew his reign was coming to an end, and he created the Barlowe as his sanctuary, since the Dominican Republic is a nonextradition country. I think he was embezzling money from all over the world and used visa sponsoring as a front to try to pay people on the inside in case he ever needed falsified documents to escape to a different country."

"Oh God, this is all so crazy," I say.

"Yeah, but we did it. We got him." He sighs. "Hey, if you ever want to put your psychology background to use at the FBI, just let me know. I'm sure I can put in a good word after today." He chuckles.

I laugh. "Thanks, Dad. As much as I would love to live out my *Criminal Minds* dreams, the survival skills I acquired as a woman in the twenty-first century are what broke the case, not any diagnosable disorders. I think I'll stick to what I got going on." I smile.

"Okay, kiddo. You got it. I'll let you go. I got more work to do on my end."

I nod to myself, ready to say goodbye, until a thought comes rushing to the forefront of my brain. "Dad, wait. Now that this is over, can you please tell me your last name?"

I feel Tony tense next to me as I hold my breath.

I've waited my whole life to know my real last name. Spent decades hating the constant references made to *Die Hard*. Or people teasing me that Bruce Willis was my dad.

I hear my dad groan, and then he says the name I've been holding out for my entire life. "Smith. My last name is Smith, sweetheart."

Tony's chest starts to vibrate.

It takes me half a second to put it together.

"John Smith. Your name is John Smith? Are you fucking kidding me?"

Tony's laugh finally bursts out of him, and he covers his mouth with his large hands.

"Yeah," my dad says, sounding sheepish. "I never claimed to be clever. I probably didn't need a fake name, did I?"

"The two most common names in the world? And yet you come up with McClane?" I shout, dumbfounded.

Tony grabs the phone from my hand. "Congrats again… Mr. Smith." He chuckles. "We'll let you get back to work." He ends the call and drops the phone onto his nightstand. He pulls me onto his lap so I'm straddling him and kisses my head.

"Can you believe that? Nikki Smith." I shake my head.

Tony cradles my head in one hand and lifts my chin with the other. His eyes bore into mine for a moment before he speaks. "One of these days"—he kisses me softly—"your last name will match mine. And you'll never have to second-guess who you are or who you belong to." He kisses me again, awakening a blazing desire in me.

I pull back to catch my breath, then smirk. "Oh yeah? If I take your last name, what will you take from me?" I jut my chin in his direction.

His eyes devour me whole as I feel him hardening beneath me.

"Everything."

48

NIKKI

We spent the morning tangled beneath the sheets, only making it out of the bedroom by noon. Which gave me more than enough time to carry out my Valentine's Day plans.

Tony said he had a quick errand to run and was out the door before I had a chance to question him. He probably ran out to get me flowers and chocolate for today. As sweet as that gesture is, it will in no way top my surprise. I will crush Valentine's Day this year and spoil Tony just as much as he spoils me.

I'm scrolling through my phone to kill time and figure that now is as good a time as ever to finally look at the email my mother sent me a few weeks ago.

I make myself comfortable on the couch as I brace myself for what I'm about to read.

My dearest Nicolette,

I know that actions speak louder than words, and I vow to make good on my promise of being a better parent to you. While I work on myself, I thought that it might help you understand me better if I open up to you about my past.

I'll try to keep this letter brief, since I would love to discuss these matters in person, but long story short—I struggle with what I now know to be abandonment issues. When I was a little girl, my father, the man I loved most, left me and my mother for his secretary. I don't think I've ever recovered from that betrayal and sense of loss. When I met your father, it was the first time I let my walls down. And as you know, I instantly fell madly in love with him. Only to have history repeat itself.

When I gave birth to you, I felt this overwhelming sense of love. So much poured out of me when I held you in my arms. You were and have always been the very best thing to happen to me, and if only one thing resonates with you in this letter, please let it be this. There is nothing and no one on this planet that I have loved more than you.

But that also became a double-edged sword for me, because it meant that you held the power to be my biggest heartbreak ever. I know it sounds silly, now that I'm actually writing this down, but I always had a feeling that at some point in time, you would do the same as your father and grandfather did and leave me. Every person I loved had, so why would you be any different? What terrified me even more was that my love for you as my child was exponentially greater than any love I had ever experienced, so I knew the heartache would probably break me until there were no pieces left to pick up.

I've spent decades looking for superficial love in all the wrong places as a distraction. This is why I always felt it was safer to keep you at a bit of a distance. Almost like if I kept space between us, it would spare my heart from crumbling. But in reality, I was wrong, and I heavily regret the pain that my actions have caused you.

As you know, I'm currently working on myself, and I know that will take time. And if you still need time away from me, please take it. My issues aren't something that should guilt you into a relationship with me.

But if or when you're ready, please let me know, and I'll be on the first flight out of Miami and into your arms.
Love,
Mom

I silently wipe a tear away as I reread the email three more times. I feel like I'm meeting my mom for the very first time in this letter.

My chest fills with an array of emotions. This is in no way a clean slate or an excuse for the years of pain and neglect I felt. The damage is done. My personality, strengths, and flaws have been carved out of the actions of my parents. And though I desperately wish my childhood had been different, I can't change the past.

My mom and I may never have a "normal" mother and daughter relationship. Just like my dad and I may always have those awkward lulls in conversation during lunch. But something I now have, that I never had before, is a chance.

As much as I would love to put up a front and act as though I'm indifferent to my parents, I can't. I still feel like the little girl who grew up in Miami, wondering why she'd never met her dad or why her mom never showed up at her school activities.

I know, especially in my field of work, that it isn't easy to accept accountability or to take that very first step toward redemption. And although that still doesn't take the pain away, I think I may benefit from a bit of healing that only my parents can help facilitate.

I don't give it much thought as I pull up our text message thread and quickly type.

Nikki: Read your letter. Hope you're ready to experience New York City in the middle of February.

Her response is immediate.

Mommy Dearest: As long as I get to hug you, it'll be the warmest place on earth. I'll look at flights now. Love you, Nikki.

I might have to look into changing her contact name.
My chest feels lighter as we coordinate dates and plan for her to come up next week. This emotional rollercoaster was not something I had planned to go through on Valentine's Day, but in honor of the holiday that boasts about love, it feels good to spread a little of it with my mom.

Tony comes back an hour later with bagel sandwiches. No flowers or chocolate in sight. I would harp more on it if I wasn't bursting at the seams to show him his gift. We eat quickly and make our way into the frigid New York city streets.

Tony pulls me closer to his right side to keep me warm as we wait on the curb for the Uber I ordered. It's way too cold and not as romantic to take the subway on this slow Saturday afternoon. "Where are you taking us, and why did we have to leave the warm apartment where I could keep you naked all day?" Tony mutters into my ear.

I giggle as our ride pulls up in front of us, and we get in.

He pulls me back into his arms as soon as we're seated. He raises an eyebrow as he notices the direction we're going in.

For the past few weeks, Evan and Tony have been working with a real estate agent to look for spaces to lease for his brewery. I know Tony had his heart set on a specific one in Brooklyn, although he would never admit it out loud. Nope, instead I would catch him at least once a day staring at the building specs on his phone.

He tried and failed to hide how devastated he was when Evan called to tell him that the owners had gone with another tenant.

Too bad he doesn't know that I asked Evan to make that call and lie.

Because not only is Tony getting the brewery of his dreams, but he'll also be the sole owner of it, not the leasing tenant.

When I asked Evan to give me a heads-up on any leads for that brewery, he jumped at the opportunity to help surprise his friend. What I didn't expect him to do was buy the brewery... and the entire block along with it.

As we park in front of the massive structure that now belongs to Tony, I bolt out of the car before he can ask any questions. I make it to the front door before he stops me. "Nikki, what are we doing here? We lost out on the lease for this place." I can see him looking up and behind me, longing clearly written all over his face.

"You are correct. You are not the tenant of this establishment." I turn toward the front door and enter the security code provided by the realtor.

I push open the heavy doors and send a silent thank-you to whoever had foresight to turn on the heating in this place.

Probably Amelia, since she helped me set up the decorations yesterday.

Since I'm familiar with the inside, I move to the right and switch on the lights on the underside of the bar.

Tony has only seen this place online. Now, for the first time, he gets to admire the forty-foot ceilings with the exposed-wood beams. The bar that runs along the right side of the building with seating for sixty. And the glass wall at the very back with a clear view to the production line of the brewery, which hosts six industrial-sized fermenting vessels to create the beers of Tony's dreams.

Tony's brows are furrowed as he takes it all in.

He's so engrossed in the details that he fails to notice the obnoxious "Congratulations" balloons that line the bar.

He sucks in a deep breath. "Why are we here, Nikki?" he asks, his eyes still roving over every inch of the space.

I pull on his open coat to get his attention. "Just wanted to give you these." I dig out the building keys from my coat pocket. "And be the first to say congratulations, boss. You are now the proud owner of this fine establishment." I smile widely, struggling to hold back the tears that threaten to spill over.

Tony's eyes snap up to the keys in my hands, then back to my eyes. "What did you just say?" he whispers.

I decide to put him out of his misery and give him the full rundown quickly so we can pop the champagne and start celebrating. "Evan bought the place, so you don't have to lease it. Actually, he bought the whole block."

Tony tenses. "He did what?" He closes his eyes briefly. "I told him I'd be okay with him investing, but not bankrolling the whole thing." He shakes his head roughly.

He starts to back up, but I stop him. "He knew you would say that. So he wanted me to relay this message." I pull out my phone and look at the last text Evan sent me, then read out loud. "If Nikki is reading this, it's because you have your panties in a wad." I giggle as Tony puts his hands on his hips, clearly unamused. "So I'll cut to the chase. When you invested 5k into my nonexistent business, you gave me your entire net worth at the time, since you were in your early twenties and broke as shit. Today, I have invested 2 percent of my net worth into your business. We can go over the numbers when I give you the deed later this week. And if, for some idiotic reason, you fail to accept my investment, just know that I'll transfer it to Nikki's name instead. I'm sure she has better methods for convincing you to accept my offer. Until then, you're welcome, future brother-in-law."

Evan's company went public this month, and his new net worth was widely publicized. If he invested 2 percent of his net worth, that means he spent roughly two hundred million on the brewery and the rest of the block.

I look up to Tony and say, "This is a separate text." I clear my throat and continue reading Evan's message. "Also, tell the big guy that he's my best man, so he better not piss me off by getting grouchy on me about this."

I put my phone down on the bar behind me, then look back up to Tony. "So, what do you say? Are you a proud brewery owner, or just dating one?" I ask with my arms crossed over my chest.

Tony tips his head up and laughs for a few moments. He then leans down as he locks eyes with me. "You're such a little brat." He takes my face in his hands and kisses me. "How long have you known? When did Evan tell you he bought the place?"

"Actually." My hands trail up his chest until I lay them on his pecs. "I told Evan that this was your favorite location, so he bought it last week, *after* I did a walk-through with the owners to make sure it was the perfect spot for you." I wince, realizing that he may have wanted to do that himself. "I'm sorry. I hope you're not mad."

He tilts his head. "You did this? How did you know this one was my favorite?"

I smile softly. "Call it a hunch. Or maybe because you would light up whenever you were looking at pictures of this place. I only ever see you do that when you look at those you love." I shrug. "Took a bit of a gamble there, but it's Evan's millions, not mine." I laugh.

Tony's lips crush down on mine, and all traces of humor escape me as he consumes me with fervor.

I snake my arms inside his coat and around his middle, and he hisses into my mouth. I drop my arms and lean back. "What was that? Are you okay?" I look up at him, confused.

He rubs his mouth with his hand, doing a terrible job of hiding his grin. He casually takes off his coat and places it on the bar behind me. I guess it is warm in here, so I do the same.

"Nikki, I'm going to go ahead and crown you the winner of Valentine's Day."

I laugh and curtsy. "Thank you for recognizing that this could not be topped. To be fair, I'll never be able to surprise you with a place of business again, so I hope you know that in terms of gift-giving, I have peaked."

He shakes his head, his eyes twinkling with mischief. "I was planning on giving you your gift at home, but I guess now is as good a time as any." He takes his black sweater off, leaving him in a white tank top undershirt.

My eyes widen, and I chuckle nervously. "You know, I brought champagne to christen this place. I should have known that you had other plans in mind." I bite my lower lip at the thought of Tony taking me right here on top of the bar.

Tony says nothing as he reaches behind his neck with his right hand and pulls off his undershirt in one swift motion.

My eyes greedily eat up every inch of him until I gasp.

My eyes land on tape covering what I think is a bandage on the left side of his ribcage. Tony's arm is down, so I can't get a good look. Before I can take a step closer, Tony raises a hand for me to stay put. "Corazón... do you know what that word means in Spanish?"

"Heart," I whisper.

He nods once. "I've been calling you that since we were at The Barlowe. Do you know why?"

I scrunch my nose. "Because it's a pet name. Like calling me *mi amor*?"

He shakes his head. "Nope. But I hope you know that the moment I met you, you stole mine. I've walked around this earth for over seven years with my heart in the palm of your hands."

"Tony," I whisper as my eyes water.

"Yet the main reason I've been calling you corazón is because you said something that struck me while we were on the island. You said that you've always felt like you weren't a complete version of something. And up until that moment, I realized that I felt the same way too." He lifts his left arm, revealing a clear wrap around a fresh tattoo.

My tattoo.

My jaw drops as he continues.

"It's one-half of a heart." With a jagged zigzag running down the middle, just like mine.

"I know you initially got this because of my sister." He pauses, his eyes boring into mine. "But you're my best friend too, Nikki." His eyes mist. "And it didn't seem fair that you're still walking around with my whole heart… so I inked a piece of yours on myself."

I'm rooted in place, shocked to my very core.

He steps close enough for me to get a better view of his tattoo, though it's barely visible through my tears.

I fear hurting his fresh ink, so I lower his arm and bury my face in his chest. He cradles the back of my head like he always does and kisses the top of my head.

After taking a few moments to regulate my breathing, I place a chaste kiss over his heart, then look up to meet his gaze. "I love you so much, Tony."

His eyes blink for a moment longer than normal as he takes a deep breath. "I love you too, corazón." He pulls me into a tender kiss, and I can feel my heart swell with his lips on mine.

Before we get too carried away, I pull back. "Wait, there's one more thing I forgot to tell you!"

He pins me with a look. "If it doesn't involve me setting you on this bar and making you mine, it can wait."

He makes a move for me, but I put a hand on his bare chest. "I'm serious!" I laugh but hop onto the bar anyway. Not like I don't know exactly how this conversation will end. "There's a reason Evan bought the whole block." I smile widely at the idea. "There is a whole row of brownstones at the end. He said it's up to us what we want to do with them, but I was thinking we could move into one? Make it our home? That way, you could walk to work. And we could figure out if we wanted to sell or rent the others, but really, I was hoping we could move your dad into the smaller one that only has two levels. He's getting older, and it might be nice to have him close. Plus, Amelia and I already secretly schemed for her to take one as well, so we can live out our dream of being neighbors. I know she already has one on the Upper West Side, but rich people have multiple homes and all that." I laugh while trying to catch my breath. I'm rambling. "But there's this large one on the corner that has views of the city from the rooftop. And there's a cute little backyard and lots of rooms..." I cup his face with my hand. "And maybe one day we can put all that extra space to good use and fill it up with what I'm sure will be massive babies."

The rest of my speech dies on my lips as Tony slams his mouth over mine while stepping forward to stand between my open legs. "God dammit, woman. I already said you won Valentine's Day," he growls into my mouth.

I giggle and wink. "Just making sure I maintain the top spot." I pepper his jaw and cheeks with kisses. "So what do you say, caveman? Wanna make a new home with me?"

"I wanna do forever with you." And he seals our fate with a kiss.

EPILOGUE
FOUR MONTHS LATER

ANTONIO

I must have the patience of a monk.

Because I haven't proposed to Nikki yet, even though I was ready to do it on New Year's Eve at the Barlowe.

But Nikki has been wrapped up in Amelia's wedding planning process, and I knew she wouldn't want our engagement to overshadow her best friend's wedding. So for months, I've held on to the engagement ring I bought the week after her disastrous dinner with Justin and his family. Seeing another man get down on one knee for Nikki tested my sense of morality, but I kept it together.

And now, it's been a week since Evan and Amelia's wedding. They're honeymooning somewhere in Europe while I look at my future bride, who's standing in the kitchen of our newly remodeled brownstone home.

We moved in immediately after Valentine's Day but have been slowly putting our touches on the place.

The brewery, *Caveman Cerveceria*, opens up next month. Nikki tossed the name around as a joke, but I immediately knew I would be keeping it. The name went well with our no-frills vibe and rustic décor. We'll be offering Dominican tapas and over fifty beers on draft. And at the moment, we are working on two IPAs, a cider, and a pilsner. My hope is to get the formula right so we can distribute to liquor stores nationally.

A surprising side effect of quitting my job and creating my own business was the reparation that happened to my relationship with my dad. After I quit the force, we had a four-hour conversation at his apartment. With the help of my therapist, I was able to successfully convey the emotions that I have been struggling with for the past fifteen years. My father sat back and absorbed it like a sponge. I knew my father never really believed in therapy, so color me surprised when he revealed that Mom had roped him into getting mental health help before and after she died too.

Two Dominican men, sitting down and speaking about their traumas and emotions, was a sight I'd never thought I'd live to see. We laughed, we cried, and we drank… a lot. But by the end of the night, I walked away with a better relationship with my father. And for the hundredth time, I send a silent thank-you to my angel up above, my mother, for always knowing what she's doing and setting us on the right path.

Yet now, as I stare at my other angel, mi corazón, I send up a quiet prayer that I don't mess this up and that Nikki will say yes to our forever.

Nikki

I'm sorting out takeout containers on our kitchen island as Tony continues to look at me funny.

He's been in one of his hyper moods all day. I should have known that today would be an eventful day when I woke up to

Tony dancing to Tina Turner's "The Best" in nothing but black boxer briefs.

The biggest surprise of being with Tony is how much he loves music. All music. I never imagined that moving in with Tony would entail daily dance parties in my pajamas. From rap to reggaeton to merengue to salsa.

Home used to be a place where I went to rest after work. Now it's a place where I live my life between handling my responsibilities.

We already had a sex marathon this morning, so if he's thinking of going at it for another round, he's sorely mistaken. Sorely being the keyword. After he treated me to my very own version of a Dominican *Magic Mike* performance, I pounced on him. But he's still giving me this look from across the room like he's up to no good.

He saunters his way toward me, wearing a black Henley stretched across his expansive chest and gray sweatpants. He leans against the kitchen counter as I continue to unload the absurd amount of Italian food Tony ordered.

"Are you going to decant the wine, or are you going to continue to ogle me?" I ask while keeping my focus on the stacks of containers.

"I need you to promise me something," Tony says tenderly.

My head snaps up at his tone. "What?"

His right hand cups my cheek. "I need you to promise me that we'll always be like this."

"Like what?"

"Together. Happy. Content doing the simplest of things, like eating takeout."

"Where's all this coming from, love?"

His thumb caresses my cheek. "I'm not naïve. I know we'll face hardships down the road. I know that we'll go through seasons of life that'll test us, that'll make us question every-thing around us. But promise me that we'll never question the love we have for one another." I open my mouth to speak, but he continues. "Promise me that we'll try for kids in the future. It's not a guarantee that we'll get pregnant. I know that it's not a given, but promise me that we'll try for a family, in whatever form that may look like, and I'll promise to change every dirty diaper and handle every morning drop-off. Promise me that you'll put up with my crazy work hours, and I promise to prioritize our date nights. Promise me that you'll taste test my beers, even when they suck, and I promise to watch all your Bravo shows with you. Promise me that you'll always stand by my side, and I'll promise to spend every day from now until my dying breath making sure you never doubt the love I feel for you. Can you promise me that, corazón?" He exhales deeply.

My sweet man.

I don't know how I got so lucky. To be loved by a man like him. To be given these affirmations of love on a regular Tuesday night over takeout containers.

I smile softly and say, "I pinky promise." I lift my left hand with my pinky extended.

Tony's face breaks out into the biggest grin I've ever seen.

"I was hoping you'd say that."

Tony lifts his left hand, pinky extended, only for me to notice that he has a freshly tattooed *N* on his ring finger.

He must have removed his right hand from my face, because in the same instant, he slips a diamond ring on my extended pinky finger.

I'm frozen in place, rendered speechless by the stunning princess-cut diamond, as he continues. "Nikki, we've been living off pinky promises. How do you feel about turning them into wedding vows?"

His smile stays firm as he drops down to one knee while his eyes silently plead for my answer.

"Tony! Oh my God, yes! Yes!" I shout.

He quickly slides the ring off my pinky and onto my ring finger, where it shall stay forever.

He stands and lifts me off the floor as he pulls me into his arms, kissing me senseless. "Fucking finally," he mumbles into my hair as I break out into a fit of giggles. "I've been waiting forever to propose to you."

"Oh yeah?" I smile into his neck and place a quick kiss there. "And when did you get the time to get that tattoo on your finger?" I poke him in the chest.

He sets me on the counter. "Perks of small tattoos. The whole process takes twenty minutes or less, mi amor."

I should have learned from the last secret tattoo he got for me.

"Good thing you said yes. I promised our little Moana/Ariel/Cinderella/real name Anna that I would marry the princess and live happily ever after." He laughs.

"No way! That was the last pinky promise you shared with her?" I gasp as I realize what that means. "But wait, that can't be right. You knew then? That you wanted to propose to me?"

"I knew the very first time we met," he whispers over my lips.

How this man manages to raise the bar when it comes to making my heart soar will never make sense to me.

I kiss him tenderly as my mind slowly starts to absorb the fact that we just got engaged.

"I'm going to have to text Isabella to get tickets for a game this season, because I need to thank our sweet little Anna in person." I kiss Tony's cheek.

I lean in and wrap my arms around his neck and pull him to stand between my legs that dangle off the counter. I stare at the sparkling diamond in awe. "Nikki Nuñez," I start, already buzzing with energy at the idea of finally having a last name that feels right. "Mrs. Nuñez, mi amor, corazón…" I count the names off with my fingers. "I don't know, Tony, I'm racking up a long list of names for you to call me now," I tease as his lips hover over mine.

"I already have a favorite." His words fan over my lips.

"Oh yeah? Which is it?" I ask eagerly.

"My wife."

The End

ACKNOWLEDGMENTS

First and foremost, this book would not have been completed if it weren't for the love and support of my husband. Hugh, thank you for always championing my dreams, and for always putting our family first. I love you more than Antonio's tree trunk thighs.

I would also love to thank my family, but I'm really banking on them not reading my first open door book, so I'll move this along.

Hannah Bonam-Young, I want to thank you for being my friend and writing buddy during this book. But more importantly for flying down to Florida to attend the Taylor Swift concert with me. Core memories were made. Taylor Torres, I'm so lucky to have found a fellow Latina author friend in you. But if the facetime transcripts between Hannah, Taylor, and I ever go public, please know I will have to enter the witness protection program.

Sam Palencia, I absolutely adore you. Thank you for always creating the most stunning covers for me.

My beta readers are my literal lifesavers! Carolina Capunay, Carla Peterson, Johanna Burgos, and Lela Del Mar. Special shout out to Nyla Lillie, who not only beta read, but also proofread as well. You guys made this story ten times better, and I will forever be indebted to you. To my incredible editor, Beth

Lawton, thank you for taking my manuscript and turning it into an actual book. This process can be so stressful, yet you were able to make my editing process so enjoyable. Please take this as my official request to keep you for life.

And lastly, to my insanely passionate readers. You guys are making this Latina woman's dream come true, one page read at a time. Every tag, share, and DM fill my heart with so much happiness, and I can't thank you enough for embracing me and my characters as fiercely as you have.

Thank you, thank you, thank you.